BY ANY MEANS

OTHER BOOKS BY BEN SANDERS

The Fallen

BY ANY MEANS

BEN SANDERS

HarperCollins*Publishers*

This is for my brothers Joss and Tom.

HarperCollins*Publishers*

First published 2011
HarperCollins*Publishers (New Zealand) Limited*
P.O. Box 1, Auckland 1140

HarperCollins*Publishers*
31 View Road, Glenfield, Auckland 0627, New Zealand
Level 13, 201 Elizabeth Street, Sydney NSW 2000, Australia
A 53, Sector 57, Noida, UP, India
77–85 Fulham Palace Road, London W6 8JB, United Kingdom
2 Bloor Street East, 20th floor, Toronto, Ontario M4W 1A8, Canada
10 East 53rd Street, New York, NY 10022, USA

National Library of New Zealand Cataloguing-in-Publication Data

Sanders, Ben,1989-
By any means / Ben Sanders.
ISBN 978-1-86950-877-7
I. Title.
NZ823.3—dc 22

ISBN: 978 1 86950 877 7

Cover design by Priscilla Nielsen
Cover images by shutterstock.com
Typesetting by Springfield West

Printed by Griffin Press, Australia

50 gsm Bulky News used by HarperCollins*Publishers* is a natural, recyclable product made from wood grown in sustainable plantation forests. The manufacturing processes conform to the environmental regulations in the country of origin, New Zealand.

■ ONE

The bullet had entered the bus through the front-right side window and hit the driver in the head. It made contact with the tip of his chin and removed his lower jaw.

Sudden massive blood loss makes standing a challenge. The driver had made it up out of his seat and through the open door onto the footpath. Witnesses said he was panicked. Probably an understatement. Pavement spatter showed a flurried, crimson scramble. Collapse came seconds later, an Albert Street gutter his finish line.

Friday rush hour, six-oh-five p.m. — horn blare and the white scorch of headlamps, a chip packet fluttering beneath a blood-daubed sleeve.

Paramedics were on-scene within five minutes. They didn't attempt to resuscitate. They proceeded straight to sheet-drop. Six-ten — clots of pedestrians and static-backed radio chatter. A plain white shroud, a newly minted homicide statistic.

Six forty-five p.m.

I was on the pavement, near to where the bus was still parked, twenty metres south of the Albert/Victoria Street intersection. The entire block had been cordoned. Lights were still signalling faithfully, but stopped emergency vehicles constituted the only traffic. Blue-and-red light rippled north and south, delineating the high-rise corridor. Patrol cars formed a crooked nose-to-tail queue, like a memento of evening jostle.

My phone rang. It was my supervisor, Claire Bennett.

'What's it like?' she asked.

'He'll be a closed casket.'

'Any clarification on what happened?'

'The bus was stopped at a light when it happened. Witnesses are unclear on the origin of the shot.'

'How unclear?'

'I'm working off second-hand info, but someone thought the shooter fired from across the road. Someone else thought the round came from a passing car.'

'And what do you think?'

I looked across the street. Beyond the opposite footpath, development vanished; the grade fell sharply to the Elliott Street Carpark. A billboard offered discount life insurance.

'There's nothing across the road, so it can't have come from a building; he was either on foot or in a vehicle.'

'What sort of weapon?'

'Nobody saw, but from what I gather it was too loud for a handgun.'

'So shotgun or rifle.'

'Shotgun, probably. Firing slugs, not buckshot.'

'Wonderful.'

'Yeah. Are you going to come and have a look?'

'I'm getting there. I'm stuck in traffic.'

I had the driver's wallet in my back pocket. I removed it and thumbed it open so the plastic card-protector housing his licence was visible. Robert St George, born April 1979, had required correcting lenses while in control of a motor vehicle. While still attached, his jaw had been prominent and bisected with a visible cleft.

'Who else have you got there?' she asked.

'Some patrol guys and a Scene of Crimes unit. I'm the only detective.'

7

'What are you doing?'

'I've got patrol holding a perimeter, Scene of Crimes taking photographs. I'm going to try and get some security footage and find a shell casing.'

She said nothing. The battery hummed in my ear. The bus was an old Mercedes, with a double wheelbase at the rear end. The odometer probably had a million ks on it. The front passenger door was agape. A fishhook of blood passed through it; a haphazard stroke of death's brush connecting sheet and driver's seat. Inside, Scene of Crime technicians were silhouetted by arc lamps set up on the footpath below the windows. A patrol officer emerged from the rear door and stepped towards me, poised for chat.

I pocketed the wallet. 'I'm going to have to dash,' I said.

'OK. I'm not too far away.'

'You can come and help find his jaw.'

She ended the call. I found a cigarette in my jacket pocket, lit up and drew deep. It was August, and warm for early evening, the heat of an earlier hour rising free of the pavement.

The cop's frown betrayed a smoke aversion. He stayed upwind. 'They think his jaw's disintegrated,' he said. 'As opposed to torn off.'

'OK. So definitely a shotgun.'

'Yeah. Probably.'

I glanced up and down the street. Firemen and paramedics were still lingering; patrol cops were clustered together in groups at random intervals. Gun-toting police were out in force and camera flashes stretched wild shadows.

'Where have you got my witnesses?' I asked.

'Crowne Plaza.' He pointed south up the road.

'Are they separated?'

'More or less. They're in a conference room. We told them not to talk to each other until you got there.'

I stepped left and surveyed the front end of the bus, but the digital window above the windscreen had died. I tapped ash on the footpath.

'What's the route number?'

'Eighty-seven,' he said. 'Express.'

'Where does it end up?'

He shrugged. I took a pull of nicotine. The bottom floor of the building behind me was an Automobile Association office. A dairy occupied the northeast corner. On the northwest side, a low-rise complex was backed by more high-rise.

'I need the surveillance footage from the intersection,' I

said. 'Start a walk around, see if you can get me any video. Go five hundred metres south and north of here, and a block east and west to begin with, and we'll go from there.'

He didn't answer. I turned and looked over his shoulder at the street south of the parked bus. I could see a forensics van about thirty metres away. Far off, a truck horn blared.

'I'll go and talk to forensics,' I said. 'If you could get me some footage, that would be great.'

The Officer in Charge of Scene of Crimes was a woman named Ellen Stipe. She enforced a strict no-cigarette mandate. I guttered the smoke, and she ushered me through the rear door of the bus. She was probably touching thirty-five. Mid-length dark hair, trim build — she looked like a jogger. She probably thought smoking was a filthy habit.

She eased her way past me and led the way down the central aisle to the driver's console. The bullet had passed through an open window, so there was no broken glass, just streaked blood spatter. It was beginning to dribble, ponding on the sill below the windscreen. Stipe stopped me when she reached the front-most passenger seat.

'We've just done the photography,' she said. 'ESR will have to deal with the blood.'

I nodded, despite the fact she was turned away from me. 'Was the front door always open like that?'

'Yeah, apparently. I don't know why.'

'You did a check of the exterior?'

She turned and looked at me. 'Not in any real detail. We checked the gutters for a shell casing. Didn't find one yet, but we haven't been here long.'

'OK,' I said.

The windscreen spatter had arced wide. It originated at the centre of the right-hand panel and terminated near the top left. More on the floor, interspersed with solids. It had been warm outside, but the air from the open doors and the window right of the controls felt suddenly chill. The keys were still in the ignition.

'You find an exit point?' I asked.

'On the driver?'

'On the bus.'

'Above the door.'

I looked as directed. There was a rough, craggy fissure about thirty centimetres across, centred on the line where the wall of the bus met the roof.

'Shit,' I said. 'It packed a wallop.'

Stipe said nothing, but I saw her mouth form the word *wallop*.

'What about trajectories?'

Her hair was tied back with elastic, and she tossed her head to clear a rogue strand from her eyes. 'The round came in through the open window, so the only contact point we've got is the hole in the wall.'

'I just need something approximate.'

She shrugged. 'The debris's been driven straight back, which suggests the shot was fired from a position perpendicular to the bus. To have entered the window, clipped the guy, then come out at the top of the wall, I'd say whoever fired was somewhere across the street.'

'Shotgun?'

'Ten- or twelve-gauge, yeah.'

I nodded. Seat backs bore graffiti. A gem of contemporary prose: *Life's a shithouse*.

'You got a lot of background in ballistics?' I asked.

She smiled. 'No, just a lot of common sense.'

'We'd get on like two peas in a pod, then.'

'No doubt.'

I turned away from her and headed towards the rear exit. 'Thanks for your time. I'll be outside if you need me.'

My car was at the corner of Wellesley and Queen. I retrieved a torch from the boot and began a gutter search.

I started at the corner of Albert and Victoria and worked south. Ellen Stipe hadn't lied to me. The gutters had been checked, and they were empty of anything of investigative merit. I walked back north, stood on the eastern kerb and looked across the street. An empty stretch of bitumen ten or fifteen metres long paralleled the bus in the southbound direction — everywhere else occupied by stationary police cars. Horn blasts came from a couple of blocks over, where neighbouring streets seethed, oblivious. I flicked my torch off.

The witnesses had been unhelpful. Whether the shot had originated from a moving car or a pedestrian was still in question. Understandable. Following the blast, people's attention would have switched to the driver, and the fact a large portion of his face was now AWOL. I positioned myself level with the front of the bus. A shot from the footpath seemed unlikely. It was a question of intended targets. If you want to kill a bus driver, you don't do it on Albert Street, during rush hour, from twenty metres away across a busy street with a twelve-gauge shotgun. Not if discretion is needed. Not if you want to be sure you'll hit the guy. You can always find somewhere more secluded than the central business district.

I stepped onto the road and looked at the gap in the

southbound lane. I imagined a car pulling out from behind the stopped bus, punching hard through the opposite lane, one shot as it passed the driver, north onwards through the intersection and away. Quick and clean, traffic permitting. Three seconds, tops. Fast enough and traumatic enough to leave the idle observer in doubt as to what had happened. Shocking enough to make the idle observer fabricate an alternative scenario.

I checked my watch. Six fifty-nine. Fifty-four minutes since trigger-pull. I needed the initial triple-one calls, I needed video surveillance and I needed to know why someone would want to top a bus driver.

I re-summoned my drive-by scenario: car threads out, pulls alongside, one shot and away. Not an easy thing to pull off. Shotguns are temperamental creatures. They thrive on inaccuracy. Hitting a static target from a fast, laterally moving origin is difficult. It raised the possibility that the bus driver was merely collateral. That he had taken a round intended for someone else. Overhead a helicopter rotor thropped and for an instant a searchlight draped me in gold. On the hunt for tomorrow's above-the-fold photo.

I flicked the torch on again and knelt and fanned the beam across the road. The low angle cut the texture deep.

Pricks of white light shone against the black; ground-level mimicry of the view above. So much for forensics checking the street: shards of glass were scattered across the southbound lane. I stood up and turned the torch off. The shot had broken a window. Meaning: it had almost certainly been fired from a passing car.

Drive-by theory confirmed.

■ TWO

JOHN HALE

The girl had good taste.

John Hale watched her order Corona; bottle, no lemon. Pocket change settled the tab. Coins rang and spread wide and shivered before settling. She took a mouthful and seated herself left of the door, one elbow propped on the table.

K Road, just west of the Queen Street intersection. The upper storey of a double-level unit, probably sixty years old. Timber floor with a rippling dark grain, a tall counter, and a scatter of wooden tables. MC Escher on the walls and a murmuring stereo. The smell of smoke, alcohol and the dusty odour of old wood.

Hale was seated outside, alone at the far end of the

balcony. The position afforded him a view of the interior, plus a two-hundred-metre stretch of street. He wasn't a regular, but a footpath chalkboard's offer of three-dollar lager lured him. He went up and claimed the balcony seat. It was a good location. He liked the night vibe — the red-and-white montage of the traffic below, the general hum of urban motion. In terms of free city panoramas, one could do worse.

Clientele ran light. Inside near the bar, a woman in her late thirties flipped shots of dry vodka. At the opposite end of the balcony, a guy in his early fifties worked his way through a bottle of Merlot. Hale watched the girl appraise them carefully. Frequent mouthfuls punctuated her assessment. She was younger than him, not much more than twenty-two or twenty-three. Dark roots peaked below hair scalded bleach-blonde; make-up flaked her jawline and she wore faded jeans below a thin cotton T-shirt. Glow from a fireplace to the right of the bar jostled her shadow.

He looked away and took a swig of Heineken from a bottle resting on the railing. Across the street, old two-storey buildings occupied the view. Façades, built to different heights, kept adjacent rooflines out of level. This part of town had always appealed. The stereo was playing a Grant Lee Buffalo album called *Fuzzy*. The current track was 'Wish You Well'. Hale hadn't heard it in maybe fifteen years. Complemented by Escher and a cold beer, it was a welcome return.

He worked the beer down to half-tide. It took him until eight minutes after eight. Which, as chance had it, was the exact time he glanced back inside to witness two guys arrive via the staircase on the far side of the room. The first man in saw the girl: an easy glance, then away. A flick of the head beckoned his companion. They paused and surveyed carefully. Shot lady, wine man, Hale.

He stared back neutrally, saw an oblivious bartender stocking lager. The two guys moved right, fluid and confident. They were not small men. Six-two, eighty or ninety kilos, dark clothing. Vaguely similar in a superficial sense. One was blond, short-cropped hair and beard buzzed to the same length. The other wore a peaked cap, the nose below it doglegged, like a kicked downpipe. They took the two remaining chairs at the girl's table, leaned in shoulder to shoulder, a broad wall of flesh, forearms stacked on the woodwork in front of them.

No other staff on duty.

Merlot man pinched a dribbling cigarette between two fingers, eyes wistful as he considered the street, legs crossed beneath his table.

The blond guy scraped his chair round a fraction, so the three of them were spaced equally. He mirrored the girl's pose, one arm propped on the bar, his chin cupped in his upturned palm. He mouthed something inaudible to Hale. The position of his palm distorted his mouth, ruling out a lip-read.

Hale saw the girl shake her head emphatically. Her hair rippled. Hale had more Heineken.

The blond guy delivered another distorted mumble. The girl shook her head again. She'd placed her drink on the table, and pushed back tight against the wall. Above her, Escher's *Waterfall* presided. Quiet suddenly, as the stereo found the next track, golden light touching loose strands of her hair. Hale was the only one observing the situation. The remaining two customers had eyes only for alcohol. The bartender pushed through a door to the back of the shop. The blond guy noted his exit.

A moment's pause, and then a third man came up the stairs. He was older, pushing forty-five. His short haircut matched the blond guy's, except his was grey. He was tall, square-built. A hard, angular face, slightly gaunt, his features etched deep. He entered the room and joined the original two guys, his back to Hale.

Hale stood up. He finished his beer. The third guy's

hand dipped in a pocket, produced something Hale couldn't see. A moment later everybody was on their feet, moving as a tight cluster towards the door and down the stairs.

Neat and discreet. A three-man persuasion to vacate, bartender absent, no hubbub. Hale was only halfway across the room. He waded through tables to the stairs and trotted down to the ground floor. Chill air, solid throng of pedestrian traffic. He looked east and west and couldn't see them. To the right, a wide concrete pad sloped away from the street. He moved out of the doorway and rounded the corner. An indigo Subaru sedan was idling against the bar's eastern wall, nose aimed uphill. Its headlamps were burning, tail tinged crimson by brake lights.

The car's right rear door was open. The older guy was pushing the girl into the back seat. She was struggling, hands taut with sinew clawing the edge of the roof. An eye wide with panic found Hale across the top of the door.

'Help m—'

The car's interior snatched the rest as she was forced inside. The guy shoved her across the seat and climbed in next to her. A glimpse of prison ink: a crude rose encircling a burning arrow on the back of his hand. His door thunked.

The guy with the hat was already in the car. The blond guy blocked Hale's path. The door closure left him stranded. He looked back and forth between Hale and the Subaru, weighing up options. Hale cut his decision time and moved forward. He swung the empty Heineken head-high. Tempered glass made solid forehead contact. The guy tottered but stayed upright, took a knee in the gut and ended up prone. Not fast enough to stop the car, though.

It shot past him with a squeal of torque from the rear tyres and bounced out onto the road, leaving only the smell of exhaust.

The guy on the ground was under the weather but still conscious. Hale slow-turned as he made the triple-one call on his cellphone. Groups of onlookers were precipitating out of the through-traffic. He relayed the details to the operator and ended the call, then knelt beside his victim and rolled him onto his side. The bottle-knee combo was an unprecedented manoeuvre, but it had risen to the task. He frisked jacket pockets quickly but found them empty. He moved south to trousers and discovered an arsenal: a box cutter, a Victorinox Swiss Army knife, and a switchblade mounted in a black plastic release. He pocketed the box cutter, ran out of trouser space and slipped the switchblade and the Swiss Army knife down the side of his shoes. He found a wallet with eighty bucks' cash, as well as an EFTPOS card. No ID, but bystanders were getting too agitated to allow him to question the guy. He palmed the EFTPOS card, stepped to the footpath and shouldered across to the kerb. Urban kaleidoscope; red lights heading left, white lights heading right. The car was long gone. He caught snatches of cellphone chat: '… hit the guy in the face with a bottle.'

Exit time.

He buried his hands in his pockets, ducked his chin to his chest and strode east. People's interest dwindled once he'd put twenty metres behind him. He crossed to the opposite side of the street when he reached the intersection with Queen and headed north, swift on the downhill gradient.

He wasn't aware of the patrol car until it was upon him. It blipped its siren once and popped its lights, then mounted the kerb in front of him, blocking his path.

■ THREE

The bus passengers were of minimal use. At the moment prior to the shooting, their thoughts were idle. It was six on a Friday. They'd called full-time on needless concentration until Monday at nine. Testimony switched from fact to speculation. It was a three-second event dropped at random amid the evening monotony, and nobody had been on the lookout for it. Details proved elusive.

I made calls and requested traffic camera data. Intersection feed was available for Albert/Victoria, Customs/Gore, Hobson/Cook, Queen/K, Symonds/K, Union/Nelson, Victoria/Nelson and Wellesley/Mayoral. I asked for it all and was told I could have it by tomorrow morning. I said it was urgent. I was told the most I could have right now was the Albert/Victoria data. It was better than nothing. Night-shift officers were sent to inspect the original recordings, with copies to be sent to CIB at Cook and Vincent Street.

By eight thirty, I was back there myself. I dealt to a coffee, and then some preliminary scene-report paperwork. I hit computer databases. Robert St George was law-abiding. He'd never been in prison. He had no police record. His driver's licence was free of demerit points. Immigration had no quibbles with him. He was unmarried and without children. It raised questions of greater tragedies: which is worse, a victim from a loving family, or a lonely one fated for anonymity?

At ten before nine, DVD copies of the traffic recordings between six and seven p.m. arrived. I accessed the file. Trigger-pull had been six-oh-five and the video file started at six. The film was monochrome, but crisp, split four ways to cover each intersection leg. The recording consisted of single frames captured at brief intervals, pedestrian motion made random and disjointed. I concentrated on the southbound view. When the bus appeared, it would be framed right of shot.

1801.

Like an image from a textbook: *Figure 1: This is a rush hour.* I dragged the progress tracker at the bottom of the screen and the clock advanced to 1802. I looked around. Still nobody for company. Major crime often leads to low office head counts.

I clicked the footage forward to 1803. My phone on the desk buzzed with a text message. Armed Offenders Sergeant: *Abandon perimeter yet?* I replied with a message telling him to call Claire Bennett and ask her.

1804.

Bus appears at far right of screen, the northbound lane nearest the kerb — 87X LONG BAY. I could see the driver through the windscreen. No passengers in the front row of seats. Stationary northbound: the right-hand lanes remained unchanged for a fourteen-second stretch. Southbound traffic had a green light, and the cars occupying the left lanes were substituted at each frame change.

I hit pause.

The western footpath was dense with foot traffic, but the eastern side, where the shot originated, was empty. There was a cyclist hugging the gutter, but it's difficult to hide a large-bore shotgun beneath Lycra. The bus was boxed in on all sides by traffic: an Audi sedan, a Mitsubishi Diamante, an early-nineties Nissan Skyline.

I hit play.

The time tracker resumed its patient chronicle. I watched the front of the bus. Four minutes and thirty seconds after six and Robert St George still had a jaw. It was still attached at four minutes and forty seconds, and still there at four minutes and fifty seconds.

Facial integrity ceased four seconds into the sixth minute. The camera hadn't captured the event itself, merely the transition from a transparent bus windscreen to one rinsed with blood. I paused it again, not quite ready to invade what happened next. I incremented the video back by fifteen seconds. 1804:49 — a bus with a clean windscreen, an Audi sedan, a Mitsubishi Diamante, an early-nineties Nissan Skyline. I jumped forward five seconds. No change. Forward again, to 1805:04, and the bus windscreen turned opaque. A guy on the west footpath was shielding his face with an arm, trouser cuffs jerked to mid-calf by the crouch he had adopted. The centremost southbound lane was occupied by an old C-Class Mercedes sedan, heading north, which had apparently pulled out to overtake stopped traffic.

I let the recording run. The Mercedes vanished as it shot below the south-facing camera. It dipped downhill towards the harbour and left the shot. The light controlling northbound traffic apparently changed to green, and the

Audi disappeared. Robert St George emerged from the open side door of his bus, hands cupping his lower face. He wasn't upright for long. Eight seconds more saw him prone.

I cycled back the feed and wrote down the Mercedes' licence plate. I hit pause and leaned back in my chair. My eyes felt as if I had salt trapped beneath the lids. A sure sign of dedication. Or maybe just a sure sign my eyesight was packing in.

A further two seconds, and the Nissan Skyline in the lane adjacent to the bus pulled a U-turn and disappeared south. Four more, and the sight of a dead man had induced congestion: gridlock. People were abandoning vehicles and dialling one-one-one, panicking because the switchboard was overloaded and they couldn't get through. Robert St George's constituent matter advanced north in fluid form.

I paused the video and dragged the progress bar back, then relived the sequence. Blood on the windscreen. The northbound Mercedes overtaking. Robert St George stumbling outside. The Nissan's U-turn. Blood in the gutter.

I closed the window and dialled Claire Bennett's cell, on the off chance she'd pick up. She did.

Too late in the day for phone etiquette: 'What've you got?' she asked.

I removed Robert St George's wallet from my pocket and dropped it on the desk. 'I haven't pinned a shooter,' I said. 'But at the moment of the shot, there was a Mercedes sedan overtaking the bus, heading north through the intersection. Few seconds later, another car parked next to the bus pulls a U and heads back south.'

'What was the other car?'

'Nissan. Skyline, I think.'

'The witnesses didn't mention it.'

'No, you're right.'

'Or the Mercedes.'

'No.'

'Are the licence plates visible in the video?'

'I've got the Mercedes.'

'Check the other one.'

I let the feed run. The Nissan stayed idle, then as Robert St George hit the gutter, it pulled out across the street and headed south. The rear body was in full view of the camera. The licence plate had been removed.

'The plate on the Nissan's been removed,' I said.

I could sense her pinch the bridge of her nose.

'The shot was fired from a low angle,' I said. 'Maybe

a shotgun round from the back of the Mercedes caught a window before it clipped the bus driver. Explains the glass on the road.'

'Is the muzzle flash visible?'

'No.'

'You think the Nissan was the target?'

'Maybe. The fact it was at the scene of a homicide without a plate makes it worth checking.'

'So what do you have in mind?'

'I'll hit the databases, try and track it down.'

'OK, do it,' she said, and clicked off.

■ FOUR

The arrest was rapid. They cuffed him and shut him in the back of the car. No dialogue. No seatbelt, either. He braced his feet either side of the drive shaft for stability, leaned forward to prevent his wrists being crushed against the seat.

They took a roundabout route to book him. Queen to Wellesley to Albert to Mayoral Drive, then up to the station at Cook and Vincent. Some sort of emergency further north, pulses of red and blue contributing to the evening light show. They took him in the Cook Street vehicle access and led him to the booking window. A tired little sergeant in his forties sat behind a Perspex sheet, swivelling his chair back and forth through a short arc, forearms braced on his desk. He took Hale's measure with red-edged eyes. The uniforms signed him in. They pat-searched him and took his pocket contents, did a drug-check of his shoes and confiscated the switchblade and the Swiss Army knife. He was fingerprinted and led to a holding cell the size of his kitchen pantry.

The door and locking mechanism were well oiled. A soft click announced imprisonment.

It's not just the dimensional minimalism that ensures holding cells are unpleasant — it's the lighting. Hale's cell was painted white concrete block. Illumination was courtesy of caged halogen tubes, à la Guantanamo. Closing his eyes simply lessened the assault. The architecture was severe. Concrete and steel construction boxed a blurred, echoing acoustic of rambling shouts and cool heel clicks.

He considered himself an oddity, as far as tenancy was concerned. The number of previous occupants with Yves St Laurent business shirts and a fresh three-back-and-sides haircut would be a low count. If he'd had a marker with him, he would have added his name to the visitor log. *John Hale, August 2011, jailed for the pursuit of righteousness.* As a graffiti tag, it would have been admirable.

He was lucky, though — his punishment was short-lived. At eight forty-nine a uniform motioned him to the bars. He was cuffed via the rectangular wrist gate, then waved out into the corridor, like a parody of airport tarmac protocol.

'Sergeant wants to see you,' was the guy's only explanation.

'I don't want to see the sergeant,' Hale said.

The uniform didn't reply. Clearly, he didn't take Hale's comment on board though, as they eventually arrived at the sergeant's office. It was a poky little alcove off the central patrol suite, walled with cork bulletin boards crowded with curled paper. A compact man in an off-the-rack uniform sat behind a desk with his back to the opposite wall.

He looked up as Hale entered and motioned for him to take a seat on the opposite side of the desk. Hale did as directed and the uniform stepped out into the corridor, but left the door ajar. Hale stretched out, crossed his ankles and shook his wrists to try and alleviate the pressure from the cuffs. His wrists were too wide to comfortably accommodate long periods of detention.

The guy looked at him and said nothing. In the absence of air conditioning, an overhead fan spun lazily, a bloated floor shadow tracking the motion. The desktop was choked with stationery. It looked as if the guy had gone to a stock-clearance sale and bought as much as he could and dumped it all on his desk. Hale waited. The guy smiled. His head was bright red and over-filled, like the top of a balloon when you grip the bottom too hard. He wasn't overweight, but his shirt was open two buttons to accommodate the girth of his neck.

'I've never had a cop in handcuffs in here,' he noted.

'I'm not a cop,' Hale said. 'I've been out three years.'

The guy shrugged and rolled an unseen drawer in and out, as if resignation letters were of no consequence. 'Tell me you remember me,' he said.

'I don't,' Hale said. 'Sorry.'

'No offence taken. I don't remember you either. Fortunately, the computer did.'

Hale said nothing. Books of refill and sheets of loose A4 and the odd paperclip occupied the space in front of him. He raised his hands and rested his wrists against the edge of the desk.

'Have you been advised of your rights?'

'No, I haven't.'

The guy reeled the spiel: the right to silence, a telephone, a lawyer. Hale listened patiently. He stifled a yawn with his fist.

'Would you like to be released?' the guy asked.

'That would be splendid.'

'So tell me why you clocked a guy outside a bar on Karangahape Road earlier this evening.'

The fan shadow beat at two a second. He let three pass before replying. 'He was engaged in a criminal endeavour.'

The guy's chair was on rollers. He looked at the door and gripped the edge of the desk and coasted himself in and out a couple of times. 'Describe the criminal endeavour.'

'I already told the emergency operator.'

'The emergency operator wasn't a sworn police officer. You'll need to tell me.'

'Can't you just pull the tape?'

'You're not helping yourself.'

Hale watched the guy roll himself in and out a couple more times, and then he gave him the story, told for the second time that night.

'He wasn't badly injured,' Hale said.

'How did you reach that conclusion?'

'I deduced it. Based on the absence of blood. You can see for yourself.'

'I can't. He'd left the scene by the time officers arrived. We haven't found him.'

The cuffs were too tight. Hale twisted his wrists to relieve pressure.

'You hit him in the face with a bottle.'

'It was the only thing available.'

'It was excessive.'

'It was necessary.'

'No one reported the assault on the girl.'

'Probably because it was a kidnapping.'

'Nobody noticed.'

'I did. I tried to prevent it.'

The guy didn't answer. The fan beat on. He arched back and leaned sideways, ducked his chin to his chest and rolled open another drawer, removing a transparent zip-lock bag with the contents of Hale's pockets. In such an untidy room, it seemed inconceivable the bag had been in a drawer for any other reason than the dramatic effect of revealing it. He broke the seal and inverted the bag. Hale's wallet, cellphone, the EFTPOS card and the box cutter found a place among the desktop detritus.

The guy raised the box cutter, extending seven centimetres of naked, pristine blade. He laid it on the desktop in front of him.

'What do you carry this for?'

'Street collectors wanting donations.'

'It's an offensive weapon.'

'It's more than just offensive.'

'Why did you have it on you?'

'The guy was carrying it.'

'Why did you take it?'

'He had no immediate need of it.'

'Remember you're trying to convince me to uncuff you.'

'There's no reason to have me cuffed at all. Nobody's pushing charges.'

'Three people dialled one-one-one saying they'd seen a tall man with short grey hair hit another man in the face with a bottle.'

'Did anyone ring to say they'd seen three other men kidnap a blonde woman in her twenties?'

The guy didn't answer. Hale clinked his cuffs then dropped his hands off the edge of the desk into his lap. The door to the corridor closed a fraction further, narrowing a band of light that fell across the desk.

The guy said, 'If you're telling me the truth, why did you leave the scene?'

'I was looking for kidnappers. And their kidnappee.'

'When the patrol unit picked you up, you were walking.'

'I would have been running if I'd seen them.'

The guy didn't reply for a moment. He tamped a thin stack of papers square with his index fingers then ran a palm over a widow-peaked buzz-cut. 'How long have you been out?' he said at length.

'Three years. I told you.'

'Final rank?'

'Constable.'

'Did you exit on your own terms?'

'Essentially.'

The guy said nothing. He palmed the buzz-cut again, as if checking for uneven growth.

'Our chat's over,' Hale said. 'I'd like a phone.'

They didn't take him back down to the holding cells. They left him seated in an interview room on the same floor. His wrists were shackled to a bar set in a shallow dish cast in the table in front of him, cuffs crimped tight.

His stifled yawn earlier had been subtle theatre. It concluded a slick two-part manoeuvre: a lowly paperclip, smuggled desk-to-hand, then hand-to-mouth.

He tongued it out onto his bottom lip. Hand-to-mouth had been easy. With anchored wrists, mouth-to-hand would require slightly more finesse.

He checked the door. It bore a single square of peep-glass, but there was nobody keeping watch. He pushed his chair back and stood up, leaned in across the table from the waist. He pursed his lips like blowing a kiss and the paperclip flittered free and landed on the table by his left hand.

Hale shouldered a spit-line off his chin and sat down again. With the door closed the room was warming fast. He blinked sweat off his lashes, checked the window was still empty.

He twisted his left wrist inside the cuff and levered the paperclip off the desktop with judicious use of thumbnail. Saliva had left it slimy. He prised out a ten-mil length of wire, awkward damp fingertips-only.

Sweat speckled the table. The angle was poor but a couple of blind jabs got the wire in the barrel of the cuffs. He ducked low, saw his breath fog the polished table surface.

He watched the window. Random shadows blipped across it. The left cuff mechanism clicked. The bracelet arched open and liberated one cramped wrist.

He paused and flicked some circulation back. He rattled the cuffs from beneath the anchor bar and dropped them in his lap. Forty seconds since barrel insertion, maybe another minute to go. Sweat burned his vision. His face crinkled and he closed one eye. The right cuff was more awkward. Left-handed picking wasn't his strong suit.

It took him ninety seconds. The right cuff popped open and left a scarlet band in its place.

The need for dramatic effect made him leave the restraints swinging limply from the armrest of his chair. He pocketed the paperclip, then palmed sweat off his face and opened the door to the corridor. No reason to lock it when he'd been left anchored. Foot traffic dribbled back and forth. Nobody noticed him. His attire quashed notions of illegality.

He took the stairs down to the ground floor and walked away towards Mayoral Drive.

■ FIVE

By midnight I had a headache nudging migraine territory. Unfortunately, I hadn't made much progress, either. The Mercedes had been a '91 C-Class, the Nissan a '92 Skyline. The C-Class was operating with plates stripped off a blue Honda Accord registered in Hamilton, so finding its driver would not be straightforward.

I browsed records. The list of Auckland Skyline owners ran to five pages. The Mercedes list weighed in at two and a half. The record of these models reported stolen in the last six months was still long, but at least it fitted on one page. I was hoping for an alert telling me one or both of the vehicles had been stolen within the last couple of days. But on an evening when headaches prevailed, cigarette packets were empty and the coffee machine was out of beans, I had no such luck.

I pulled Department of Corrections records and collated lists of violent offenders released within the last two months. I hit the central computer and searched for shotgun-related offences that had occurred within the last year. Mistake. The list outstripped the Nissan records by a couple of pages.

I packed it in at half-twelve, made a hard copy of everything I had found and left it in a meeting area designated as the case situation room. I could have purchased a small, beachside house for what it cost to print everything. The coffee machine was the only one still awake. *Select product*, it instructed. Latte or cappuccino. No tramadol.

At least the drive home was easy. Tamaki Drive was well-lit but quiet at that hour. The rear-view mirror dangled a stern message: *Quit Smoking or You'll Get Cancer!* I promised it quitting would begin tomorrow. I pulled into the driveway of my Mission Bay home at five before one in the morning. The security light blinked on obediently as I pulled into the carport. The security light's always pleased to see me.

I locked the door behind me as I entered. My home is a white, two-bedroom unit probably designed for old people. My rationale is it'll accommodate me for the next sixty years. My headache was telling me bedtime, but duty still called.

Good things come in twos, but unfortunately murders sometimes do as well. I'd agreed to review the case file of an incident from Monday night; the death of a woman and her young daughter. The bodies had been discovered by the woman's husband, who had arrived home in the early hours of Tuesday morning, and found his wife and her eight-year-old daughter from a previous marriage dead, each with a single gunshot wound to the head.

The fridge gave me a Mac's Gold and I carried it through to the living room, and set the stereo to work on Richard Hawley's *Truelove's Gutter*. The rear-view mirror forbade smokes, but tolerated beer and music.

The case file was balanced on the arm of my recliner opposite the stereo, pages tamped, no loose edges. About as appealing as police case files can ever hope to be. I sat down and turned to page one, migraine monster rearing its head as I started reading.

The deceased's names were Carolyn and Amy Lee; Carolyn's husband was Ian Carson. The deaths occurred at the family home on Hurstmere Road, North Shore. Comms logged Carson's initial emergency call at twelve fifty-two a.m. Tuesday. The first patrol unit arrived eight minutes later at one a.m. The responding officers found the front door of the residence closed but unlocked, and went in. They searched the house front to back. They found a woman in the master bedroom upstairs, shot once in the head. They found a young girl downstairs in a bathroom adjoining another bedroom, also shot. Last of all, they discovered Ian Carson, in apparent shock, in a foetal position beneath his desk in the house's study.

I drank some more Mac's.

Comms had supplied a print-out of the status codes radioed in by the responding unit. Arrival had been confirmed by a ten-seven at precisely one in the morning. The unit had radioed in an eleven-ten, the offence code for homicide, at one-oh-four, followed by a request for immediate assistance.

An ambulance arrived at one-fifteen and coaxed Ian Carson into a more regular state. The senior medic recorded Carson's heart rate as eighty-six per minute, his blood pressure 132/84 — mildly hypertensive, but essentially calm. At one-thirty a CIB patrol unit turned up. A gun was found in the hand of the victim in the master bedroom, but the serial number had been chemically erased. At one fifty-seven a.m., Takapuna Police yielded control of the case to Auckland Central CIB.

At the outset the case looked like a murder–suicide. At approximately twelve a.m. Tuesday, Carolyn Lee had apparently entered her daughter's bedroom, chased her into the adjoining bathroom, and shot her once. She had then returned to her bedroom and taken her own life.

Holes formed quickly. Friends and family could offer no insight into a possible motive. Carolyn Lee had no history of mental illness. She'd never admitted ownership of a firearm. After allegedly claiming her daughter's life, she had then taken her own while sitting upright in her bed, beneath the covers. The evening of her death, she had brushed her teeth and flossed. When officers arrived, she was found clad in her nightwear.

Amy Lee's life had ended in a bathroom en suite adjoining her bedroom. She had locked the door in order to escape her killer, but the door had been kicked inwards, breaking the lock, something that would require a considerable degree of strength. Combined with the fact the house exhibited no signs of forced entry, attention turned to Carolyn's husband, Ian Carson.

I turned to the Persons of Interest section. Carson occupied the first page after the divider. He was forty-three years old, Caucasian, five-foot-nine, and eighty-seven kilograms. His driver's licence photo showed a rounded face topped with short blond hair. His eyes were crinkled at the edges, as if a smile was imminent. Hardly a trait of callousness. He'd graduated from the University of Auckland in 1992 with a first-class honours degree in chemistry. Somehow a science degree had led to property investment. He bought and sold and got rich, amassing assets valued in the low eight figures.

I downed some more beer.

Carson was a quiet millionaire. Wealth did not necessitate public prominence. Despite the science background, he served as one of four directors of a finance company that had managed to survive the recent industry collapse. He had no assault record, no accusations of fraud, no drink-driving offences.

The only black mark against him was he claimed to have been absent when the deaths of his wife and her daughter occurred. Which was fine, except he couldn't explain where he *had* been.

I finished the beer.

My phone rang, the alert deadened by the pressure of the seat cushion. It was after half-past one in the morning. My courteousness always runs hot, and I picked up.

'Anything on our shooting?' Bennett asked.

'Not really. I printed some stuff. You can read it in the morning.'

'OK. You at home?'

'Yeah, I'm reading the Carson file. I haven't seen the scene, but I'm going to check it out tomorrow. But what's this *our* shooting?'

'It's yours too. You can't just abandon ship.'

'I might have to delegate. Depends how sticky Carson is.'

'We'll see. How's it looking at the moment?'

I rose from the chair, stepped to my stereo and cycled the CD back to track four: 'Remorse Code'.

'If he can't offer an alibi, he's looking pretty good for it. Even just reading the file it looks as if the wife's in the clear.'

Keyboard patter from her end: the sound of an office all-nighter. I sat back down.

'How's our luck so shit we ended up with two homicide cases in one week?' she asked.

'Don't know. It's not *us* with the shit luck, though.'

'No. You're right. I've set up a meeting with everybody for nine tomorrow morning.'

'OK. I probably won't be there.'

'Right,' she said flatly. 'Sleep well. I won't be.'

She ended the call and I went back to my file.

■ SIX

Hale spent the night in a motel off Gillies Ave. Blinds down, the room was still indigo after sun-up. Seven in the morning, he flicked lights on in preference to admitting the morning, then dialled a number on his room phone. It was a number he'd left un-rung in eight years. Remembering it was a feat of mental excellence.

'I think I'm owed a favour,' he said, when the call was answered.

'Shit. John Hale?'

'Yes indeedy.'

Sound of paper being rearranged, but no reply.

'I need a card traced,' Hale said.

'What sort of card?'

'EFTPOS.'

Dead air for a beat. 'Yeah. OK. What for?'

'Because you owe me.'

A breathy, nervous laugh. Hale closed his eyes and conjured more mind wizardry. He relayed the card number and the bank it was registered to, from memory. He heard a keyboard recording faithfully.

'What exactly do you need?'

Hale watched the window. The sun hung shy behind the blinds. 'Owner's details,' he said. 'Anything and everything.'

'Name, date of birth, that sort of thing?'

'Yeah. An address would be helpful.'

A drawer was slid closed. 'OK, sure. I'll see what I can do.'

I read until three in the morning. The crime scene chronology was detailed.

As a precaution while the scene was secured, Carson had been placed in handcuffs. They'd come off at one-thirty a.m. and official interviews commenced at two a.m., when Carson's lawyer arrived. Carson's statement did little to lessen his importance as a suspect. He had left the house at quarter to ten the previous evening. He'd returned to the house at twelve forty-five. He made no response to queries about where he had been during the crucial time.

Saturday morning offered cool air and light cloud. I rose early and drove into town to the station at fifteen minutes to eight. The postmortem for Carolyn Lee and her daughter had already been conducted. I had none of the associated reports, so I placed a call to the pathologist assigned to the case, and arranged a meeting with her for midday. I retrieved a key to the Carson residence, then drove north across the bridge to the North Shore.

Ian Carson's property on Hurstmere Road was about a kilometre north of central Takapuna. Hurstmere runs through a narrow north–south gap formed between Takapuna Beach and the eastern end of Lake Pupuke. It's top-end real estate. Carson's address was on the eastern, beach-facing side of the road, marked at the kerb by a parked patrol car. I cruised north along the street then U-turned and parked across his driveway. The house couldn't have been more than ten years old. It was a double-level minimalist structure of floor-to-ceiling glass and concrete panelling. Tall hedges bordered the property, yielding to a wrought-iron gate across the driveway. The gate was standing open, substituted temporarily by emergency tape.

I trapped the file under my arm and got out. I retrieved gloves and disposable shoe-protectors from the boot, then went to speak to the officer in the patrol car. He was a young guy. Officers assigned to guard four-day-old crime scenes are normally young.

He squeaked his window down. Breakfast time: he was spooning dry cereal out of one of those little sampler packs that come in your mail.

'Anything happening inside?' I asked.

'Not for a while. You going in?'

'I am. If forensics turns up, let them know I'm in there. I don't want to get shot.'

He gave me the attendance log and I signed myself onto the scene: *Det. Sgt Sean Devereaux (AKX6), 0813.*

I ducked under the tape and approached the house. I paused under the eave to don the protective gear, then unlocked the front door and went in.

A small entry alcove floored with polished concrete greeted me with a cool, grey silence. To the left, a corridor walled with glass disappeared to the front of the house. To the right a staircase led to the first floor. Carolyn Lee had died in the master bedroom, which I knew was upstairs towards the rear of the house, her daughter in a bathroom at ground level.

I did a ground floor reconnoitre first. A series of three doors led off the right-hand wall of the corridor, but I ignored them and made my way to the back of the house. A secondary wing was occupied by a living room to the left and a combined kitchen and dining area to the right. The flooring was a warm timber and the back wall was glass, framing calm water lapping a shoreline lumped with volcanic deposits, like mounds of cooled tar. The living room furniture was cream leather, with a ceiling at roof level making the place feel cavernous.

I checked the kitchen. Polished granite and stainless steel. No dishes. Flat surfaces dusted with print powder. I turned towards the front of the house. Preliminary estimates had indicated both victims died between twelve and twelve-thirty.

I opened the last door in the corridor. The polished concrete gave way to thick cream carpet and neutral cream walls brightened to a light shade of pink. Girl's room. There was a four-poster bed in the far left corner, long edge parallel to the door. The sheets were wrinkled and the covers had been thrown back. There was another door in the wall to the right of the bedroom entry. The panelling beneath its handle was cracked — where it had been kicked. The lock tongue had punched through the adjoining frame, leaving jagged splinters.

I toed the broken door open into a small en suite

bathroom. Grouting around the tile work at the left-hand end of the tub was darkened, as if recently stained with fluid. A small, circular indentation emanating a spidery network of cracks marred a nearby tile. Bullet hole. I stepped back out to the corridor and headed upstairs.

The first-floor layout was similar to the ground. A corridor occupied the left-hand side, with doors branching right. The first door I tried was a bathroom. The second was the master bedroom. The cleaners had been through: linen had been stripped off the bed, floors had been scrubbed and steam-cleaned. Remnants of stains were still present on the mattress and carpet; wide, irregular smudges that would always remain. The house's form of memory retention. There was a desk to the right of the door, with a laptop computer and a separate mouse attached to the left.

I went back downstairs. The first door on the right of the corridor led to another small living room. The second was an additional bedroom. Pristine, unlived in. From the doorway I could see into an open cupboard, packed with children's toys. A pink trolley sat on the floor, a yellow teddy bear spouting white stuffing was in apparently well-earned retirement on a shelf above. I moved back to the girl's room. At the foot of the bed was a small dresser topped with loose coins and a framed photograph of a young girl with shoulder-length brown hair and a pale face, cut by a grin set to full wattage.

Whoever had killed her had seen the same picture, but the underlying message had gone unread. They'd seen the photograph, seen youth personified in eight-by-ten form, ignored it, and shot the subject of the photo in the head. That's depravity. That's evil in the most undiluted sense.

I pulled the door to the en suite closed again and stepped out into the corridor.

Key photographs taken on arrival by Scene of Crimes were sectioned together near the front of the file. I examined them back in the car. Carolyn Lee had died from a single gunshot wound to the side of the head. The trajectory had been approximately thirty degrees to the horizontal. The 9 mm bullet had entered her skull through her right ear canal and exited near the top of her cranium. The exit wound was about the size of a grapefruit. Her right hand was shown limply cradling the handle of a black Glock 17 pistol. Another photo showed a spent brass shell casing in situ in the open doorway.

Amy Lee had suffered worse. The back of her skull had

been depressed, most likely due to impact trauma suffered from contact with the tiling around the bath. She had a 9 mm entry wound through her left eye. Interpretation: the bullet had killed her, a subsequent backwards fall had inflicted the damage to the rear of the cranium postmortem.

The initial CIB investigator assigned to the case was listed as one Detective Senior Sergeant James Weir. I called his office number and introduced myself.

'I just had a look at the Carson place,' I said.

'OK. You know what's going on?'

'I'm starting to get a good idea.'

'And what do you think?'

'It's a dressed-up suicide,' I said. 'Someone's tried to make it look like the wife shot the daughter and then topped herself. But the wife can't be suicide. There's no contact scorching from the muzzle. Must have been fired from at least thirty centimetres away.'

He said nothing.

'So what's his story?' I asked.

'Deaths occurred sometime between twelve and twelve-thirty. Mr Carson says he was out.'

'He came home and found them like that?'

'Apparently.'

'No further detail?'

'Not so far.'

'He didn't say where he was?'

'No.'

'Did the neighbours see anything?'

'No.'

'Did the neighbours hear anything?'

'Not until about quarter to one when Carson was out on his deck, screaming. We turned up and found him inside in his study.'

I closed the file and placed it on the passenger seat beside me. Hurstmere carries heavy traffic on a weekday, but Saturday morning had relieved it of its workload.

'Any other suspects?' I asked.

'No,' he answered. 'Just the one. And right now he's looking pretty good for it.'

■ SEVEN

The call back came at twenty after eleven. Hale was on the road: State Highway 1, southbound. He was travelling light. Ditching non-essentials is a prerequisite of fugitive status. Thus, glove box clutter constituted supplies.

He had a back-up phone.

A quarter-roll of duct tape.

A SOG-TAC Auto switchblade.

A six-hundred-dollar cash payment from a client renowned for writing bad cheques.

The cell rang to nine before he answered.

'I could get fired for this. Or imprisoned.'

'You won't,' Hale said. 'Someone would have to find out.'

No response. A mouthful of something liquid was swallowed.

'I found a name and address,' the guy said. 'And a workplace.'

Details were recited. The colossal memory trapped all, verbatim.

'You're not planning anything illegal, are you?'

Hale mused. Heavy northbound cloud; he squeaked the wipers to life to rid pricks of water off his windscreen.

'Not really,' he answered.

The Carson autopsies had been conducted at the Grafton mortuary. I drove south through trickle-traffic across Grafton Bridge at five minutes after twelve, the Auckland Hospital complex dominating the view ahead. These days, bridge traffic was enclosed on each side by concave Perspex shields attached to the existing concrete barriers. Prior to their existence, Grafton had been a suicide favourite: State Highway 16 was a mere twenty-metre plunge below.

I left the car in a parking building behind Starship Children's Hospital, then walked around to the City Hospital entrance.

Morgues don't fill me with joy. There are a number of contributing factors. The smell, primarily. Formaldehyde is a wonderful preservative, but its odour isn't that agreeable. The presence of dead bodies never makes for merriness, either. I'm always offered a gentle reminder from the darker sections of consciousness that one day I will be booked in for a visit.

The pathologist was a Maori woman in her early fifties named Mel Henry. I'd worked with her before. Cutting dead people never seemed to inhibit her cheerfulness. I met her in an examination room adjoining one of the primary postmortem theatres. Clad in gown, cap and facemask, she was unrecognizable. The bodies of Carolyn and Amy Lee were lying shrouded beneath blue polyethylene sheets on separate wheeled gurneys. A stainless steel extraction duct sucked patiently overhead, lessening the nostril-burn from the preservative. Clinical halogen lighting on clinical white floor tiling. Paradise.

'You tie the gowns up at the back,' Henry noted as I entered.

'I like to be able see how to take it off,' I said.

'In case you have to make a swift exit?'

'Precisely.'

'You're a worry, boy, you really are.'

The room was small, maybe a four-by-four square, with the gurneys arranged parallel to one another, ninety degrees to the door behind me. The tube lighting was on the way out; epileptic flicker making shadows fluctuate.

Henry stepped over to a control dial on the wall and twisted a small knob fractionally. The duct above the gurneys began to suck with more vigour. She moved to the far end of the right-hand table and folded the sheet back, revealing the face of Carolyn Lee. The hair had been shaved back to a buzz-cut shadow and the exit wound through the top of the cranium had been cleaned and packed with gauze. Henry stepped away.

'The extent of the powder tattooing around the entry wound suggests the muzzle of the weapon that killed her was approximately thirty centimetres away,' she said. 'Cordite traces are evident on the right hand and arm, which is consistent with the notion that the injury is self-inflicted.'

'Is it self-inflicted?' I said.

'It's possible.'

'Is it probable?'

'Not really,' she said. 'Gunshot suicides are typified by contact injuries. It's easier to press the muzzle of a firearm against the side of the your head and pull the trigger than to carry out the same exercise from thirty centimetres away.'

'And this isn't a contact injury.'

'No, it's not. Contact shots, even shots within five, maybe seven centimetres, you'll notice scorching of the skin. Basically, when you fire a gun, you get an eruption of gas that precedes the bullet, which will burn you instantly if you're close enough. In this case that's not evident. Which is indicative of someone else pulling the trigger.'

I said nothing.

'The bullet trajectory is another issue,' she said. 'You've got right-ear-canal entry and top-of-skull exit. Difficult to purposefully achieve that sort of pattern. Considering suicide, intuitively it implies the weapon was held at a low angle and the shot was fired upwards. That's a very awkward position to fire from; thirty or forty centimetres away, with a thirty- or forty-degree angle. Normal suicide approach with a handgun is a single shot through the roof of the mouth.'

'So it's likely someone else shot her?'

She nodded. 'Someone shot her from a distance of about thirty centimetres. Immediate reflex for the victim in that sort of circumstance is to lean away as far as possible. It's likely she was being restrained, and was trying to distance herself from the weapon.'

'Hence the odd entry angle.'

'Yeah. Exactly.'

I nodded. 'OK. What about the girl?'

Henry replaced the sheet, then stepped to the wall and

applied a minute adjustment to the extractor control. 'The girl's not good news,' she said.

'I know. But I've got to look anyway.'

Henry took a step left and positioned herself at the head of the second gurney. The extractor hum and light flicker maintained their monotonous rhythm. She folded the polyethylene sheet back to reveal the head of a little girl. The bullet entry wound through her left eye was patched over with thin gauze.

'There's a two-step sequence,' she said. 'You've got the gunshot wound, followed by the head injuries.'

I nodded and looked at the floor. Milky white, overlaid by thin arcs of rubbery wheel residue from multiple gurney visits.

'You OK?' she asked.

I looked up, saw the gauze over the bullet wound, and looked down again.

'Yeah. Just put the sheet back.'

She folded the sheet back into place. 'You look as if you need some air. You've gone white.'

Pearler of a migraine on the way. Seven on the Richter scale, a low-rev throb.

'I'm OK. What happened to her? Gunshot and then head injury?'

She raised her arms and sidled through the narrow corridor between the gurneys and came and stood next to me beside the door.

'Essentially. The trauma is largely disguised by the bullet's exit wound, but it's still evident. From the position she was found in, she was shot, and the subsequent fall backwards caused the skull fractures.'

'No other injuries?'

'No other injuries. Someone shot her and walked away.'

The doors were windowed and hinged inwards. I could see the exit sign at the end of the corridor. I wanted out.

'Anything else?' I asked.

'Toxicology analysis came back yesterday. The mother had high levels of ibuprofen and codeine phosphate.'

'Painkillers?'

She nodded. 'Difficult to calculate exact consumption, but we're probably talking two five-hundred milligram tablets each of Panadeine and Nurofen.'

My head pulsed. 'Is that a lot?'

'It's a fairly high dose.'

'Fatal?'

She shook her head. 'No, but she would have been pretty numb.'

'Any reason she might have been taking painkillers?'

'Not that I could find.'

'So maybe she was using them as sleeping pills.'

'Possible. They'd certainly do the trick. Once you were off to sleep they'd keep you under pretty comfortably.'

'OK. And with that fact in mind, she's alleged to have woken up at midnight, broken a locked door and killed her daughter, then committed suicide.'

'Apparently,' she said.

'Right. Where's your bathroom?'

The bathroom fitted the facility's design theme: claustrophobic, white tiled floor, stainless steel fittings, formaldehyde creeping in beneath the door. Tying the gown at the front had been a remarkable stroke of foresight. I had it off and trash-canned in less than a three-count. I flipped the lid on the toilet, knelt, gripped the rim and threw up, hard. Breakfast's toast and coffee revisited in blended form. The torrent backed off but I still felt terrible. The rim of the bowl was shaking under my grip. First instinct was earthquake, before I realized my hands were at fault. The bulb suspended from the ceiling buzzed like a dentist's drill on idle.

I rose shakily and found the mirror above the sink. She'd been right about looking pale. Deathbed white undersold it. I was talcum powder. I bent and drank tap water, then smiled at my reflection to check for teeth clingers. All clear. Still shaking though. The residual aftershock. I leaned against the door and knuckled my right eye. The throb gained tempo. I found a switch for an extractor fan, flicked it on, and palmed my breast pocket. It held emergency supplies: two cigarettes and a lighter. I killed the first in about two minutes, chained the second off the smouldering filter and managed to even out the shakes.

My phone buzzed against my hip but I let it ring through to voicemail. I breathed smoke and formaldehyde and waited for calm to return.

I got back to the station at three minutes before one, to find Claire Bennett seated alone in her office, reading file documents. Her office is windowless, airless, strewn with paper and slightly larger than a coat cupboard. I sat down opposite her, the desk separating us, and waited for acknowledgement.

'The bus shooting's not moving,' she said without looking up. 'No suspect sightings, no evidence to work with, the CCTV footage dead-ended.'

Paper crackled gently as a ceiling fan attempted to ventilate.

'What about the vehicles?' I said.

'They don't appear to be stolen.'

I said nothing. Bennett closed the file she was reading, dropped it on the floor beside her and shunted herself a channel of clear desk space.

'I spoke to the pathologist for the Carson job,' I said. 'No way was the wife suicide.'

'We knew that,' she said.

'I've ruled it out completely.'

She rubbed her eyes with the heels of her hands. A trio of murky coffee cups were arranged beside her computer monitor. 'So Carson shot the daughter and then shot the wife.'

'No, other way around. Wife then daughter.'

She rotated one of the coffee cups. A new-email alert sounded and her eyes panned to her screen and then back to me. 'What makes you say that?'

'The daughter barricaded herself in a bathroom. He had to smash the door handle to get at her. The wife would have heard something.'

'When the wife died the girl would have heard the gunshot.'

'She would have heard something loud, wouldn't necessarily have concluded gunshot. It's likely the noise woke her, she got out of bed to investigate, then ran back into her room and locked herself in the bathroom when she realized what had happened. At which point someone smashed open the door and shot her.'

She nodded and fell quiet as imagination supplied imagery. A Post-it note worked its way to the edge of the desk and pirouetted to the floor.

'Keep working it,' she said. 'I've got to keep this bus thing moving, though. See me later this afternoon.'

I could still taste vomit. I made myself a coffee with a view to oral cleansing, sat down at my desk and opened the Carson file. I had never really questioned crime chronology. Ignoring the possibility of suicide, whether or not Carolyn Lee's death had preceded her daughter's wasn't clear. I turned to the crime scene photographs section. Carolyn Lee had died in bed, wearing pink cotton pyjamas. The blankets that covered her were tucked along one edge, loose along the other. Barring murder–suicide, if Amy Lee had been shot first, the sound probably would have woken her mother in the bedroom upstairs, even with four painkillers. Potentially, she had gone to investigate the noise and been forced back into bed by her killer.

I found the photograph showing the spent shell casing in the master bedroom. The suicide theory demanded death via ear canal GSW. The easiest way to achieve this would be to turn the gun sideways. The weapon was a Glock 17. Glock 17s eject shell casings to the right. A sideways pistol orientation would cause the spent brass to discharge vertically and land close to the victim. The only way in which the shell casing discovered could come to rest as it did would be if the gun was held in the intended, upright manner, causing the dead cartridge to arc across the room. Physically possible in a suicide, but wrist discomfort would make the perpendicular alternative intuitively preferable.

I browsed further. The gun had been found in Carolyn Lee's right hand. The position of her computer mouse suggested she was left-handed. A comment from Detective James Weir noted that the alarm clock beside the bed was programmed to sound at nine in the morning. The alleged murder–suicide perpetrator had allowed for a generous sleep-in.

I checked the mortuary photographs. The digital print-out of Amy Lee's face supplied after cold-room check-in bore no resemblance to the portrait I had seen in her bedroom. The hair was still intact but the injuries rendered everything alien. The bedroom portrait had captured an instance of youthful radiance, the file photo documented wanton abuse. You could draw no parallels. Memory tiled a side-by-side line-up. I didn't know which was worse.

I finished my cup of coffee and window-gazed. Harmless to the idle glance, but urban machinations did well to camouflage the subversive and the predatory. Nooks and crannies of workforce normality, where the damned sought refuge.

I picked up the phone and dialled the forensic team at the police armoury and left a message asking them to report back with any further information gleaned from the pistol found next to Carolyn Lee. Next, I placed a call to a colleague at the Financial Intelligence Unit in Wellington, requesting Carson's earnings be nit-combed.

I put the phone down and brought up a report template on my computer. Blue text asked me to describe the nature of the incident. It told me to be concise. I selected a bold typeface and bulked the font out.

I wrote: *TRAGEDY*.

■ EIGHT

The cardholder had been identified as one Geoffrey Gage. Six-two, eighty kilos, green-eyed blond. Altogether, not an intimidating package. Hale found an Internet café and used an illicit log-in to remote-access the police system and pull Gage's Master file off the Whanganui computer. He subsequently added drink-driving, drug possession and assault to the Gage CV. A gold-plated citizen. He was listed at a Waitakere address that didn't prove a hard find.

It was the right-hand-end unit in a row of four single-level brick flats on a quiet, undistinguished street near the Mega Centre.

Hale slowed as he passed. The section was un-fenced, the building parallel to the road. A tarsealed parking bay bit the kerb. Hale continued past and parked two hundred metres further up the street. The car was a black '79 Ford Escort, lovingly restored to its original factory-line condition. Not a flashy vehicle, but Hale wasn't one for pretentiousness. Recent jail break noted, driving it was a risk. He rationalized the decision based on knowledge of a low cop quota: he wasn't likely to be picked up.

He locked the car and walked back to the target address. Cloud had lifted; the sky was now a smooth blue smudged irregularly with light grey. Gage's parking space was the only one left vacant. Hale occupied it briefly and ran his standard pre meet-and-greet assessment. The flats were a design-manual standard. Each unit had a window left of centre, with a door to the right, located above a shallow concrete ramp for disabled access. Blinds were down behind the window of Mr Geoffrey Gage's residence. It had the luxury of a side-door in the right-hand wall, presumably to the kitchen. The property was bounded to the right by temporary chain-link construction fencing. The adjoining property was a two-storey weatherboard home fronted with patchy lawn and a pair of emaciated lemon trees. Nobody outside. Altogether a dishevelled outlook. The street looked as if it had just rolled out of bed.

Hale stepped up the ramp and knocked twice on Gage's door. No peephole, which was advantageous, from the perspective of an unfriendly visitor. There was a bell-press left of frame, but operating it brought no response. He stood and waited. Television satellite dishes and UHF aerials clung to the street-facing eave in a skeletal four-deep row. Rubber on bitumen hush of nearby traffic. He knocked once more and waited another minute then picked the lock and let himself in. The front door led straight into the living room. Worn yellow carpet, stained where it wasn't scuffed threadbare. A new LCD television left of the door, a two-seater couch opposite. A toppled cardboard box spewed polystyrene pellets and transparent plastic. The right rear corner of the unit was open-plan, revealing a kitchen and dining area. The bedroom and bathroom were walled off to the left, both stinking of cigarette smoke and alcohol. He stepped to the open bedroom door: unmade double bed, discarded clothes draped limp and random. The bathroom and shower stank.

The dining table was a collage of junk mail and porn; the dishes in the kitchen sink were this morning's vintage. He moved back to the front door and re-set the lock, then slid home the deadbolt. He crossed the room and let himself out the kitchen door.

He walked back to the Escort and his in-car GPS led him on a short drive south to a semi-industrial stretch of Railside Ave. The neighbourhood was largely trade services: scaffolding suppliers, construction contractors, vehicle mechanics, metal fabricators. The buildings were compact block structures protected by wire fencing and signs threatening prosecution. Exterior windows were steel-grilled.

Geoffrey Gage's account had shown regular deposits from a Concept Welding Solutions Ltd. The business occupied a warehouse located down a potholed right-of-way behind a storage yard containing sections of a dissembled tower crane. Hale continued up the street, U-turned through light traffic, and parked, the western railway line running parallel to his left.

Information gathering can be a rewarding activity when data volume snowballs with very little initial effort. EFTPOS card number led to account details led to a name and address led to a Securities Register search for goods offered as loan collateral, which led to a vehicle make and registration number. The big three: name, address, car. Geoffrey Gage drove a green Mazda Familia. Hale could see it parked against the chain-link fence on the far side of the storage yard. Geoffrey Gage was doing weekend overtime.

He twisted the ignition off and waited. The halt didn't

bother him; he had Ryan Adams's *Love is Hell* at whisper-quiet on the stereo, just embarking on a cover of Oasis's 'Wonderwall'. Hale was of the opinion the quality of Mr Adams's version exceeded that of the original cut. Certainly, it was quality enough to render the pause worthwhile. He watched the warehouse premises. It was a light structure, panelled with corrugated metal. A roller door built to roof height occupied the left end of the street-facing sidewall. The door was open, the dark within interrupted by periodic pricks of ultra-blue light and parabolic showers of yellow sparks that leapt and scattered as they struck the floor. A dulled clang reached him as something unyielding was hammered. The hot smell of saw-cut steel leached through the vent system.

Hale waited. His watch crept around to three o'clock. Ryan Adams was finished. He tossed up between The Verve's *Urban Hymns* and *The Best of R.E.M.* He settled on The John Butler Trio's *Grand National*. The Familia stayed parked. His wing mirror maintained a miniaturized commentary of approaching traffic. Three-thirty, productivity began to break down: grille screens were dropped, metal roller doors were locked down, vehicles nosed out of driveways.

Three thirty-seven, the roller door at Concept Welding

73

Solutions Ltd slid closed. There was a four-minute interlude of inactivity, and then three men appeared from a door at the right end of the building. One man headed towards a red Toyota ute nose-in to the warehouse. The second man walked towards the road via the right-of-way. The third man was Geoffrey Gage. He walked towards the green Mazda Familia parked against the fence at the rear of the storage yard.

Hale twisted the key. The CD player muted momentarily on motor start-up. He toed the gas and watched the tach flick eagerly. The Mazda turned into the right-of-way and rolled road-bound, wheels juddering slightly on the uneven surface. It indicated, merged into traffic, and accelerated back north towards home.

Hale gave himself a three-car cushion then let the brake off and followed. The shallow blue-cast undulations on the horizon in his mirror shrunk and disappeared in reverse around a shallow bend. The Familia moved quickly, accelerated to catch an orange light and slipped through before the change. Hale stopped obediently at the red. He wasn't in a hurry. He continued on a moment later and turned into the end of Geoffrey Gage's street just as the Famila claimed its vacant space in the kerbside parking bay. Hale pulled to the shoulder, jiggled the stick to neutral and turned the engine off. The muffler ticked twice and then quietened.

He watched. Cars were good for stakeouts. Mirrors enabled twelve and six o'clock monitoring. The Familia's driver's door opened and Geoffrey Gage, six-two, eighty kilos, green-eyed blond, with assault and possession priors, swivelled in his seat and dumped his feet on the tarseal.

He climbed out, elbowed the door closed behind him and walked towards his front door.

Hale slid out of the Escort. Fifty metres away, opposite side of the street, moderate traffic; Geoffrey Gage didn't notice. Reconnaissance on the fly: the house to the right still appeared unoccupied. Hale crossed the road on a diagonal and reached the mouth of the neighbouring house's driveway just as Gage stepped up onto the wheel-chair ramp. Hale skirted the edge of the fence and weaved fast through the lemon trees for the front left corner of the house. Trespass was never a good feeling. Risk of observation was a gut-freezer; he window-watched as he walked. All clear. Fortunately, the wire fencing didn't obstruct the view next door.

Gage dipped a hand into a trouser pocket and removed a set of keys, jiggling them on his upturned palm to spread the bunch. He tossed and caught them neatly by the necessary key, and inserted it into the knob-lock. Chime of knocking metal. Hale watched. Gage couldn't get the door open. The deadbolt had seized everything up. He cussed, shook the key free, stepped off the ramp and came around the side of the building to the kitchen door.

Hale stepped forward and approached the fence. Timing was everything. He paused there, amongst the lemon trees. He heard a car turn in at the driveway behind him. Squeal of a too-loose fan belt, dulled thunk of a worn auto transmission shifting into park. He took his attention off Gage and checked behind him. The lemon trees blocked the view. He hoped the same applied in the opposite direction. He turned back and saw Gage battling the lock, his head turned. Hale saw the grimace, the relief as the lock finally gave and a split appeared between frame and panel.

Gage would have heard him vault the fence but didn't register the implication. Hale caught him from behind as he was passing through the doorframe, looped his neck with his left arm. He used his right palm on the side of Gage's head combined with a sudden forceful sideways jerk to knock his head against the frame. Gage was a fighter. Not an especially large guy, but he was in shape. He dug his heels in, tried to shout until Hale smothered him with his inner elbow. He reached behind him, clawing for Hale's face, probing for an eye socket. Hale spun him through a tight one-eighty and dragged him further into the kitchen. He switched his free hand to the left side of Gage's face, jerked suddenly and slapped Gage's right cheek against the bench top.

The resistance stopped. Cranial contents are delicate, and the quirks of physiological evolution mean human tolerance for lateral head trauma is especially poor. Gage's knees stopped working, unable to support his weight. His arms went slack. Hale lowered him carefully to the floor, stepped to the kitchen door and risked a glance outside. No spectators staring aghast. All clear. He pushed the door closed.

Gage had gone foetal: knees raised, chin ducked, arms shielding his head. Hale bent and grabbed a fistful of shirt and dragged him across the kitchen lino and into the living room, dumping him with the empty television packaging. Gage said nothing and just lay there. Hale took a seat in the middle of the couch opposite the television. He leaned forward and propped his elbows on his knees, netted his fingers together and watched Gage across the tops of his knuckles. Mild concussion. There was a purple discolouration the approximate width of a 330 ml beer bottle marring his forehead.

'Do you remember me, Geoffrey?' Hale asked.

Gage risked a glance between the raised forearms. No reply, but Hale sensed recognition.

'Don't worry,' he continued. 'You won't have to talk much. I just want to know where the girl is.'

Comprehension lagging. Gage abandoned the foetal but remained on the floor, confident for now Hale wasn't about to injure him further. His beard had grown out longer than his hair. He wore black jeans, worn and kneaded with dirt, and a heavy button-down, long-sleeved shirt beneath a black nylon jacket. His eyes were focusing out of sync. 'I don't know where she is,' he said quietly.

Genuinely apologetic. The memory of the bench-top contact was still ripe. Hale dropped his hands to his sides, pushed up out of the chair and made an unrushed survey of the premises.

'Remember fast. I notice you've got a neon light in your kitchen. Those things draw a start-up current of about fifteen amps. A zap from one of those would sting a little, I'm sure.'

Pulse of Adam's apple. 'Shit, man. Please.' He struggled

on the floor, limbs ineffectual, like some sedated animal. He was no more than thirty; a young man.

Hale made an exaggerated step over him and moved to the window. He fingered a slit in the blinds and checked the street. No issues. The Escort waited patiently. He stepped to the couch and sat down again.

'Where's the girl, Geoffrey?'

'I don't know!'

'That's a problem. You took her. Stay on the floor, or I'll start taking teeth.'

He rolled onto his back and covered his face with his hands, breath whistling between the gap in his palms. 'I promise I don't know.'

'Your credit rating for promises is a little shot.'

Gage removed his hands and raised his head off the floor, accordion-roll of skin beneath his chin. 'The *fuck* man?'

'What's her name?'

'What?'

'You're as deaf as a post. Yesterday evening you helped abduct a young woman. I want to know her name.'

He paused. He tried to remember. Hale observed bona fide difficulty.

'McLane,' Gage said.

'What was her first name?'

He closed his eyes. 'Christine. Yeah, Christine. Christine McLane.'

'Why'd you pick her up?'

'I … Oh, God.' He pushed up on his elbows. 'I don't even know.'

'Would you remember if I broke both your legs? Stay on the floor.'

Gage stayed on the floor. 'I got a call,' he said. 'We just had to find her, nab her.'

'Who called you?'

'Cedric.'

'Who's Cedric? Was he there last night?'

The foetal position again. 'No. Cedric just does the calls.'

'Why did you take her?'

'Jesus I don't *know*. OK? We just had to pick her up. It was just like, find her, snatch her, whatever. Two hundred bucks or some shit.'

'So where is she now?'

'I don't know. I didn't leave with them. I was with you. On the pavement. I just split by myself.'

Hale said nothing. He pushed off the couch again and knelt and pat-searched him. Cellphone in his left

trouser pocket. He cycled through the inbox. The aforementioned Cedric had dispatched a text message at four
the previous afternoon: *Small job. Pickup at yours at seven.*

'They collected you from here?' Hale asked.

'Yeah.'

'And then what?'

'Then we cruised her place.'

'Where's her place?'

'In town. Like, up Nelson or Union or something. An
apartment building.'

'She wasn't there.'

'No. Nobody was there. We hit K Road, figured we'd
find her eventually.'

'Pity you found me, too.'

'Well, yeah.'

'How did you know to search K Road?'

'We had her cell number. I just called it and said *Where
are you?* and she said straightaway she was at this place on
K, even though she doesn't know me.'

Hale fell quiet and linked his fingers. The smell of
the place seemed to have been amplified. A breeze from
somewhere set the security chain on the front door ticking
against the frame. Television a window to a black liquid
parallel.

81

'Had you met the other guys on Friday?' Hale asked.

'I knew the guy in the hat. I didn't know the older guy.'

'Who's the guy in the hat?'

'His name's Jamie.'

Hale picked up the phone and address book-searched, found one Jamie Kilcullen.

'I'm keeping your phone, OK?' he said.

Gage said nothing. Hale pocketed the phone.

'What're Cedric's details?'

'Shit, I don't know. The details are in there.'

'In the phone?'

'Yeah.'

'You ever contact him?'

'Shit no. You don't ever talk to Cedric. He hates that shit. That's a real sweet way of getting yourself done. That guy would waste me, no question.'

'So how come you've got his number?'

'It's not *his* number. It's like a cutout, or whatever you call them. But it's like *we call you, you don't call us.*'

Hale said nothing.

Gage gestured weakly. 'Hey, I'm sorry man. I never done this sort of shit before. All I thought I was doing was picking up some lady. I didn't know it was going to get all … you know.'

'Illegal.'

'Yeah. Illegal.'

Hale paused again. Gage watched him from the floor, chest rising and falling as if the conversation required significant exertion.

'Have you been honest with me, Geoffrey?' Hale asked.

Gage nodded. Hale saw his eyes go to the neon light in the kitchen and believed him. He watched his reflection in the placid sheen of the LCD as he spoke.

'I don't want to have to come back, Geoffrey,' he said. 'I don't think you want me to come back, either, do you?'

Gage shook his head, short hair scrubbing against the carpet.

'I'm going to leave you now. Don't leave town. You don't want me to have to find you.'

Gage said nothing.

'If you give me reason to come back, you're going to be very sorry I visited you. Even more sorry than you are now.'

Gage looked at him as if he were receiving an unquestionable truth. John Hale, giver of gospel.

'The universe does not operate with randomness, Geoffrey. There is a constraining degree of balance applied to everything. Everything is evened out. You take part in a kidnapping, karma sends me after you. Get out of line again, it sends me after you like rats on a dog carcass.'

Gage didn't reply. Hale stepped to the door.

'Keep your nose clean. I'm gonna be watching you. I'm Mr Universe.'

▪ NINE

Four-thirty Saturday, and nobody from forensics or financial intelligence had rung back with information. I went home, making a supermarket detour for pasta ingredients. The rear-view mirror signage still forbade tobacco-related products, but I bought one pack of Marlboros. For emergencies.

Dinner: the pasta, with mince and a tomato sauce. Probably palatable. The Checks provided background music. I helped myself to a Mac's Gold and seated myself in my armchair to eat.

I heard The Checks right through and sat with speaker crackle afterwards. The walls muted to dull purple as evening advanced. No television, but we didn't mind. The house and I were accustomed to quiet. This was our time. Vanished daylight and thoughts of vanished lives.

I touched my breast pocket out of habit. The stitching was pulled near the top. The flap gaped like some unfed creature. It missed holding the box. I missed the box, too. I gazed at my bookshelf in self-pity. Garage-sale paperbacks choked it, floor to ceiling. No space left vacant, I'd stuffed its sagging face with the best of Steinbeck, Maurice Gee, Cormac McCarthy, Philip Roth. It was a crinkled yellow pig-out of dog-eared excellence. The smell of smoke was still in the air. Maybe the room missed the familiar white tendril, the lazy orange ember curled lovingly towards finger.

I claimed a second beer from the fridge and dealt to it from my armchair. Cigarette withdrawal made for shaky sips. Deep shadows settled, forgiving of the décor. Late evening silence that only the clock dared to break. The eternal plight of the unaccompanied. I sat in the quiet and worried on behalf of those who no longer could. Oh for nicotine.

Hale found a motel room in Mercer, south of Auckland. There was cheap eating aplenty, but he drove north to Pokeno in search of dinner.

Small-town dining at this hour was always a difficult call. By now café food would have been neglected to oven-fester for the better part of ten hours, and bar menus were often severely inadequate.

He went bar. He found one on the main drag. An open front door spilled a low internal murmur. Outside, smokers chatted and toed spent butts. He parked and went in. The carpet was deep red, matching the vinyl coverings of the stools fronting the counter at the back of the room. Through an open door, he could see the bright electric hue of slot machines. Their edge-of-seat patrons paid him no heed, his arrival as insignificant as the drop of the last coin.

He ordered chilli con carne and took a table for two in the corner, right of the door. The place was probably half-full. Two little girls about five or six sat cross-legged on the floor outside the door to the slot machines, so bored by now the carpet was starting to look interesting.

He felt separate from it all, as if what he saw bore a false glaze that kept him distant. It was the after-effect — the shock of smashing a man's temple against a bench top. And then doing it again.

The chilli was scabbed with a helmet of tasteless cheese. He picked the whole thing up like a biscuit and deposited it on a napkin, then worked his way through the meat and rice. Disgusting, but the distancing glaze extended to his tastebuds and he got the meal down. He couldn't help but relive the Gage procedure — the overwhelming odour, the striped light from the curtained windows. That neon tube in the kitchen. He wondered to what lengths he would have gone if Gage hadn't talked. He'd seen electrocution victims — it was a coin-toss as to whether he could have gone there.

He kept coming back to the guy's face. That wild look from the floor; cheeks bloodless, eyes wide behind a mesh of fingers. It was a look that focused beyond flesh and bone and saw the threat of violence — something irrational, immune to pleading.

Hale finished his meal, settled the bill with cash and left. It was dark out. Storefronts threw cuts of yellow light across black bitumen empty of traffic. He slid into the car, started the motor and backed out onto the road. Brake lights cast puddles of red in the view behind. He watched himself slip past in storefront windows, a shapeless smudge of shined black, preceded by white and chased by red.

He found the motorway and drove back to Mercer. It was a purely functional little establishment. There were fast-food outlets, a petrol station and some basic accommodation clustered under the curl of the southbound state highway off-ramp. Ideal for long-range freight trucks, but not much else.

He parked the car behind his motel, out of view of the road, and walked back around to his room. He let himself in the front door and locked it behind him, slid the chain and lay down on the bed running beneath the front window. The curtains were thin, and the light that filtered from outside patterned the roof in a fine grille, which elongated with distance. He pondered the guilt. It was the prolonged proximity that induced it. It was knocking the guy's head around and then lingering to witness the result. Seeing that expression of fear — an expression evoked in response to the wicked, the morally void. He was loath to categorize himself likewise.

Irony: he lay there and planned his next violent excursion.

■ TEN

Sitting got old. The Carson thing was bothering me. I called Ellen Stipe, the SOC officer at the shooting.

'It's Sean Devereaux,' I said.

'I know. It's called *caller ID*.'

'Have you got a minute?'

'Depends. Business or pleasure?'

'Business,' I said. 'I've got the Ian Carson case.'

'I don't,' she answered. 'So I'm probably of no use.'

The room was still dark. Light from the kitchen pawed the doorway carpet. 'I'm going to look at the house,' I said. 'I thought you might want to tag along.'

'Right now?'

'Uh-huh.'

'Tag along? What, to provide professional assistance, or just for a casual nosey?'

'Well. The former, primarily.'

She laughed. 'Are you joking? It's nine o'clock at night.'

'I'm trying to quit smoking. Inactivity makes me crave nicotine.'

'There're probably better cures than snooping murder scenes.'

'I don't know. Objective analysis is therapeutic.'

'Disciplinary hearings aren't.'

I didn't reply.

'Well,' she said, 'to answer your question, no I'm not interested in tagging along. Maybe another time.'

'OK,' I said. 'There's something I need to look at, so the offer still stands.'

I gave her the address in case she changed her mind.

'I'm all the way over in Ellerslie,' she said.

'I'm all the way over in Mission Bay,' I said. 'It's not that far.'

She ended the call.

I did the dishes and left. It was a cold, dry night. The on-shore breeze as I drove along Tamaki Drive was laced with the smell of the ocean and fluttered softly in my open window. Confident full moon. Not enough to lift the harbour out of the inky expanse, but sufficient to outline the spidery lines of silver foam that marked the shoreline.

The city was its picturesque nocturnal norm: adorned with yellow orbs, smog layer temporarily cleansed.

I followed the road around the foreshore to Mechanics Bay, past the cargo cranes and their anorexic silhouettes. Quay Street was quiet, too. A fine night for silence. I left the stereo off in celebration.

It took me fifteen minutes to get across the Harbour Bridge to the Shore. I left the motorway at Esmonde Road and stopped outside the Carson residence moments later. The crime scene tape jiggled listlessly. A marked patrol car was parked on the verge behind the footpath, but when I flicked my lights it offered no acknowledgement in return.

The gate was closed, and beyond it the house was black and formless. I dropped the passenger window and heard the hushed sigh of gentle waves melting on a high-tide mark. The crime scene tape ticked rapidly with no discernable rhythm. A yellow Fiat Punto hatch was parked a few metres up the street. Ellen Stipe got out and squinted past my high beams. I raised the window, doused the lights, then popped the boot and slid out.

'I hoped you might change your mind,' I said.

She made a sarcastic face and spread her arms. Street lamp glow edged her thinly. She was wearing a navy forensics jumpsuit and white trainers. 'Ta da.'

'You even beat me here. That's keen.'

'I think you can class this as strange behaviour.'

'You're here, too. Pot, kettle.'

I went to the rear, removed my torch and closed the lid.

'Nothing better to do on a Saturday night?' she asked.

'Not really. What about you?'

She smiled. 'Oh, definitely better things to do. But it was either come along or report you.'

'And you were too nice to report me.'

She didn't answer. I crossed the road towards the gate. Stipe followed.

'There's no rule that says you can't do these visits during daylight hours,' she said.

'My sudden revelations tend to hit me after sundown.'

'Right.'

'You ever get those?'

'Sudden revelations? Yeah, but I tend to postpone any action until nine o'clock the following morning.'

The gate was secured by a padlocked chain. I freed it with a file key I had taken on Friday, links ringing heavily as they collapsed on the concrete. Stipe bent beneath the crime scene tape and pushed through the gate. I followed her, then replaced the chain and locked it behind us.

She led the way to the front entry. The security light flashed on and provided me with sufficient light to find the door key.

'I feel a bit illegal,' she said.

'I wouldn't worry. It's a victimless crime.'

I stepped to the door and unlocked it.

'We're not wearing gloves,' she said.

'Oh shit.'

'You didn't plan this very well.'

I stepped outside. I'd forgotten gloves and shoe-protectors. Stipe dug in a zippered pocket. 'I've got two sets of protectors, but only one pair of gloves.'

'You have the gloves. I won't touch anything.'

She passed me the shoe-protectors and I hopped about in the pools of gloom in front of her, trying to put them on. The standard crime-scene one-foot ballet, but observed with cynicism. Stipe was more adept and mimicked the process much more elegantly.

I elbowed the door fully open and stepped back inside. The house seemed to exhale through the opening. Relief at renewed occupancy. I removed the torch from my pocket and clicked it on. The beam streaked white into the hollow of the corridor; magnified and scattered by the polished floor, the geometry of the space distorted.

Ghostly bleach versus black. I turned right up the stairs.

'We should turn the lights on,' Stipe said.

'Someone will think we're burglars.'

'Your torch looks more suspicious.'

'We'd better be quick then.'

She was following me on the stairs, but I couldn't hear her footfalls.

'What are you looking for?' she asked.

Terse tone, but I reasoned if she was truly disgruntled she wouldn't have driven all the way from Ellerslie.

'I don't know. I was here this morning. It didn't look right.'

I reached the upstairs landing and turned right into the master bedroom. It was as I had left it that morning. Walls oscillated as I flicked the beam around. The quilting on the mattress switched between stark and non-existent. Nothing fresh to examine. I walked to the end of the corridor to Carson's study. The door was standing open. I went in and stood beside his desk and looked out over the water. The moon peaked between a faint overlap of cloud, like a bulb seen through torn lace. Below it, Rangitoto Island formed a dark, blunt mound beyond a flat expanse of harbour. Stipe entered behind me but stayed near the door.

'You said there was something you wanted to look at,' she said.

'I thought there was, too.'

'That's a little vague.'

I didn't respond.

'Why did you come out here?' she asked.

'Because I visited this morning and looked at everything and it made me throw up.'

She was quiet a long time. I flicked the torch on and off, watching the image of the bulb vanish and reappear in the window in front of me.

'Carson's little girl was shot. I saw the results close-up. I couldn't get to sleep on that sort of thing.'

'She wasn't his little girl. She was his wife's.'

'Would it make you feel any better, if you were in his position?'

I heard her let her breath go. 'What do you normally do?' she said.

'What do you mean?'

'When you see something like this. What you saw this morning.'

'I forget it. I smoke a cigarette, listen to music, try and blank it out. It doesn't always work though. Some stuff tends to linger.'

She didn't reply.

'You ever get that?' I asked.

'Yeah, but it fades after a while. I stop remembering it.'

'I don't think you do. I think stuff like that scorches pretty deep.'

She was quiet a moment. 'So what's happened?' she asked.

'They think Carson shot his wife and daughter. They think he's dressed it up as a murder–suicide on the wife's part.'

'But you think differently.'

'I've got doubts.'

'They must be fairly considerable for you to be out here at nine at night.'

'Well. Yeah.'

'Stop flicking the light at the window.'

I turned the torch off. The room adopted a shade of grey in its absence. I turned and slipped past her to the corridor, where I flicked the torch on again. The door next to the master bedroom led to the upstairs bathroom. I kneed it open, cast the beam around without really looking for anything.

'You smell like beer,' she said.

'I'm not surprised.'

She made no reply. I walked to the end of the corridor and headed back down the stairs. I walked towards the kitchen at the rear of the house, then turned right into Amy Lee's bedroom. The gouged en suite doorframe was the most obvious thing out of place. The torch beam swung there without thinking. I heard Stipe on the concrete outside, brush of bootie on carpet as she entered the room behind me.

I checked the dresser at the foot of the bed, examined the scatter of coins I had seen that morning. I moved into the en suite and looked at the handle. The lock button was still depressed, the tongue trapped in the extruded position. I stepped back into the bedroom. Stipe turned the light on. I winced at the sudden clarity.

'I don't think he did it,' I said.

She made no reply. She took a step towards the bed as if to sit down, but then rejected the thought and remained standing. The bright light didn't seem to bother her.

'The girl died in the bathroom,' I said. 'She locked herself in there; the door was kicked inwards.'

She traced the base of her forehead with the back of her wrist, depositing a small trace of talcum from her glove in the process. 'How does that rule him out?' she asked.

'The door handle isn't key-locked. It's got a curved slot

on the exterior surface so you can open it with a coin.'

I pointed to the dresser. 'Busting the door probably took a good couple of goes. He wouldn't have made the effort if he knew he could get in with a coin.'

'Maybe he didn't know that. Maybe he left the lights off and didn't see them. Maybe he was in such a state he didn't think to use them. You can't rule him out based on pocket change.'

'Yeah. Maybe. It still makes me doubt stuff.'

'No one else seems to doubt. The papers think he's guilty. The television thinks he's guilty.'

'I don't have a television. I'm unbiased. I like to think people don't slaughter their own children.'

She nodded, as if it struck her as a fair assertion.

I pocketed my torch. 'What's the time?' I said.

'Fifteen after nine.'

'You want to get a drink or something?'

She looked at me. 'Don't go getting any naughty ideas,' she said drily.

'It wasn't a euphemism.'

She smiled. 'Yeah. OK then.'

We went to GPK, further along Hurstmere in Takapuna Central. Parking was swamped. We left our cars at the bottom of Earnoch Ave in the beachfront lot and walked back. By nine-thirty mealtime was approaching its conclusion and the place was occupied primarily by drinkers. We ordered beers and sat outside at a table for two and watched traffic congestion.

'You don't look that good,' she said.

'That's not very nice.'

'I mean you look kind of sick.'

She'd abandoned the jumpsuit to reveal a hooded sweater and black jeans. You could class them as rag-tag, and against a backdrop of high fashion she looked a bit out of place. She wasn't bothered. I placed an elbow on the table and propped my head against my palm. My temple fluttered. Blood pressure didn't like crime scenes.

'The girl's bedroom made me feel sick,' I said.

'Scale of one to ten?'

'About a six. Between queasy and nauseous.'

'You get that a lot?'

'Not really. I don't know. I've seen violence to kids before, normally I'm OK with it.'

She arched an eyebrow.

'Not OK with it, but you know what I mean. I saw the girl at the mortuary, though. That wasn't good.'

'I can imagine'

'It's strange. I saw her and it made me remember things and I think it made me realize she was someone's daughter. You can forget that when you're just looking at a photo. The fact that kids end up in those sorts of places, and they all belong to someone.'

She just watched me and took a small sip, levering the bottle from the neck with two fingers. Beside us, traffic navigated Hurstmere with the rapidity of cold treacle. She shunted the glass ashtray with her bottle, unsettling the half-dozen or so butts it held, then threaded her hair behind her ear with her pinkie. Scientist's trait. Too used to having the index fingers occupied.

'What would you do?' she asked.

'What would I do when?'

'If it was your child. Or your wife?'

'I don't have a child. Or a wife.'

'For the sake of argument then.'

'I reckon I'd find whoever did it and clock them out early.'

'You think you'd just ditch the system and go vigilante?'

'Probably. I think if your family was murdered, it would shake up your priorities. Revenge might end up transcending black-letter law.'

'You reckon you could do it?'

The footpath was crowded where the restaurant tables had created a bottleneck. Passing thighs brushed my upper arm. The movement rippled my beer. There was a gas fire burning inside, the light from it orange and irregular on the side of her face.

'I'd like to think so. It's not something I give much thought to, though.'

'Is family not on the Sean agenda?'

'Not really. I never really planned on wife and kids.'

She took another small sip, cut a pattern in the bottle condensation with her fingernail. 'How come?'

I shrugged. 'I don't think I'm made for it. Plus the only other woman I know is my boss, and she's fifty-eight.'

'That's a bit defeatist.'

'Maybe. There's always the chance that ten years of smoking will get me with a stroke before I'm fifty-five.'

'You can't write your life off based on that.'

'I'm not writing my life off. We seemed to reach the conclusion just now that losing a child would be pretty terrible. I think the same can be said for losing a parent. Whatever, most of my worry-time is devoted to either cancer or emphysema. I don't really want to leave dependants when I cark it.'

She laughed. 'My grandmother's ninety. She's still a pack-a-day lady.'

I didn't answer.

'So how did you end up doing this?' she asked.

'I don't know. Misfortune.'

'But do you enjoy it?'

'I don't know. I'd probably miss it if I quit.'

'Put that on a recruitment poster: *I'd probably miss it if I quit.*'

I took a mouthful. 'And what about you? How did you end up here?'

'Studied chemistry, did a post-graduate course in forensics, then, whammo, here I am.'

'Whammo. You're pretty bright then, are you?'

'Most chem grads are.'

'Including Ian Carson.'

'I'd assume so.'

'Which begs the question why he couldn't rig a crime scene to look like anything more than just a murder dressed up as a suicide.'

She made no reply to that. Her eyes panned to the street, focused on a thought she seemed unlikely to share.

▪ ELEVEN

Hale placed his call to Cedric at nine forty-five, using Geoffrey's confiscated phone. He was still lying on the bed below the front window. Drapes drawn, only light the disjointed wanderings of television glow.

The receiving phone ran to voicemail. No message, just the beep. Hale hit redial. He got the beep a second time, redialled, and was picked up after three rings. No greeting, just the absence of the electronic tone and a gentle exhalation, coarsened by several layers of digital transmission.

'I want to talk to Cedric,' Hale said.

A lengthy pause. He could sense the mental acrobatics: the surprise at the unfamiliar voice, the outright request. Maybe the fact it was almost ten at night. Silence laden with activity.

'He's not here.'

'I suggest you find him.'

'Who is this?'

'Someone friendly. I promise.' He drew out the last syllable. Something ominous in that sibilance; an implied paradox.

'How'd you get this number?'

'Not easily. Tell Cedric I want to talk to him.'

'About what?'

'Friday. I figure he owes us more than was arranged.'

'I don't know what you're talking about.'

'Cedric will. Find him. I can guarantee he doesn't want me to have to.'

The long pause again. The laboured, quiet weighing up of options.

'I think I'll take a pass on that,' the guy said. It was a brush-off gesture, but he didn't hang up.

'He's got until tomorrow morning at nine to ring back,' Hale said. 'Otherwise, I'm tying him to the kidnap yesterday evening.'

Quiet as the guy assessed the threat. It was a three-second affair: 'Answer your phone,' he said.

And then he was gone. Dead air. The television flickered. Hale sat up and placed his feet on the floor, dropping the phone on the quilt beside him. The television was muted, but he watched it anyway. Late-evening mind-trash: free nationwide delivery, via cornea. It kept the brain-slate thought-free. Advantageous, in that it sterilized the second-guess-yourself germ. He watched reruns. Boredom on an unprecedented scale. He persevered, worried that if he reconsidered the details he might reconsider the sensibility of the whole thing.

The call came at twenty after ten. A tinge of blue across the roof, a dampened buzzing as the phone squirmed its way towards the edge of the bed. Hale picked up.

'You know the liquor shop near Gage's place?' Male voice, but not the same person he had spoken to earlier.

'No,' Hale said.

The guy gave him an address.

'There's a service lane in behind,' he said. 'Be there in twenty minutes.'

'I can't make it in twenty minutes.'

'When can you make it?'

'An hour.'

A pause. 'OK. An hour. You know the rules?'

Hale said nothing.

'You show up with cops, we'll shoot you. You show up with a crew, we'll shoot you. We hear any radio chatter we don't like, we'll shoot you. You try to diddle us, we'll shoot you.'

'OK,' Hale said.

'Keep your phone on you,' the guy said.

The drive north was a blessing. Wide, almost desolate expanses of highway, the monotonous hum of tyre on bitumen. He'd read somewhere it had been proven to induce sleep. No argument there; an even more powerful sedative than television. He kept the stereo off. The world collapsed to a thirty-metre illuminated strip of tarseal and he worked hard to retain the mind blank, lest he reconsider.

He stayed on SH1 all the way to Central Auckland then turned west onto SH16 at Grafton. The harbour lay to his right, sullen and perfect as crude oil. Nothing above, just the same dark that lingered beyond the reach of headlamps, and in his face when his reflected self returned his glance in the side window.

The drive out was less than half an hour. The GPS took charge of navigation once he got off the motorway and turned south on Lincoln Road. He visited Gage's place again, just to recalibrate his sense of geography. The light was on behind the window in Gage's flat, and the green

Familia was still in residence. He paused at the kerb and fed the address he had been given into the GPS unit and U-turned back the way he had come.

The liquor store was a quick find. It was part of a small retail cluster, east of Railside Ave. It was the centre premises in a row of three, shoulder to shoulder between a takeaway shop and butchery. There was a backlit façade at roof-level displaying the company logo in egg-yolk yellow. He made a left turn out of sparse traffic into the parking lot out front and made for the far end. The light from the sign gave him a jaundiced reflection.

He flicked his lights to high beam and drifted to the left end of the parking lot. He nosed around the corner of the takeaway place and emerged into the narrow service lane running behind the trio of shops. To his right, the rear ends of the buildings were sheer and featureless, save for corrugated roller doors. To his left, the rear sections of a tight row of residential housing lay behind a steel-mesh fence topped with razor wire. His headlights funnelled his attention more or less directly ahead, but he could still make out a series of security light brackets fixed at mid-height on the adjacent wall. All had failed to activate. In terms of safety, it was about as far from ideal as he could have hoped. He brought the car to a stop but left it in gear with his foot on the clutch, doors locked, one eye on the rear-view mirror. He pondered the likelihood of becoming a future case study: *Example one: A poorly informed choice of rendezvous.*

The phone went. He picked it up off the seat and answered.

'Where are you?' the voice asked him.

'The liquor store,' Hale said.

'OK good. You sound a little nervous.'

Hale said nothing.

'OK, stay on the line with me,' the guy said. 'I need to give you some instructions.'

'I'm all ears.'

'Good. There's a gas station near where you're at.'

Directions were given.

'Think you can manage?' the guy asked.

'Probably,' Hale said.

'You've got two minutes. Be on your best behaviour, or I'll shoot you. I promise.' Emphasis on the 's'. Reciprocation of Hale's earlier threat.

He dropped the phone on the seat beside him and crawled out into the parking lot. Two lefts got him to View Road. The relief hit him like an intravenous shot: the simple lack of constraint, the reassuring sight of headlights queued behind him. Fenced in was never a good feeling. He checked his mirrors for a chase car. All clear, unless thugs now drove airport shuttles. Left onto Railside Ave. Nothing of sightseeing value. Single-level homes shoulder to shoulder on narrow lots. He saw a car stranded wheel-less, a temporary awning erected in a front yard, tarpaulin skin rolling under the light breeze.

He turned right against a red light at the intersection with Bruce McLaren Road and saw the petrol station immediately. It was situated on the left-hand side of the road, set well back from the kerb. He slowed for site inspection. 'Former petrol station' was probably a more telling description. There was a rectangular concrete forecourt marred with fissures and oil stains, sheltered beneath a roof supported on a pair of sturdy concrete columns. No sales office; its sheared-off foundations beyond the roof's overhang the only testament to its prior existence. Hale waited. The ground surrounding the concrete was lumpy and grassless and glazed hard under his headlights. A once-sealed access way from the street lay in jagged pieces.

He turned in off the street, onto the ruined access lane, headlamps creating chasms of black in the disjointed remnants. There was a disused carwash in the rear right corner of the section. Headlights awoke dimly from within it as he turned off the street, before a gleaming black Ford Explorer SUV emerged onto the uneven surface, its body wallowing awkwardly as it approached the sheltered concrete pad.

They parked nose-in to each other in the lee of the massive support columns. The Explorer's lights cut, the fierce head-on blaze diminishing to a feeble orange glow from the filament. Hale switched off the Escort's ignition and climbed out, the open door shielding his lower half. The SUV's motor ran at a high idle for a long moment, before it died to be replaced by the distant muted hiss of vehicles much too far away to help.

The Explorer's driver's door opened. A tall Polynesian man in his late twenties slid out and circled the rear bumper to Hale's side. His gait was loose, shoulders rolling exaggeratedly as he moved. His hair was in dreadlocks, all of them stiff with grease, rising free of his head, like the outstretched limbs of some sightless creature. He pulled open the rear passenger door and stepped back. The Explorer bucked on its springs and then a pair of boot-clad feet lowered themselves to the ground. Thick fingers gripped the outside edge of the door and a huge man stepped out into the glow of the Escort's headlights.

He was tall, his frame padded with massive rolls of fat. It swelled his neck, extruding it beyond the edge of his jaw, so that everything above the line of his shoulders looked like the tip of a missile, draped with flesh. At his midriff, his bulk extended uniformly in every direction, giving the impression of a regular person with a hula-hoop trapped inside his beltline. He was maybe forty, his dark T-shirt and circus-tent pants partially obscured by a leather coat, which hung to his knees. His crown was bald, the hair that remained in patches on the sides of his head light blond.

'We could have just met at a Burger King,' Hale said.

The fat guy was impassive. The younger man with the dreadlocks just smiled.

'Which one of you is Cedric?' Hale said.

'Neither,' the younger guy said. 'Turn your lights off.'

Hale recognized his voice from the telephone. 'We won't be able to see,' he said.

He was still standing behind the Escort's door. Instinctive positioning, even if it would only provide a nominal degree of protection against a man who probably weighed more than the car.

As if sensing Hale's consideration, the fat man dipped a ballooned hand into his coat pocket. It emerged swaddling the handle of a Colt Anaconda pistol. The hand stayed at his hip, but the wrist swivelled through a ninety-degree vertical arc, so the barrel found Hale's chest. Hale looked at it. He looked at the street. There was nobody about. He was still in the semi-industrial part of town. Trade services closed up at five in the afternoon. There'd been nobody around for the last six hours.

'Turn your lights off,' the young guy said again. 'Or the first shot will be through your kneecap.'

Hale watched the gun. Anacondas are manufactured with either a four-, six-, or eight-inch barrel. The item in question ran to eight. Only six-round capacity, but the cylinder is chambered to accommodate the .44 magnum cartridge. With 300-grain ammunition, the muzzle velocity can clear four hundred metres a second, which is enough to outstrip an up-to-speed commercial passenger jet by a margin of about five hundred kilometres an hour. In street terms, it meant a hole you could comfortably pass an arm though. Or a knee injury even the best surgeons would consider irreparable. Which in present terms corresponded to a prompt decision on Hale's behalf to kill his headlights.

The forecourt went dark. In the time that lapsed until his night vision built, all he had was the image of the streetlight-lit road receding into soulless sulphur yellow. He moved sideways and kneed his door closed. The dreadlocks guy appeared out of the gloom and gripped his shoulder. He turned Hale and pushed him against the side of the Escort and frisked him quickly. Satisfied, he grasped a fistful of Hale's shirt and propelled him back towards the open passenger door of the Explorer. He was pushed inside to the far door. A second later the obese guy, preceded by the raised gun, squirmed his way onto the adjacent seat. His body pressed against the bunched coat, in the way a sack of garbage bulges when coaxed into a can too small to contain it. There was a pause and then the second man came around the rear of the SUV. He climbed into the driver's seat, started the engine, backed away from the Escort and drove calmly onto the street.

A measured conclusion to an outwardly civil piece of business.

■ TWELVE

It was nudging eleven by the time I made it back over the bridge to the city. Light traffic, and a periodic commentary of nocturnal drama courtesy of the radio scanner. I had the Carson file on the passenger seat beside me. I needed Nurofen and bed, but the presence of the file made work a compelling alternative.

I caught the red light at Fanshawe Street and used the pause to file-rummage for Carson's whereabouts. With his house presently unliveable, his contact address was listed as his lawyer's: Mike Lindley, QC. It was a Parnell property, more or less on the ride home. I figured I may as well stop by.

Parnell is an up-market suburb comprised of older housing holding out against a growing population of more modern designs. Mike Lindley, QC's home was in the latter category. It was a single-storey, timber-clad structure crowned with a roof of dark tile, located on an exclusive stretch of Crescent Road, about ten minutes up the hill from Quay Street. My watch was showing eleven-fifteen when I parked the Commodore on the road beside his driveway. The property was protected from the curious by a brick wall and iron gate, currently closed.

I got out of the car. The air smelled of cold ocean; I knew this side of the street dipped towards the harbour. There was an intercom mic mounted on a pillar at the right-hand side of the gate. I stepped up to it and pressed 'talk'.

'Is Mr Carson in?' I asked.

'Who is it?'

It was a woman's voice. Maybe Mrs Mike Lindley, QC. The response was more or less instant. Maybe my arrival had tripped some sort of sensor. Or maybe the media had been proving especially troublesome and the occupants of the house had taken to perpetual window-watching.

'My name's Detective Sergeant Sean Devereaux,' I said.

'It's eleven o'clock.'

'I know. I was hoping Mr Carson was still up.'

'If you want an interview you'll have to wait until tomorrow.'

'Could you just tell him I'd like to speak to him?'

'It's late.'

'Tell him I don't think he's a murderer.'

That made her pause. I stood there in the cold while she thought about it. I could hear the chirp of the scanner in the quiet. 'Have you got a number I can call to confirm who you are?'

I gave her the landline for the desk at the station. She clicked off, presumably to dial. It was probably a well-rehearsed routine. Defence barristers get visits from all kinds of characters worth checking up on. At length she came back on and told me to come straight down to the house. A motor started up and the gates separated fractionally, granting admission. I slipped inside. The property was beautiful. Streetlights revealed a trim, emerald lawn, and a neat arc of concrete driveway stretched through to a double garage to the left of the house.

The front door was bordered by a strip of frosted glass across the top and down both sides. I rang the bell and the door was opened a moment later by a tall man in a grey suit. He was late forties. His hair was short and boxed neatly around his ears. It was the same colour as his suit, which was high-end, but crinkled as if he'd been in it since five a.m. He was in shape and radiated sunbed tan. His expression said I didn't meet his expectations.

'You want an interview with Mr Carson,' he said, 'you ring and arrange a time.'

'Sorry,' I said. 'I was on the way home. I wanted to talk to him.'

'This isn't like visiting the fruit shop,' he said. 'You can't just stop by.'

'I figured he'd like to know I don't think he killed his wife and daughter.'

His expression softened by a few degrees of eyebrow rotation.

'Are you working the case?' he asked.

'Sort of.'

'What does that mean?'

'It means I'm reviewing things for the purpose of generating a second investigative opinion.'

He put his hands in his pockets and rolled a tongue behind sealed lips. 'Let's see some ID.'

I showed him my laminated photo ID and my silver

118

detective's crest. Difficult to pull off simultaneously, but I'm quite a skilful person.

'You can have ten minutes,' he said. 'I'll listen in. You try anything funny and you're out, understand?'

'OK.'

I went in. He closed the door. I followed him through a short corridor into a living room full of bookshelves and red leather. Thick, bound documents draped over a sofa arm. He led me through the kitchen, out a set of glass doors to a deck at the rear of the house. The property sloped gently down to a belt of trees that marked the top of the cliff leading down to the harbour. I could see a faint glow of streetlights filtering up from the reclaimed land that carried Tamaki Drive around the coastline.

Ian Carson was standing with his back to us beside a turquoise lap pool, gazing out into the emptiness. He turned when he heard our feet on the boards. His mouth was ajar, a cigarette sloping off the corner of his lip.

'What's his name, Mike?' as if I wasn't there.

The man I assumed was Mike Lindley said, 'Sean Devereaux.'

Carson's eyes panned as he drew on his cigarette, as if he was trying to place the name.

'You want me to stay?' Lindley asked.

Carson hesitated. Dimples in the surface of the pool put ripples across his face. 'Cheers, Mike.'

Lindley looked at me a moment then turned and took up post beside the door, ready to interject if legally pertinent. I stepped off the deck and walked towards the pool. It was framed by a thick margin of concrete. Carson was standing at the near end, his cigarette almost at the filter. A regular-looking guy, he was wearing boat shoes, blue jeans and a striped polo shirt. His hair was sandy and widow-peaked; he had a paunch and a slight flush. The epitome of the outwardly unremarkable.

The light outside was dim. The glass doors to the kitchen provided the only illumination. Even so, he claimed to recognize me. He poked the cigarette in my direction and said, 'I've seen your face before, maybe on TV or something.'

No formality. I raised the casualness bar even further and just shrugged in response.

He indicated my left ear with his cigarette. The lobe had been missing a year now. 'Birth defect or meat cleaver?' he asked.

'Twenty-two calibre hard-nose.'

He inhaled the last puff off his cigarette and tossed

the dead butt on the grass. 'I bet that makes a good story.'

'Not really. A little boy had been kidnapped. Two other people were shot.'

The response didn't deter him. 'I guess that's when I saw you on the telly.'

'Yeah, probably. It's pretty cold out here. Maybe we could talk inside.'

He ignored the suggestion. 'You want a cigarette?'

'No thanks. I'm trying to quit.'

He laughed. It was the false, bare-bones tone of a man who didn't have a wife or daughter any more. 'You got the shakes?' he asked. 'Or the headaches? Or the desperate, desperate want just to hold one in your fingers?'

'No,' I lied.

He considered my face and then he considered the pool for a little longer. He looked towards the edge of the property, where the trees swayed as if in some drugged stupor.

'Why are you here at eleven at night?' he asked.

'Because I wanted to meet you.'

'You said you don't think I'm a murderer.'

'I'm actually still on the fence on that one.'

He put his hands in his pockets. Maybe the cold had finally hit him. He looked at the pool. 'I didn't kill anyone,' he said. It wasn't a very impassioned claim of innocence. 'And you could have just called.'

'Maybe. I wanted to tell you in person that you're going to end up in prison unless you can explain what you were doing the night your wife and daughter were killed.'

He didn't answer for a moment. He spoke at length and chose his words carefully. 'What evidence is there to suggest that I *didn't* do it?'

'Not a lot, other than the fact I think you're probably smart enough to have produced something a little more authentic.'

He didn't answer for a beat. 'Would your supervisor be happy if they knew you were here?'

'I don't expect so. But all I'm doing is telling you to come up with an alibi.'

'You've told me you don't think I did it. You've lost your impartiality.'

'Nobody has impartiality. Everyone has an opinion. And I've reached a professional judgement based on objective analysis.'

He went quiet.

'I'm not driving this case,' I said. 'I don't have big involvement. But if you want to avoid prison time, you need to explain where you were the night it happened.

Stargazing won't help your case.'

'I'm not stargazing. I'm considering things.' He gave a slight smile. 'Wondering why God's abandoned me, and all that carry on.'

I looked at him and said nothing.

'Not a believer?' he asked.

'No. I don't believe in God. Or the Easter Bunny, or the Tooth Fairy.'

'A lot of people attempt to denigrate religion by comparing it with childhood hokum. I think it's a sign of insecurity and lack of understanding, because a lot of the time they can't explain why they don't believe in something all-powerful.'

'Your cherished deity can't be all-powerful on the one hand but at the same time lord of a world characterized by violence.'

'Violence is the result of man's shortcomings, not God's. He awarded us choice.'

'OK. What about famine, disease and burnt toast?'

'You can't question God's reasoning.'

'I guess not. But I think the main thing that prevents my acceptance of religion is the fact that a supposedly loving God could be OK with the prospect of his subjects being condemned to eternal hell.'

Ian Carson shrugged again. 'Bertrand Russell posed that argument,' he said. 'Have you got anything original?'

I didn't answer. He stargazed. 'A supposedly infinite universe,' he said. 'Infinite possibilities, and I ended up here, in these circumstances.'

He glanced at me, looking for a reaction. I shrugged back at him. 'I don't believe in infinity,' I said.

He half turned and started a slow clockwise loop around the pool. 'I haven't heard that one before,' he said. 'I'd better hear it, give me food for thought while I'm out here pondering things.'

'Infinity only exists in an abstract sense. Numbers are infinite, but you can't find a physical example. Time can't be infinite, or else we wouldn't have got here yet, because we would have an infinite past. And space can't be truly infinite, because that would require an infinitely long time to create it.'

He completed the loop before replying, a small frown on his face as if he was considering the philosophical merit of my statement. 'Maybe you're on to something,' he said. 'Or maybe you've only got a feeble grasp of physics. Are you familiar with Zeno's paradox?'

'No,' I said.

He shrugged. 'Doesn't matter. I've come up with a

sort of temporal analogy for it. Consider this: you and I are talking to each other. I'm sure you would concur that at some point in time our conversation was half complete. Again, if you continue that line of reasoning, at some stage it was a quarter complete, and before that an eighth, and before that a sixteenth, and a thirty-second, and a sixty-fourth and so on. So my question is, if you can keep dividing a stretch of time into smaller and smaller segments to an indefinite extent, surely the implication of that is in order for our conversation to be over, it must have spanned an infinite number of infinitesimal segments of time. Yet despite covering an infinite quantity, it will still end.'

'Wow,' I said. 'Deep.'

'Yeah,' he answered. 'That's the sort of drivel, the sort of shit I think up while I'm waiting for you to find who killed my family. That's the only thing I can think about.'

I stepped off the path. The grass crunched faintly. 'You need to explain your whereabouts,' I said. 'Otherwise you'll go down for it. Two murders, you'll have a minimum seventeen years of quality, undisturbed thinking time.'

'I didn't do it,' he said.

'Someone did. So if it wasn't you, who hates your wife enough to want to shoot her?'

No reply.

'We need something to work with,' I said. 'Who have you pissed off so much they'd do something like this?'

He didn't answer. I walked back to the deck and Lindley opened the door for me and I moved into the house.

■ THIRTEEN

They headed north, retracing Hale's route in. Nobody spoke.

The driver watched the road.

Hale watched the rear-view mirror.

The big guy watched Hale.

The windows were tinted, and no effort was made to keep the gun below sill level.

They turned back onto the motorway and headed east. Traffic had dwindled. An occasional white beacon tracked past in the opposite direction, but the city-bound lanes were mainly vacant. The big car nudged the one-twenty mark. Hale faced forward, hands on knees. He felt kennelled. It was the windows — the tint job had turned the glass near-opaque. They reflected the SUV's interior funhouse-mirror style, accentuating colour gradients:

deep black ravines where his fingers bit the material of his trousers. The gun kept him cooperative. Never had he heard the phrases 'Colt Anaconda' and 'minor flesh wound' occur in conjunction.

He window-watched and tried to stay calm. The inner-city office block panorama grew more refined. Swathes of light clustered to form a lumpy blanket of yellow beneath the spire of the Sky Tower.

The Explorer turned onto SH1 at Spaghetti Junction and accelerated south. The driver's dreadlocks held the headrest in loose embrace, swinging left and right as he turned his head to check side mirrors. He was worried about picking up a tail. The change of mind about the pick-up location was a neat precaution. Switching him from the liquor store to the gas station would have undermined any efforts he had made to position a back-up team. So the gun and the expensive car weren't purely show items. There was some degree of know-how underlying it all. He looked at the pistol again. The muzzle looked back, patient and comfortable in its podgy surrounds.

They exited the motorway at Gillies Ave and worked south to SH 20. 'Airport', the signage announced help-fully. Maybe they were going to fly him out of the country. They stayed on SH20 for another few minutes, then turned right onto SH20A, skirting the northern edge of Auckland International Airport. Another layer of precaution. The mirror-checking ensured they were without ground-level company; a short deviation into regulated commercial airspace eliminated the possibility of helicopter pursuit. Arguably overkill at this hour, but Hale guessed in the area of work his two companions were engaged, no safety measure was superfluous.

The dreadlock driver made a left onto Puhinui Road and accelerated the big car eastwards, streetlights irregular against that anthracitic dark. The roadside architecture looked bleak and, at times, uninhabited, like some rural outpost depopulated by monetary drought. He saw tiny trailer-home-like buildings on fenceless and naked sections. Doors and windows buttressed with plywood, as if whoever lived within did so as a prisoner.

They turned back north for a stretch then made a right onto Flat Bush Road. State house territory. Patch gangs and the breadline were within cooee. The Explorer stuck out like wings on a horse. The driver backed off on the pedal and the big car slowed as it approached a group of vehicles occupying the right-hand side of the street up ahead. They were a pick 'n' mix of shit-outs. There was a massive boat-like sedan pitted with rust, which he picked as a '58 Oldsmobile, crookedly straddling the footpath. Beside it a tray-back Holden ute, parked on the grass verge. Further on, a white-painted Pajero SUV, its bodywork scalloped by grazed divots, surrounded by a handful of other vehicles, all in varying degrees of misalignment. The congregation had formed in front of a long single-level home, positioned perpendicular to the road. Two-metre-high construction fencing fronted it. There were maybe thirty or forty people crowding the front yard. He saw beer bottles clutched in fists. Splayed legs doddery with alcohol, toddling beneath gently swaying torsos.

The Explorer bumped up onto the kerb and parked beside the ute. The young guy got out and navigated his way through the frond-like swaying of the drunken, and unlatched a gate in the fence. He stepped back to the SUV and opened Hale's door, gripped his shoulder and tugged him outside onto the grass verge. The car rolled and squeaked on its suspension as the fat guy squirmed his way outside. The air stank of alcohol and cigarette smoke. The massive tubular forms of high-voltage supply lines striated the view above, bowing between steel support towers, faint amidst their ink-spill surrounds. A stereo pulsed from inside, breaking the ramble of a crowd made loud and uninhibited by liquor consumption.

He saw movement through the front window of the house. Two guys emerged from a side door and dodged through the festiveness and made their way over. One was a Maori guy in his fifties, short, with a heavy frame as solid as packed clay. A grey moustache dripped thinly from the corners of his mouth to a trim beard. The other was in his thirties, closer to Hale's age. He was shirtless and wicker-thin. His chest was concave, ribcage stark beneath skin stretched so taut it could have been a rubber membrane. Scabs ridged his narrow shoulders and scar tissue matted his inner forearms, which were coiled by kinked blue nests of veins almost as thick as the limbs that supported them.

The skinny guy grabbed him. He didn't resist. The Colt was still in the picture. He heard an exchange of dialogue over his shoulder, skinny guy to dreadlocks:

'OK?'

'Yeah, man. 'S'all good.'

He heard the fat guy panting in pursuit. The Colt was in full view, but it didn't merit anything more than an extended glance. This was nothing out of the ordinary. Gunpoint antics were a common event. They led him around the far side of the house to another door. The back of the section was a dump. Grass reached waist-high. The rear fence was timber, the panelling slouching off its rotted frame. A clothesline lay toppled and cancerous with rust.

The skinny guy darted in front of him, pulled the door open and pushed him inside. A single naked bulb hung from the ceiling, illuminating a small, trash-heap kitchen where a buzzing mass of flies made flitting zigzags. The air carried the putrid organic stink of rotting food. A circular dining table in the centre of the room was piled high with greased plastic plates and empty food tins, insides still slickly sauced by their former contents. The floor was gritty lino, dog-eared at the edges, strewn with more used plates. A stove against the far wall was heaped with pots and iron trays. Shelves above it holding aerosol cans of fly spray, oven cleaner, packaged painkillers and maybe a dozen boxed-up light bulbs. Products for meth-making. Or, in the case of the light bulbs, products for meth-consuming.

The skinny guy entered behind Hale and crossed the room, disappearing through an open door beside the stove. The fat guy laboured inside a moment later and brought the gun up. He was breathing hard, chest lifting the front of that great marquee of a shirt. His breath was pungent and warmed the room sourly after only a couple of cavernous exhalations.

'Stand still,' he said.

It was the first time Hale had heard him speak. The voice surprised him. He was taken aback by its normality: a grossly disproportionate body suggested a voice equally bizarre.

Hale did as directed. The fat guy kept the Colt raised, frame tilted sideways as per the rap-video-approved norm. He closed the outside door and backed through to the adjacent room, floorboards flexing and squealing, barrel maintaining its alignment with Hale's chest cavity.

He could hear an exchange of voices. A debate, maybe. Or instructions followed by request for clarification. The second tone seemed more deferential. Regardless, it wasn't good. Escape was prevented by a number of factors. The gun, primarily. The door behind him. The wire fence. The fact he didn't have a vehicle. The crowd was fifty-fifty. Certainly, nobody was going to actively aid his escape. It was simply a question of who could be counted on to re-apprehend him. He could feel sweat beading out of his hairline, snail-trailing his forehead to the shelf of his eyebrows. He swiped it clear.

The gun was still on him. The fat guy's missile head was turned, listening to whatever was being said. Hale took a step forward. The fat guy didn't notice. Hale took another step forward. He was level with the heaped dining table. The door leading outside was directly behind him. The door to the adjacent room was directly ahead. The gun barrel floated chest-high, muzzle ring a black peephole to purgatory. The stove was just to the right of the doorframe.

He took another step forward. The missile head swivelled on its immense base.

'I told you to fuckin' stand still.'

The water balloon fingers readjusted their grip and the guy's thumb levered the hammer to full cock. It sounded menacing. A heavy metallic grind. It yielded a practical benefit by allowing the first shot to be discharged quicker by halving the firing pin's travel. Faced with that sort of ballistic potential, a quarter second doesn't tend to make much of a difference. But in the event of wavering victim compliance, the sound alone tends to enforce good behaviour. Perhaps not in this case. Hale had reached the conclusion that inactivity now could lead to a painful, fatal injury at a later stage. The stove's wall switch was on. There was a cast-iron skillet on the front right element. Everything else was obscured beneath the teetering mountain of pots.

Missile head swivelled back to the conversation. Hale reached up and removed a can of fly spray from the shelf above the stove and set it on the skillet, in about the time it takes to turn your head.

The fat man didn't notice.

Hale reached out and twisted the far-right dial clockwise by one notch, and set the element beneath the skillet holding the pressurized can of aerosol fly spray to 'low'.

Missile head turned Hale's way and used the gun barrel to beckon him into the adjoining room.

The skinny guy had been lingering just beyond the doorframe. He grabbed Hale by the upper arm as he stepped through the door. He shoved him hard to the right, then sat him down on the far side of an old sofa that was backed up against the adjacent wall. The guy kneeled on the threadbare cushion beside him, emaciated claw fingers maintaining a vice-grip on the rear support, staring at Hale in profile.

There were four other people in the room. Fat man with the Anaconda, standing in the corner to Hale's left. Moustache man had propped himself in the far corner to the right. Dreadlocks and another Maori guy in his mid-forties occupied a second sofa positioned directly opposite, a metre clear of the back wall. To the right, a window veiled thinly by a worn curtain looked out into the front yard. A coffee table was positioned beneath it, adorned with a pyramid of empty beer cans and a glass ashtray swamped with the tan butts of used cigarettes. Flaky tips still dribbling ash, like final exhausted exhalations from their crinkled forms.

Overhead, a bulb hung from centre ceiling, its glass shade shadowing the room with a crisp, horizontal line along each wall. Hale leaned back fractionally. It put the skinny guy in all his resplendent skeletal glory within the bounds of his periphery. The Maori guy on the couch counteracted the movement, and tilted forwards, directly opposite Hale. He wore faded blue jeans, and a red flannel shirt beneath an unzipped leather jacket. His hair was long and reached his shoulders, and his lower face was heavily bearded. His eyes were shielded by a pair of black sunglasses with large, circular lenses offering a glossed and elongated reflection of the situation. His elbows were propped on his thighs, hands hanging loosely between his knees. A lit cigarette smoked patiently in his left hand. Unusual grip: he balanced it across thumb and middle finger, index draped across the top. Decreasing length would make the arrangement increasingly difficult.

'Nice place,' Hale said.

The guy looked around, as if validating the claim. 'Not actually mine,' he said. 'We sort of gate-crashed it so we had somewhere to bring you.'

His tone was low and calm. It seemed to imply an intention to keep things relatively civil. He took a drag off the cigarette and tapped ash on the carpet.

Hale said, 'I want to know where the girl is.'

'What girl?'

'She was snatched on Friday. I saw it happen.'

The guy nodded slowly and drew in ponderously on the cigarette, considering the assertion. Hale's eyes circuited the room. Nobody moved. The guy held the cigarette in his mouth and grinned to expose the full length of the barrel. He propped his elbow on the rest beside him and said, 'We'll be civil about everything. I'm Cedric.' The cigarette softened sibilants: Shivil, and Shedric.

'Who's everyone else?'

A lopsided grin that raised and lowered one sunglass lens. 'It's just you and me talking, Bud. You don't need to know who they are. But I'd quite like to know who you are.'

'I'm nobody,' said Hale.

'You look like a cop. Are you a cop?'

'No.'

'My guys tell me when they picked you up, you didn't have any wallet or anything with you.'

'Is that OK?'

He made a little motion with the cigarette. A lacy grey fume traced its path. 'I find it hard to trust a man with empty pockets.'

Hale said nothing.

Cedric raised himself up off the couch and beckoned for Dreadlocks to do the same, and the pair of them shunted the sofa a fraction closer and sat down again. The fat guy and the moustache man came in from the corners. Claustrophobia heightened. It was the classic non-contact offensive. The net-tightening technique, employed by all facets of nature, from leopard to legal prosecutor. The intimidating approach. It needed an equally significant and psychologically laden response. Hale lifted his right foot off the floor and placed it neatly across his left knee. A fine retaliation. The fluidity suggested a sort of blasé bemusement, although the sweat on his forehead possibly undermined any sense of calm the movement was intended to convey.

The black lenses held his face. The cigarette fume meandered ceiling-bound. 'Two issues,' Cedric said. 'How did you get my number, and why were you calling it at ten o'clock at night?'

Threat containment. If he wasn't a cop, the risk of police involvement had to be mitigated. So: interrogation time. Probably a two-step methodology. Phase one being the relatively friendly elicitation of info, phase two being the forceful gleaning of details. Hale didn't reply. He was hoping the question was rhetorical. The skinny guy on the couch beside him took his hand off the rear support and gripped Hale's upper arm. It wasn't a restraining hold. The guy was just kneading his bicep, massaging it between thumb and fingers, as if he was taking Hale's measure. Or maybe just idling away the time, like some wasted creature devoid of perception, for whom that one movement was the last strange thread to the living.

Hale glanced over at the ever-vigilant barrel of the Anaconda. Fastest trip you'll ever make. Thrust from the quick to the dead in the time it takes to apply finger pressure. And that muzzle. It was like a sneak peek of the abyss.

'Geoffrey gave it up,' Hale said. 'He needed some persuading, though.'

Cedric smiled. It was an expression made genuine by the sudden realization he definitely wasn't dealing with a cop. This wasn't a cop approach. Cops were very much all or nothing. It was either covert surveillance or a rapid, forceful arrest, guns drawn. So this was unofficial. Vigilantism as opposed to undercover ops. He pushed the cigarette between curled lips and took a long, slow drag. Nobody moved. Sweat pooled above Hale's eyebrow and dripped down through his eyelashes, diffracting his vision. His chest was set to marathon. He wondered how long it could sustain it before lapsing into coronary failure.

'You know what that gun can do?' Cedric said. Meaning the Anaconda.

Hale paused. He'd heard that line before. People with guns loved to trot it out. It was a good way of consolidating any pre-evoked dread.

'The shot will be heard all the way down the street,' Hale answered. 'The muzzle flash will keep us squinting for a while.'

Cedric grinned again and used the same unorthodox three-fingered sandwich grip to remove the cigarette from his mouth and place it on the arm of the couch. He stood up and reached around to the small of his back and freed a snub-nosed .38 revolver from the waistband of the jeans. He knelt in front of Hale, reached forward and gripped the back of his head with his left hand, and jammed the muzzle of the gun into the soft flesh beneath his jaw. Hard. It was going to indent a red ring point three-eighths of an inch in diameter. The forceful gleaning of details was under way.

The guy grinned. Hale saw twin reflections of his own face. The breath that reached him was rancid with alcohol and nicotine. Each yellowed tooth in his leering mouth was framed by a strip of slightly darker yellow. 'Yeah,' he said. 'Get clever. I'll give you a couple of rounds out through the top of your head.'

Hale thought about it. Jaw penetration would be inevitable. With low-powered ammunition and a misfire, there was possibility of cranial lodgement without a clean through-and-through. Still, not enviable.

'I'm a bleeder,' Hale said. 'I don't want to get your couch dirty.'

The guy got a fistful of hair and gripped hard. The skin on Hale's face was pulled back taut, like some cosmetic work-over, thug-style. 'You're not going to be this lippy when I cut your tongue out. I want to know the full story. Who the fuck *are* you?'

Nobody moved, except the skinny guy, still at it with Hale's arm. The collective held breath must have been considerable. Dreadlocks was forward in his seat, seemingly keen for a living room homicide. The fat guy and moustache man also looked poised for a shooting. Hale said nothing. He was thinking about physics. More specifically, thermodynamics. The behaviour of vaporized matter can be described with a reasonable degree of accuracy by the ideal gas law, which essentially states that pressure is directly proportional to temperature. The more heat you apply to something, the greater the pressure that something exerts on the vessel constraining it. In other words, heating a gas makes it expand. The aerosol can of fly spray had now been warming for the better part of ten minutes. He pictured the relentless, efficient transfers: the scalding element heating the iron skillet. That in turn increasing the temperature of the thin metal walls of the can and their pressurized, highly volatile contents, increasingly eager for violent, rapid release.

Hale smiled and tried for more candour. He figured he could keep the patter up until the can intervened, hopefully for the better. There was a large margin of uncertainty, though, in that his scientific education had terminated at the end of his sixth-form high school year.

Consequently, the properties of a 750 ml aerosol can, as far as demolition was concerned, weren't especially well quantified. He figured worst-case scenario, the metal surrounds would simply flex and buckle to accommodate the expansion. Best-case scenario, the whole thing would take a section of dry wall with it when it went.

As it happened, the resulting event supplied the necessary effect: there was a bang and a flash and the attention of five people was diverted in flawless unison. Hale's wasn't. His right ankle was still arranged neatly atop his left thigh. It took him about half a second to slip his trouser cuff and free the SOG switchblade, trapped inside his shoe. Human reaction time is bell-curved around a value of about point two of a second. Point two of a second to respond to the explosion, maybe another point two processing possible explanations, another point two to react to Hale's sudden motion. Perhaps point six of a second, all up. By the time the black lenses chopped back from the kitchen door, Hale had a fistful of the back of the guy's head and the blade jammed into the base of his throat.

Nobody moved. The knife-draw froze the moment. Dreadlocks was in a forward tilt on the edge of his seat, the need to investigate the noise conflicting his need to check Hale didn't kill someone. Moustache man and the fat guy seemed similarly afflicted. The skinny guy still had hold of Hale's arm.

Hale moved first. He gripped the back of Cedric's head hard, mimicking the face-lift technique. He placed his still-raised right foot on the floor and forced the other man backward, so that Hale was now leaning forward in his seat. The skinny guy released his grip.

Cedric's gun was still hard beneath Hale's jaw, but the switchblade was tight in against Cedric's neck. Grasped hairdos locked them face to face. Hale waited. The shot didn't come. The knife blade was nudging carotid. A sudden slip could mean a breathless and bloodied two-minute journey to loss of life.

Perhaps three seconds passed. Then decisiveness regained its grip. Moustache man went to the door and ducked his head into the adjoining room.

'It stinks of fly spray,' he noted.

Nobody answered, as if further dialogue could nudge the situation from its teetering equilibrium. The fat guy had the Anaconda up in a two-handed grip. He went to the window above the coffee table and looked out. The outdoor status quo was intact. The fat man turned back to the room. Hale saw his eyes run left and right in hurried assessment. The Colt panned vertically through a short arc and found Hale's head. The fat guy approached. One step and then another.

'Don't come any closer,' Hale said. 'You'll be surprised how fast I can get this thing bone deep.'

The fat guy paused. Cedric was grinning with the strain. Hale's face was blank. The lens reflections helped. They'd signal immediately if the deadpan was wavering. The fat guy took another half step closer. Hale pushed the switchblade forward a fraction. Cedric's skin bowed apart as if it had been unzipped. His jaw bulged and the grin went more grimace-like. Creases appeared on the skin ridging his cheeks below the sunglass lenses. A crimson dribble began an uncertain zigzagged path towards his collar line. He gave a long excruciating hiss and Hale caught more liquor breath.

'Just stay there,' he said. 'Keep the damn gun on him.'

The skinny guy said, 'Drill the bastard.'

'Yeah,' Hale added. 'Drill the bastard.'

Nobody had left the room. They seemed to have picked up on the implicit threat that an early exit would mean an early death for someone else. Hale re-audited the scene. The Colt was still in play. He had an assumed-loaded .38 under his chin. A safe getaway didn't seem imminent. He just watched those lenses. There was nothing in there. They blanketed any hint of whether the guy was closer to blowing his head off or backing down. He gripped Cedric's hair harder. The ears retreated a fraction. He could hear a dull metallic grating sound, which he knew was the first incremental rotation of the .38's barrel, lining up the next round. It was a hell of a sound. Like teeth grinding. Like paranoia itself.

'Do it,' Hale said. 'I'll die without feeling it. You won't.'

Slick banter, but he was terrified. His circulatory system was about ready to call it a night. He watched his reflection, applied facial adjustments to optimize the blank. Cedric did nothing. The solution to his problem was just some extra finger pressure, but he couldn't do it. The knife blade was two or three millimetres into his neck. Hale was leaning forward. If Cedric shot him, another ten millimetres of involuntary knife travel would mean a lacerated carotid artery. High stress situation, stratospheric systolic blood pressure, spraying would probably occur. So he did nothing.

Hale glanced right. The fat guy still had the Colt on him. Two guns still in the picture, but optimism combined with a small measure of similar experience and an innate understanding of gunpoint diplomacy told him things were looking up. Close to a full minute of inaction, and they weren't showing signs of mounting an offensive. They understood the delicacy of the situation. A mistake would be irreparable. So, in the absence of immediate opportunity, all they could do was wait for an opening of lower perceived risk. But in the meantime, Hale was free to capitalize.

His eyes panned clear of the lenses and found the fat guy's face. 'Put it down,' he instructed.

The guy did nothing. His eyes went to the window, flicked back left towards Cedric, seeking instruction before taking action. Cedric said nothing. Outwardly, it appeared he hadn't even heard. He was cable-taut — his neck sinew so prominent the effect resembled kindling wrapped in latex. The grimace was still on display, lips pulled back from teeth meshed so tightly they seemed moments from buckling at the root.

Hale checked his reflection in the lenses and adjusted Mr Nonplussed. Beautiful. Still on even keel.

'Tell him to drop the gun,' he said.

Cedric didn't reply. The .38 was still at Hale's throat, but the creaking sound of the cylinder had stopped. Trigger pressure wasn't increasing. Hale let the knife blade probe a little deeper. Another millimetre. Streams of breath hissed between nozzles of teeth.

'We're in artery territory, now,' Hale said. 'Have you ever tried to plug a garden hose with your fingers?'

'OK, OK, OK. Just chill.'

'I am chilled. Can't you tell?'

'Put the gun down,' Cedric instructed.

The fat guy paused a moment then dropped the gun to his side. He leaned forward awkwardly from the waist and placed the weapon on the floor at his feet.

'There,' Hale said. 'Now I feel a lot better.'

'I can still top you.'

'You won't. Not if you've ever seen a headshot victim. It's not the sort of thing you want to look at this closely.'

Cedric said nothing. Hale turned his head a fraction and looked at the skinny guy, to his left. Torso as brown as soaked wood, pectoral muscles so thin they could have been constructed from laminated newsprint.

'Where's the girl?' Hale said.

Cedric paused. No immediate denial. The knife blade calling on his carotid probably made truthfulness a compelling option. At length he said, 'No idea. I took the call, put the crew together, gave them the details, the rest was their responsibility.'

'You're just the middle man, then?'

'I'm just the middle man.'

'How'd the call come?'

'Why don't you just put the knife down?'

'I'd rather not. How did you get the call?'

'On my phone.'

'Cell or landline?'

'Cell.'

Hale slackened his grip and the release in tension allowed Cedric's ears to extend fractionally.

'Where's your phone?' Hale asked.

'In the kitchen.'

Hale released his grip on Cedric's head. Hair sprung into its natural, unrestricted state. He reached for the gun beneath his jaw and grasped the frame and turned it slowly away from him. Danger of the purest variety. If trigger-pull was still on the cards, now was the hour. But nothing happened. The tension in Cedric's arm lessened to accommodate the motion. The gun came to a halt with the muzzle sighting the vacant space between Hale and the skinny guy on his left.

'Tell the rhinoceros to get it,' Hale said.

The dynamic had flipped. Five on one, but with the guns out of the picture Hale had the high ground.

'Someone get my phone,' Cedric said. His tone hadn't

changed since Hale had entered. It was as if the exchange of authority was merely temporary, soon to be rectified. The opportune moment just had to be found.

The fat guy sidled away from the Colt and plodded awkwardly towards the door, disappearing through to the kitchen. Shadows mapped his movement, huge and bloated on the living room wall. He re-emerged a moment later, a cellphone in his hand extended in Hale's direction.

'Chuck it on the couch beside me.'

The fat guy drew his arm back, lining up the toss. The phone drifted back through a short arc then swung forward and freed itself from the damp, meaty grasp and went airborne. Five pairs of eyes tracked it. It was a peculiar phenomenon. High-stress, clench-jawed negotiation with moderate likelihood of bloodshed — and five guys paused to observe the lazy parabolic tumbling.

Hale struck mid-flight.

Conditions were optimal: the Colt was grounded. The .38 was sighted on dead-air. Everyone was watching the phone. He removed the knife from Cedric's neck, twisted left from the hips and threw the skinny guy a straight right, catching him on the side of the head. He whipped back right and swung the switchblade handle for Cedric's nose.

Tension skewed his aim. He missed nose, got solid forehead contact. Cedric fell backwards, glasses askew, face like an overdose. Hale grabbed his wrist and twisted clockwise and stripped the .38 free of his grip. The room was suddenly a manic flurry of motion. The phone hadn't stopped bouncing. The skinny guy was collapsing back against the seat cushions. Dreadlocks was powering up off the couch. Moustache man was charging in off his corner. The fat guy was attempting an awkward snatch of the Colt, legs splayed in an A-frame, bending forward over that immense girth, stocky fingers as smooth and jointless as luncheon sausage scrabbling for the floor.

Hale got his finger through the .38's trigger guard. He extended it at arm's length and swept the barrel.

Everyone stopped. They watched the gun. It looked eager for a target. The fat guy abandoned his quest for the Colt. He levered himself upright with an effort that blushed him choke-red. Hale was standing. Cedric was kneeling on the floor at his feet. Hale juggled the switchblade on the flat of his left hand, thumbed the blade shut and pocketed it. He bent down and reclaimed a fistful of Cedric's hair and lifted him to his feet. The guy was as heavy as wet sand; it was hard not to twitch and ruin the blank face. Quick appraisal: his circulatory system had survived, but was still running north of normal. No bleeds. No bruises. His face bore a sheen of damp, which undermined Mr Nonplussed, but a perfect scorecard was rare.

He looked down at the skinny guy. The returned look was one of fascination. Mr Nonplussed's performance implied mythic qualities.

Hale said, 'Bring the truck in through the gate and park it next to the house. Engine running, door open.'

'Which truck?'

'The one I came in.'

The guy's eyes swivelled back and forth, listless in an otherwise static body. Dreadlocks dipped a hand in a pocket and removed a heaped bunch of keys. He tossed them in a jangling, flickering arc into the skinny guy's lap. He recoiled at the impact, then stood and left the room. A moment later Hale heard the outside door open and close.

He held the .38 in his right hand and hooked his right elbow around Cedric's neck from behind. He dragged him in a hands-and-feet shuffle across the floor to the Colt, bent and pocketed it, along with the switchblade. Back to the couch, and he claimed the cellphone. Everyone watched, as if he was some rare, live motion exhibit. He guessed this was an as-yet unwitnessed spectacle. No one bettered Cedric.

He heard the squeak of the gate in the fence being pushed back. He heard the labour of the Explorer's engine, the squelched slithering as thin tyres searched for purchase on slick earth. Time: half midnight. The crowd outside was still oblivious. Indoor happenings merited no interest. Hale dragged Cedric in an awkward reverse stagger towards the door, blood droplets marking the move. He still had the .38 aimed at Cedric's carotid. Nobody tried to intervene.

He walked backwards into the kitchen. The air was putrid. The graceful black silhouette of a flame was scorched into the paint above the stove. He heard the big car draw to a stop outside. The driver's door opened but didn't close. The engine tone maintained an easy idle. He made it to the door. The other three siphoned through from the living room one at a time: Dreadlocks, fat guy, moustache man. They followed patiently. At some stage the power balance would flip again, and they'd be on hand to grasp it when it did.

He emerged backwards into the rambling smoky dark. The Explorer's headlamps blazed white into the beyond. The skinny guy rejoined the other three. They closed up in a rank of four and watched him contemplate his entry to the car. He dragged Cedric backwards until he felt his head knock the roof. Now things got tricky. As soon as he let the guy go they could rush him, reclaim the .38.

The engine idled. Hale contemplated. All he had to do was drop backwards and he'd be in the driver's seat. He leaned left a fraction and placed his shoulder against the inside of the open car door.

'Cheers, fellas,' he said. 'You've been helpful.'

Nobody spoke. They were tense with the thrill of dawning opportunity.

Hale said, 'Buzz the window down.'

Cedric paused. Then he scrabbled awkwardly with his left hand, found the necessary switch and lowered the glass into the doorframe with a quiet electric hum.

Hale eyed the fat guy. 'Stay trim,' he said.

Then he grabbed Cedric's head by the hair with his left hand and smashed his face against the top edge of the door. The guy slumped. Hale let him fall. He raised the .38 and extended it one-handed. The four others flinched instinctively, a quick duck, hands shielding heads.

Hale squeezed the trigger, firing above their heads, and put six quick rounds through the side of the house.

The four guys stayed down. Front yard, instant panic.

People scattered like dust under a fan. The six crisp cracks preluded crisp screaming. Hale tossed the spent .38 across onto the passenger seat. He climbed in behind the wheel and pulled the door closed.

The four guys and Cedric stayed down.

He found reverse and cut a fast J-turn right there on the lawn. He selected 'drive' and floored the gas. Tyres scrambled, desperate for traction. He looked left.

The four guys and Cedric stayed down.

He lined the headlamps up on the gap in the fence and fishtailed towards it, party-goers forming streak lines left and right. He made it through the gate and tumbled down off the footpath onto the road. He glanced in his mirror.

The four guys and Cedric stayed down.

■ FOURTEEN

I made it home by midnight. Supper was Panadeine with a Mac's Gold chaser. It worked a treat. I slept until half-past four in the morning, at which point some subtle chemical imbalance pulled me awake and set me down in the dark. Cold, dense, empty even of birdsong.

I wanted a cigarette. I gave in and executed a clumsy bedside table forage. But the me of days past had planned ahead and purged my bedroom tobacco cache. My hands were shaking. It was either nicotine withdrawal or Parkinson's onset. Hopefully, the former, but with no smoke, my only substitute narcotic was crime solving. Homicide investigation trumps nicotine gum.

I showered at five and consumed a breakfast of toast and caffeine, then drove into town. Auckland was still safely asleep. The urban choke was dormant. It made for a quick and stress-free drive.

I cruised along to a desolate Quay Street and turned left up Albert. When I passed the Victoria Street intersection, I pulled a U-turn and stopped at the light. Austere Auckland. Window frost blurred a dark and lonely vista. Traffic lights hung as scattered red smears against the black. To the right, Victoria Street dipped east towards Queen, rising again towards the pebbled arch at the entrance to Albert Park. A bedraggled old guy in a scavenged outfit coaxed a loaded trolley uphill, yellow streetlamps holding back dull surrounds. To the left, a parked taxi marked the scene where someone had fired a shotgun round through the window of a bus and killed the driver.

Video footage had shown a Mercedes sedan heading north through the Albert/Victoria Street intersection after the shooting. Broadly speaking, escape-by-vehicle meets one of two categories. Category one, the getaway car is abandoned as soon as possible. Category two, it isn't, and the detective has work to do.

I didn't know where my bus shooting fell. Surveillance suggested the shot had been fired from the Mercedes, targeting a Nissan in the adjacent lane. Following the shooting, the Mercedes had continued north through the lights, the Nissan had pulled a U-turn and disappeared in the opposite direction. In terms of the Mercedes' escape, that scenario suggested category two. Category one was ruled out: the local area had been searched and the Mercedes was yet to be found, and good car drop-off points need good initial planning. My shooting seemed to be the product of a two-car, Merc–Nissan chase, and as far as chases go, you can't plan at all. You follow the other car and see where it takes you. Certainly, there's no guarantee you're going to end up in an inner city environment, on Albert Street, at the corner of Victoria Street West. You follow the other vehicle and, when an opportunity emerges, you take it.

Then you consider the getaway.

But it's a heat of the moment, on-the-fly-decision thing. You're in a setting you haven't envisaged, so evacuation is governed by chance, instantaneous decision and subconscious logic. You don't have a safe, pre-established location to dump a car, so the chance of said car being immediately abandoned becomes small. The chance of a mild, indecisive panic, with the underlying objective of generating as much distance as possible, becomes increasingly likely.

The light went green. I crawled downhill. I didn't

believe the Mercedes had headed north for long. Driving north on Albert Street at rush hour on a Friday will get you nowhere very quickly. If you're patient, eventually you'll make it down to Customs Street, then a stop-start trip along Fanshawe through half a dozen sets of lights to the Northern Motorway. Far from ideal if you're in need of a rapid exit. The most promising option is to turn as quickly as possible and follow Hobson back uptown to the Southern Motorway.

I rolled on. The district court approached on the left, the City Centre parking building slid by on the right. Drop-off point? Probably not. Too close to the Victoria Street intersection to make it likely. I stopped at the red light at Wyndham. Albert Street's a mix of design. At the Wellesley Street end it's got the Crowne Plaza Hotel, and Quay West down towards Customs Street. The stretch between is an indiscriminate mix of high-rise, mingled with some older two- and three-storey places that have fallen into disrepair, ground-floor walls gummed with paste-on advertisements peeling like leper skin. The light stayed red. The APN building was on the opposite side of the road. Surely some journo would have had the sense to point a camera out the window shortly after hearing a gunshot?

The light went green. Garish window signage announced souvenir shop tenancy. I went left. It made sense if exiting the CBD was priority one. Turning right wasn't an option. Auckland CBD is a bigot when it comes to right turns. And straight ahead on Albert Street would eventually land you in a static choke point at the eastern end of Fanshawe. Not good. So, left, on Wyndham. I cruised downhill, and made another left at the light onto Hobson, headlight reflections flashing me as I turned. Signage forbade me making a right, which had probably put the parking garage diagonally across the intersection out of the picture for my misdemeanant Merc man.

I accelerated south. Hobson Street's bland: all high-rise office space and medium high-rise living. The Department of Corrections uses some of it. Violent offenders typically need somewhere cheap that's near their parole officer and distant from any schools. As a result, Hobson has seen its fair share of criminals. I kept it very slow. I pretended I'd just blown an innocent man's lower jaw off with a twelve-gauge. Was I worried? Probably not. Paramedics had taken five minutes to show. Police hadn't put in an appearance until slightly after, so I probably couldn't hear sirens yet. Motorway onramps were close by. The prospect of closing down city blocks

160

was still a good half an hour down the to-do list. So I was probably riding an adrenaline high, a little breathless, but still managing to think things through. I was trying to be rational, trying to decide on the best rush-hour exit route. The southern end of Hobson gave me three options. I could turn left up Pitt Street to K Road, I could stay in my current lane and head south on SH1, or I could jump across two lanes and get on the North-Western Motorway.

I stopped in the empty intersection and weighed options. Headlight glow spilled wide. Heading south was the easiest solution. It required no awkward switches across choked lanes. But realistically, the car could have gone anywhere. A big, big gamble.

I headed straight and hit the SH1 onramp.

Sunday, six o'clock in the morning. Motorways are rarely more vacant. I kept to a conservative eighty. It allowed time for sightseeing, so I turned the stereo on again. Maybe I was wasting my time. A statistician would tell me I was more likely to win first division Lotto two weeks in a row than stumble upon an abandoned car. A logician would tell me careful, structured reasoning might get me somewhere.

I went with the logician.

My southbound escape theory was patchy, though.

Motorways at rush hour serve as the bountiful hunting grounds of Highway Patrol cops looking to boost their ticket quota. Consequently, if an alert message was circulated, the risk of being spotted by a traffic officer would be moderate to high. Cops don't tend to match the paunchy, dim-witted typecast posed by TV — for the most part they're alert and competent as far as spotting homicide suspects is concerned. And if my Mercedes driver was of the same opinion, he might have felt inclined to exit fairly quickly. I hoped he hadn't turned off at Gillies Ave, or Market Road, or Green Lane East. Gillies and Market were unlikely, but Greenlane was an option. I slowed and pulled left when I reached the exit, looped clockwise around the ramp and headed west. There's a big shopping complex sprawled out just east of Great South Road. Among other things, there's fast food and a supermarket. Fast-food outlets and supermarkets generate traffic. Traffic creates a sense of anonymity, and possible appeal for someone wishing to discreetly rid themselves of a vehicle. I cruised the parking lot. At quarter past six in the morning, it was completely empty. Just a perfect expanse of smooth asphalt dotted with lampposts, naked and useless for the next few hours. I got back on the motorway.

Southbound SH1 runs light as far as good ditching spots are concerned. Within greater Auckland it's channelled by stout concrete barriers, with secluded grassy rest stops few and far between. Consequently, I was never going to find a vehicle on the motorway itself. I had to check exits. Common sense told me I wasn't going to find anything at all, but cruising quelled nicotine craving.

I started at the Tecoma Street exit, and quartered empty, unremarkable residential streets. No Merc. I paralleled the motorway south and linked with the Ellerslie–Panmure Highway next to the Ellerslie Domain. I got back on SH1 and headed down through the industrial area north of Penrose. I put Robbie Robertson in the CD player, cycled it to 'American Roulette' and wound the stereo to within an inch of its life. It was worth it for Robbie.

I got off at the South-Eastern Highway and trawled more empty streets. I did the same at Mount Wellington, and Frank Grey Place. Not a brief process. It was nine o'clock by the time I drove back north and exited at Khyber Pass Road. I turned south and got off again at Gillies, hopped across to SH20 and took a trip down to the airport. I trundled packed parking lot aisles and peeped long term sections. Sensibility and rationale insisted patiently that I would find nothing. They weren't wrong. Airport checks are a massive job. I gave up, headed north and drove out along Redoubt Road and found suburbia and then some lifestyle blocks. Nothing pursuant to an active homicide.

Eleven-thirty in the morning. Five hours frittered needlessly. I wound my way back to SH1 and went north. Traffic had resumed its normal arterial pulsing. It was reassuringly typical. Nobody cared, end of story. Maybe that shouldn't be a comfort.

Eleven-forty. My phone rang. It was a police dispatch operator.

'We've found that car you were after,' the guy said.

Timing doesn't get much better.

'Which one?' I asked.

'The vehicle wanted for that shooting on Friday. Patrol unit picked it up just now.'

Three cars ahead, a courier van switched lanes and snarled traffic flow. Brake lights filled my view. I slowed and jolted against my belt.

'Where is it?' I said.

'Highbrook Drive. It's definitely the one you're after. They tried to hide it.'

I trapped the phone with my shoulder and fumbled my

glove box map. Highbrook Drive was just off the motorway, south of Otahuhu. I reviewed progress: Tecoma, Ellerslie, Penrose, Mount Wellington, all checked. Highbrook was essentially the next best southbound option. It looked semi-rural, therefore it had probably been dead at six or seven p.m. on a Friday. It was about twenty kilometres south of town. Maybe a thirty- or forty-minute drive at six on a Friday. A feasible drop-off point for my Merc man.

The operator was still talking. I'd zoned out and asked him to repeat himself. He gave me directions, said there was a patrol car marking the location. I couldn't miss it.

Getting there took close to thirty minutes. Highbrook Drive traces the southern edge of a shallow inlet from the Hauraki Gulf. I exited left off the motorway then swung east on an overpass and made another left onto Highbrook. To the south, power pylons convened in a ragged cluster around a fenced-off electricity substation. To the northeast, trees formed a barrier between the road and the inlet. Traffic was very light, the road two lanes each way, separated by a narrow grass median.

It was after midday. Overhead was a hemisphere of light grey. I followed the road all the way around to a bridge spanning a crooked subsidiary inlet. There was a patrol car parked on the edge of the road, two silhouettes

165

side by side up front. Twin curves of black rubber marred the road behind, evidence of an anxious screech-skid. The driver's window was down, a forearm propped along the top of the door, a hand hanging limp at its end.

I parked on the skid marks, got out of the car and circled the hood, looking down towards the foreshore. There was a car parked amongst the trees. Not a Mercedes. It was a Nissan sedan, empty, nose-in to the foliage.

■ FIFTEEN

Hale drove the Explorer north and then west. He dumped it, keys in, windows down, stereo on, midway along Bruce McLaren Road. Then he walked back along to the petrol station and reclaimed the Escort.

The second point on his to-do list was the purchase of a two-way radio unit. He found one in a second-hand store on Lincoln Road, then set out to find himself another motel.

The car was grey. It looked like a '92 Nissan Skyline and its rear plate was missing.

The officers in the patrol car had print-outs from the Albert/Victoria intersection footage, which confirmed make, vintage and criminal history of the vehicle at the bottom of the hill. They had responded to a call about forty-five minutes ago from a man who had seen the Skyline when he pulled off the road to take a leak.

There was a wire fence paralleling the road. I went along to where it ended just before the bridge and walked down the slope towards the car. As far as concealment went, the job lacked effort. The rear section south of the passenger seat was jutting out clear of the tree line. Your classic ditch-and-dash.

I pushed branches back and worked my way down the right-hand side. They'd tried to burn it, dousing the front seat with accelerant. The heat had blistered the paint on the roof and driver's door and busted the window. There was no further damage, though — the fire had inexplicably lost interest. I walked back up the hill and collected gloves from the boot of the car. I called Comms on my cell and requested a Scene of Crimes unit and a tow truck. Cell calls to Comms are always safer than radio. Journalists with frequency scanners can mean a premature press release.

I relocked the car and went back to the Nissan. I sidled in down the left and checked out the passenger side. It was defect free. The glass on the road on Albert Street had suggested a broken passenger window, but everything was intact. The car had been locked after the fire was started, which seemed illogical. I went back around to the driver's side and reached in through the vacant windowpane. I opened the door, then leaned down and popped the boot lever. Nothing exciting back there: a spare tyre, stripped panelling and exposed copper leads. Maybe a new sound system project that hadn't quite got under way.

I moved back to the front and leaned in. I couldn't touch the seats for fear of disturbing potential forensic material. I didn't want to open the glove box without an initial print-check. Nothing immediately useful on the floor, just plastic bags, receipt stubs and used coffee cups. I checked the windscreen. The registration card had been removed from the plastic sleeve. Car Abandonment Rule One: strip the plates and the rego sticker. I probed beneath the wheel for the bonnet lever, released the bonnet and found the chassis number after a thirty-second search of the motor bay.

I returned everything to the way I'd found it, walked back up the hill, and called Comms again. The car was registered to one Joseph Michael Te Awa, D.O.B. March 1993. They gave me his home address. I went back to the car and checked maps. Said address was only a short trip west, just across the motorway overpass.

I walked along to the marked patrol car and asked them to wait until Scene of Crimes arrived, then I got back into the Commodore, pulled a U-turn and headed for the motorway.

The address was five minutes away, down the end of a narrow unloved cul-de-sac, just west of the motorway. The housing had passed its prime. It was all single-level, weatherboard construction. My target house was white with lime green skirting and a limp little fence made out of slumped chicken wire. I drifted past and trundled along to the cul-de-sac, turned around and parked on the opposite side of the street.

It felt cluttered. The narrow road was boxed in by cars straddling the kerb. More vehicles in varying states of completeness in skewed pairs in front yards. I got out. The street was quiet. A few places down, a shirtless guy in his sixties thrashed a machete against weeds at the base of his veranda. I locked the car and crossed the street to my target house.

It was set apart from its neighbours by the presence of a television satellite hanging from its front eave. I followed a cracked concrete path to a door midway down the right-hand side and knocked. Nobody answered. I walked around the back. The set-up was dismal. The lawn grew wilder the closer it got to the back fence. A rusted open-top iron drum sat creased and buckled on one side, like a kick in the gut.

I walked back along the left-hand side and came around to the front. Windows were un-curtained, and I didn't see anybody. I knocked on the door a second time. When nobody answered, I picked the lock with a little tool attached to my keyring and let myself in.

Lino greeted me with a creak. I closed the door and stood for a second. The house reassumed its prior silence. I nosied. The lino led straight through to a kitchen. Unwashed dishes bathed in the sink. A camping table and chairs served as dining furniture.

I went left and found a living room. The carpet was brown and ran threadbare near the centre of the room. Cushions in the furniture bore foam-deep lacerations and were cupped with sags. The ceiling plaster had slump cracks. Something smelled damp.

There was mail on a coffee table. Bills, addressed to a Mr M.T. Te Awa. Nothing for young Joseph. I drifted through the bedrooms at the rear of the house, but didn't find anyone hiding in a corner. Ditto in the bathroom, where I found a well-stocked medicine cabinet and a damp toothbrush. I went back to the kitchen. The pantry was well stocked. The dishes suggested frequent inhabitancy. Someone was bound to turn up sooner rather than later.

I went back to the car to wait.

Cops are good at waiting. It's a necessity, and a skill honed by surveillance time spent in patient vigilance. I sat and watched. My angle meant the windscreen framed the driveway. I thumb-twiddled. I daydreamed. My mind unearthed some weird stuff: visual memory of Mrs Carson on the morgue slab, coupled with a heartfelt rendition of Nick Cave's 'Let the Bells Ring'.

I waited. I thumb-twiddled some more. Two-thirty approached. Two-thirty went. Machete man wheel-barrowed slashed weeds away. He flicked a wave at an orange hatchback that burbled by. Two forty-five approached, and passed uneventfully. Two-fifty, and a red '94 Corolla turned into the driveway and stopped. A dark guy in his late forties wearing a T-shirt and shorts climbed out and headed for the front door. He had a stiff, shuffling gait, arms and legs chopping in tight unison, upper body leaning forwards under the influence of a straining paunch. Too old to be Joseph. I got out and followed him to his front door. He glanced at me over his shoulder as he keyed the lock.

'I ain't switchin' churches,' he said.

'I'm a police officer,' I replied.

He got the door open. 'Somebody died?' he asked.

He wore a bland, unconcerned expression, as if luck was tilted against him and the answer wouldn't bother him one way or the other.

'Not yet. I'm looking for Joseph.'

He jiggled his keys free and pocketed them. 'Right,' he said. 'Well, better come in then.'

He squeaked in across the lino, crossed the kitchen and made a left and entered the lounge. He made a quick circuit of the room, checked furniture gashes and roof cracks, in case more had appeared in his absence. His jandals snapped crisply against his heels as he moved. He let himself down in an armchair. It buckled and drew him deep.

'I don't know where Joseph is,' he said.

I claimed a couch opposite him. 'Is he your son?'

'You can't just roll in here and start interrogating. I don't even know your name.'

'Sorry.'

He smirked. 'Yeah. Sorry makes it all better.'

173

'My name's Detective Sergeant Sean Devereaux.' I badged him. It merited a flick of eye.

'Are you his father?' I asked.

'Yeah. Why you asking?'

'I'm trying to find him.'

The smirk again. The chair pulled him closer. 'Then you're three weeks late. You're behind the trend line.'

'Excuse me?'

'I haven't seen him in three weeks. I already reported it to you lot. But nobody really gives a shit, 'cause he's turned eighteen. So I don't get why they've just picked up the trail now and sent a twelve-year-old to find him.'

'I'm thirty-three. I didn't know he was missing.'

He waved his hand. 'Yeah, whatever. I don't give a shit. He's AWOL, anyway. What's he done?'

'I don't know if he's done anything. I think he's seen something, though.'

'Like what?'

'The shooting in Auckland City on Friday evening.'

'What shooting?'

'A bus driver was killed. I think Joseph may have witnessed it.'

'Well, shit,' he said.

'Yeah,' I said. 'And you've got no idea where he is?'

'No. I told you. He's bounced. He don't care about us. He's got a mother needing a new kidney and a dad scraping the barrel and he's as good as dead.'

'Any brothers or sisters?' I asked.

'Me or him?'

'Him.'

'Nope. Just Joseph.'

'Is he still at school?'

He smirked and slashed a grin, as if I'd asked if he could take me to the moon in the Corolla. 'He hasn't been in a school so long, he probably forgets what one is.'

'He have any friends?'

'Everyone's got friends.'

'You know any of his?'

'Sort of.'

'If I found a phone book do you think you could point one or two of them out?'

He took his time answering, as if a reply would be a grudging concession. 'I don't know their names. So you're just going to have to do what it says on that badge you've got and detect him.'

He looked across at me without expression. Hooded eyes, like the cusp of an overdose. Window to a mind where the last meagre traces of caring had long since dissolved.

175

'I understand your frustration. But I didn't know he was missing. I didn't know who he was until today. But I need to find him, and I'm sorry if the people you've already asked haven't bothered. But I'm bothering, and I need you to give me a hand and think where he might be.'

The eyes scanned back and forth under the heavy lids. The rest of him lay inert, like an android flicked to standby.

'You think just 'cause you got that silver badge you're a real smooth dude. Up yours. You don't know jack shit. He disappeared three weeks ago. And doing something too late is as good as not doing it at all.'

I said nothing.

He netted his fingers behind his head. 'I hope you're a real hard-arse,' he said. 'They make them tougher than a little fella like you can cope with.'

'We'll see. Do you mind if I look through his room?'

He gave a little shrug and said nothing.

I got up and went through to the kitchen. Lino chirped afresh. The carpet in the corridor was yellow, worn back in patches to grid-mesh underlay. Photos adorned the wall: portraits of a younger and narrower version of the man in the living room, a boy aged about thirteen or fourteen who I assumed must be Joseph. Colours dulled by glass furred with dust.

Joseph's bedroom was at the end, the window framing the feral backyard. His bed hugged the left wall. There was a cheap shelving unit made of fake wood against the right wall with a small red-painted chest of drawers beside it. The floor was strewn with *Guns and Ammo* magazines and bits of clothing, arms and legs creased and pulled inside out before haphazard abandonment. Bedroom search protocol is pretty well standardized. I worked top-down. The ceiling was plaster, which left no opportunity for concealment. I found dust and a CD by Simple Plan on the top of the shelving unit. Boyhood trinkets on the lower levels: a kit-set Spitfire, a used shotgun shell, homemade nunchucks, other assorted nuggets of mischief. An unopened bank letter lay trapped beneath a cellphone battery.

I checked the dresser next. In his bottom drawer I found a small plastic bag containing about ten grams of marijuana, and a little glass bong showing residue of something much harder.

The space beneath the bed proved most promising. A twenty-deep stack of *Playboys* constituted his porn collection and a VHS copy of *Fight Club* was using a *Penthouse* as a tent. Of most interest: bank stuff. Dog-eared account statements in criss-cross repose. I gathered them

177

all up and added them to the *Guns and Ammo* shambles.

I organized. I read. All up it was a thirty-minute odyssey. Under-bed filing systems tend to lack coherency. He'd been receiving bi-monthly payments of between seventy and one hundred dollars from some place called iKonic Ltd for a period of about fourteen months. Your standard eight-hour-per-week high school job, minus the high school. EFTPOS transactions typically took the form of ATM withdrawals, which is the safest way to go when making purchases of a nature best kept unrecorded. I arranged everything chronologically and looked at the most recent statements. There was nothing dated in July, which made sense. If he'd been gone three weeks, the under-bed statement stash couldn't have been added to since then.

I picked up the sealed letter on his shelf. Warrantless envelope opening is a no-no. I bit my lip and trowelled the flap open with my thumb, found another account statement. A $5.20 transaction conducted at a Caltex petrol station was billed against his EFTPOS during the last week of July. Petrol stations mean video surveillance and possible progress.

I returned the room to its original level of disorder and walked back to the living room. Dad was still sitting.

'Thanks.' I told him.

He looked at me. 'If you find him are you going to make him come home?'

He leaned forward as he said it. His eyebrows perked. Maybe some residual hope. Maybe parental worry had wormed a crack in his earlier pretence of uncaring.

'I can't make him do anything,' I said.

He leaned back in his seat, optimism stymied. He touched a knuckle to his lip. He looked away. 'Well, can you just let him know,' he said carefully, 'that his old man misses him, and would like him to come home. Even if it's just for a bit?'

'Of course.'

He fidgeted. 'I just worry that I've spent all this time bringing him up good, and he's gonna get done by some shitbag, and there'll be nothing I can do about it, and I'll never be happy again.'

He spoke slowly. He sounded as if he was acclimatizing for the inevitable. Posing the scenario, auditioning it as a survivable prospect. Testing whether stripping away all familial support would be something he could endure for the next thirty-odd years of barrel-scraping, damp-tinged existence.

I told him I would be in touch, and left.

I went back to the car and trawled phone books. The Caltex in question was on Weymouth Road, Manurewa. More drive time. I put Wilco's A *Ghost is Born* on the stereo. I got back on the motorway and followed a three-deep truck convoy southbound through ten minutes' worth of unremarkable Auckland suburbia.

Weymouth runs west of SH1, just south of the Hill Road exit. The station wasn't a hard find. It occupied a corner site on a stretch that was primarily residential, save for a couple of shops occupying the opposite corner further up the street. There were four pumping bays on a concrete forecourt boxed in on two sides by a service garage and a sales office.

I parked next to the sales office. It wasn't busy. A lone SUV guzzled diesel. A lone SUV owner guzzled Fanta. The door binged as I went in. A bespectacled guy of about sixty was on counter duty. He wore a short-sleeve collared shirt and a tie and had a damp comb-over so severe it could have been machine-ploughed. He looked up as I came in and watched me closely on the approach. Some sort of innate salesman's sense probably told him I didn't want gas.

'What you after?' he asked. He had an Eastern European accent, maybe Russian, possibly Polish.

'Surveillance,' I answered. 'If you've got any.'

He smiled wryly. 'Policeman or pervert?'

'The first option.'

He made a little eyebrow movement that I interpreted to mean *ID, please.* I obliged.

'You don't look like your photo,' he observed.

'Should I be thankful?'

He smiled and pinched his spectacle frames gently to adjust them. 'What date you want?'

I told him. He rolled open a drawer and rummaged. They had a four-camera system, wired through to a DVD recorder. Split-feed display was courtesy of a little fourteen-inch CRT television set up on the counter behind him.

'Our filing's not that flash,' he admitted. 'But it's probably here.'

I joined him behind the counter. The archived footage was on discs held in upright slotted rows in a drawer beneath the register. Bold Vivid marker on the paper-protector denoted the corresponding date. He finger-walked his way back, chin pulled flush to his neckline, peering down over his spectacle rims, and eventually found what he was looking for. He removed the necessary disc, blew on it like a birthday wish, and fed it into the DVD unit.

Progress stalled as SUV man came in to pay for his diesel. He was chatty. He enquired politely as to the origin of the accent. Apparently, it was Latvian. I looked at the cigarette display in the interim. Marlboro, Pall Mall, Dunhill. My dear old friends. Shakes, headaches and desperate desire could be satiated by a mere seventeen dollar purchase. It was proving a difficult separation. My mental stereo backed the tragic imagery with the opening bars of The Doors' 'The End'. It played the remixed version for Coppola's *Apocalypse Now*, with the rotor blades thumping at the beginning.

The door binged. The old guy turned back to his telly. The timestamp started running.

'Stolen car or murder suspect?' he asked.

'Runaway.'

He didn't reply. He cranked it to fast forward. 'Tell me when.'

I watched the screen. Turnover occurred with dizzying frequency. Nine, nine-thirty, ten, ten-thirty, eleven. We cycled in silence. Vehicles streaked the forecourt. Patrons scurried. Eleven-thirty. Eleven forty-five.

'Stop it there.'

He hit pause and cued an on-screen halt.

At pump three, a green four-door Isuzu SUV. And

exiting said SUV: Joseph Te Awa, dressed casual in jeans and a T-shirt. I claimed control of the DVD and advanced it slowly. Te Awa didn't want petrol. He left the car at the pump and headed inside the office, reappearing two and a half minutes later with a pie and a Coke. $5.20. I paused it.

'Can you zoom that?' I asked.

'Which bit?'

'The end of the car. For the number plate.'

He thumbed a control on the player. The picture expanded. He toggled to the camera aimed end-on at the Isuzu's grille and got the licence plate dead centre for me. Pixelated, but far from illegible. I thanked him, committed it to memory, and left.

■ SIXTEEN

I called Comms and queried the plate number. They gave me a Manurewa address, which was good, because it implied a two-minute travel time. It was five before four in the afternoon. I turned the stereo off and checked maps. The plate was registered to one Lee Kyle Mikus, whose address was located on a cul-de-sac south of Weymouth. Virtually walking distance, which meant the two-minute drive turned out to be only a minute thirty. Weymouth was quiet. I passed an Indian couple walking a Doberman the size of a leopard. Further east, some workmen laboured over a busted water main. No other samples of urban living conjured for my benefit.

The house was a light-pink single-storey building on a forty-five degree angle to the street. A narrow deck stretched its full length. The green Isuzu was parked in the front yard, along with a white Hilux ute and a gold Ford Laser. They'd transformed the lawn into myriad overlapping arcs of mud. I slowed and surveyed. Nothing eye-catching to report. The Doberman and its couple traipsed across my rear view. Up ahead a yellow sign signalled the entry to a public walkway commencing at the end of the cul-de-sac.

The Isuzu and Hilux framed the front door. I parked between them and turned the engine off. I got out, stepped onto the deck and knocked on the door.

A dog barked. I heard claws scrabbling against a hard surface, a rapid clacking as it approached the entry. It paused just behind the door and barked a second time. I could hear it panting — huge frenzied gasps like bellows operating on high. A sharp command, and then footsteps approached. The handle squeaked round a fraction and the door rattled back against a security chain. I saw the dog first. It crammed its nose out through the gap and I glimpsed an eye so round and wild it looked as if it was straining to break free of its socket.

'Is Joseph in?' I asked.

The dog strained. Its lips drew back to reveal feral-looking dentistry. It barked and gave frenzied head-shakes, as if recoiling from a sting. The gap tightened about ten millimetres. 'No. Who's asking?'

'A police officer.'

The dog was a bullmastiff. Its head came almost waist high. It probably weighed upwards of sixty kilos. Breeders will tell you they're lovely animals, by virtue of fierce owner loyalty. The downside of this trait is they don't take kindly to strangers. Potentially problematic when the animal in question weighs almost as much as you do and has bigger teeth. The door closed another ten millimetres.

I said, 'Why don't you sort the dog out, open the door and come out and have a chat.'

'Chat about what?'

'A guy called Joseph.'

'We don't know any Josephs.'

I stood there. 'Maybe you should all come outside and have a talk.'

'Maybe we shouldn't. I don't want to talk to you.'

I said nothing.

'Or maybe I could send the dog out.'

'Now, now. Threatening a police officer is an offence.'

'I haven't threatened you.'

'It was implicit in the invitation to meet the dog.'

'I don't know you're a police officer.'

'I told you I was.'

'I haven't seen ID.'

'Come outside and I'll show you.'

'Piss off. If you're not gone in twenty seconds I'll set the dog on you.'

'If you let the dog out I'm going to shoot it.'

Things went quiet. The gap hovered at the twenty-millimetre mark. The chain clacked idly. Dog breath snuffled and a pink tongue slathered sightlessly. The 'we' implied multiple occupants, but the guy I'd spoken to hadn't moved from the door. The silence implied decision-making. Maybe a third party was directing operations from within the house. And multiple people of questionable character fortified in a suburban home in the company of a large dog could mean a drug HQ. Most likely P-den as opposed to tinny house. I sniffed. P-labs never smell appealing. Pseudoephedrine requires potent additives to activate it, a strong odour of hydrochloric acid or drain cleaner is not uncommon. Alas, currently absent.

The dog maintained its antics. Frequent barks punctuated a routine of retreating and rushing forward. I heard a door on the opposite side of the house open. Easy, unrushed footfalls around to the front of the property. A guy of about thirty-five wearing jeans, rubber boots and a T-shirt appeared. Silver studs traced the outline of his ears and a buzz-cut wrapped his head the way dust clings to damp wood. Not Joseph. He had a bunch of keys hanging loosely from a curled index finger. Without paying me the slightest regard he walked to the gold Laser, slid in, then started it up with a rattle and curlicue of blue smoke. He found reverse after a crunch, then backed up the little sedan, stopping so that between it, the deck, and the Isuzu and Hilux, a temporary corral was formed around the Commodore.

I watched him. He turned the engine off. The blue emission hung as a thin skein. He got out of the car and gave me an easy glance. Glacier-cool in the face of the law.

'Move the car,' I said.

He moved off a few steps and just looked at me. The keys flipped a lazy vertical loop around a cocked index finger. I jumped down off the deck and opened my car door. The dog barked. I unlocked the footlocker and removed a holstered taser and clipped it to my belt.

'I've been instructed to leave the premises,' I said. 'I can't comply with that request unless you move your vehicle.'

'Then walk back to the pig farm.'

I stepped back onto the deck. 'Cute,' I said. 'Did you get the part?'

'For what?'

'*Pirates of the Caribbean*.'

He gave me the finger. 'Fuck you,' he said, in case the gesture's meaning had been misinterpreted.

And then his eyes flicked behind me.

A subtle movement, a quick sideways cut, and I was lucky I saw it. It meant that as I turned to follow the line of his gaze, I was facing the door when it opened and the dog exploded out through the gap towards me.

I saw its massive frame, roiling with adrenaline-rinsed muscle, backed by a second shape holding a sledgehammer.

I had the taser clear of its holster before the dog reached me. I had it aimed while the animal was still airborne. I fired when the thing hit me in the chest. The taser's twin electrodes arced out and caught the guy with the sledgehammer in the chest. The shock convulsed him immediately. He managed to twist just enough so that he hit the floor shoulder-first. Dog and I were grounded at about the same time sledgehammer man keeled. The impact dumped my lung contents. The dog was huge and muscular and wild and trailed a flicking length of rope. The skin over its shoulders looked as if it had been shrink-wrapped over its flesh and its breath scorched. I braced my forearm across its throat and levered its face away from me. It had worked itself into a frenzy, both eyes looking to bust clear of optic nerve, each bark fuelled by the gleeful hysteria of the opportunity to eat my face.

I drew my knees up and pushed against its chest and squirmed backwards towards the edge of the deck. The dog came up short against its lead, front legs pedalling airborne, tethered collar cutting bone-deep. Thick ropes of spit swung slack from shining rubber lips.

The door of the Isuzu opened and someone climbed in. I got to my feet. Adrenaline saw me through the mayhem. I still functioned. Sledgehammer man had recovered. It's a key disadvantage of tasers: provided the pulse isn't excessive, victims regain complete self-control almost immediately. The guy had pulled the probes out of his chest. They're calibrated to penetrate twenty-five millimetres of clothing, so his woollen jumper had proved a weak adversary. He was up on one knee. A big guy: probably six-three, a hundred kilos. He probably liked his dog and he had his sledgehammer back. Key disadvantage number two: you don't get a second shot. The nitrogen propellant allows for one trigger-pull only. Don't miss, and don't let the other guy recover.

I jumped off the deck. The Isuzu was having trouble

starting. The pirate was back in the gold Laser. It was a three-on-one situation. And they had a dog and a sledgehammer. I slid into the Commodore and started it just as the guy with the sledgehammer landed on the bonnet. The front suspension bottomed out. I found reverse. He swung. I let the brake off. The transmission kick jolted his balance. It tightened the hammer's trajectory just enough so that it smashed my windscreen but missed my head.

He lined up for another shot. I stomped the pedal and T-boned the Laser behind us. The pirate whipped sideways in his seat like a test mannequin. The Laser rocked up on two wheels. A devil's miracle kept the guy with the sledgehammer on the car. He crouched and spread his feet on the bonnet. I slotted into drive and launched forward, crunching the deck. He tripped forwards and lost the hammer. His face whipped forwards and bounced off the broken windscreen, cracked glass speared his lips. I rammed back into the Laser, accelerated forward again and this time the guy rolled clear of the car and smashed his chin on the edge of the deck.

The Isuzu shuddered through a lengthy gear selection into reverse and then squirmed backwards out of its park with an arcing mud display. The Commodore couldn't move. The deck and the Laser behind trapped it in place. I opened my door and got out, whiskers of white exhaust fume gusting my ankles. Windscreen debris tinkled free of my jacket. The Isuzu bobbled down off the kerb into the road, paused then accelerated towards the end of the street.

Standard procedure: secure the scene, reacquire the absconded. I moved around to the bonnet. The guy with the sledgehammer was groggy. He'd bitten his tongue and blood was pooling behind a slack lower lip. The bullmastiff was yanked upright against the lead, collar crimped tight by rope stretched cable taut by an unseen anchor inside the house. White eyes lolled and pinned me, tongue outstretched like some oily, raw limb. I went around to the Laser. The side impacts had skewed the door pillar, busting the side window and trapping the door closed. The guy was still in his seat. Shards of glass pebbled a sticky head laceration that had left him hazy. I reached in through the window and cuffed his wrist to the steering wheel.

And then I ran. I sprinted hell-for-leather. I turned right when I reached the road and made for the cul-de-sac, and hit the pedestrian accessway. I couldn't hear any traffic. I ducked low to miss foliage from adjoining properties, reached the end of the path and came out onto Weymouth, just east of an intersection. I stepped out into the road. The green Isuzu rounded a shallow bend, braking and wallowing as it saw me. It would have headed east originally, but then struck the roadworks and been forced to spin back west. It swerved, then gathered speed again. Many people have no qualms about resisting arrest, but draw the line at running down police officers. I tracked sideways as it weaved. Tyres squealed. Hands blurred across the steering wheel, desperate to bring the big car back in line.

It passed me with less than three hundred millimetres to spare. The driver still couldn't get it straight. A tow truck crossed the intersection. The driver panicked and stomped the brakes. Wheels locked. Rubber vaporized. The back end fishtailed. The car hit the kerb. It bounced violently and skipped the verge before it nose-ploughed a pohutukawa and stopped very quickly. Tree limbs shivered and sprinkled a frosting of leaves.

The engine died. I crossed the street and walked up to the Isuzu's driver's side and opened the door. Joseph Te Awa sat with one hand draping the wheel, his face turned to look at me.

■ SEVENTEEN

My car wasn't a complete write-off. It needed a new windscreen, and front and rear bumper work. Its front-line service was due for a brief hiatus.

I left the scene at twenty to seven in the evening. I hitched a ride north in a patrol car, and arranged a drop-off at Joseph Te Awa's home, just west of Highbrook Drive.

The red Corolla was still in the driveway. I walked up and knocked on the front door. His father answered. He looked out at me and said nothing.

'I don't think I caught a name,' I said.

He stepped back. 'How about "Mr Te Awa"?'

I moved past him. The only lights he had on were in the kitchen. He had eggs frying in one pan and some strips of bacon popping wetly in another.

'Have a seat, I guess,' he said.

I sat down at the table. It featured a crinkled newspaper spread, open to a photograph of Ian Carson. I dumped my wallet on top of it so I didn't have to look.

The temperature had dropped a good five degrees, but he was still wearing his shorts and jandals. He bumped his head on the light shade as he went back to the stove, shadows roused until the bulb returned to rest. He probed his eggs with a rubber spatula, then stirred his bacon for good measure. TV noise leaked weakly from the living room.

'Any luck?' he asked.

'He was living with some guys a little way south of here,' I said.

He didn't answer.

'It was a drug lab. They were cooking P.'

He said nothing. He raised the spatula in a careful two-finger grip, pinkie cocked, and thumbed yolk off the tip.

'Methamphetamine,' I added.

'I know what it is. I'm not stupid.'

He flicked yellow off his finger into the sink, laid the spatula down on the bench and turned the handle of each pan so they didn't protrude beyond the edge of the stove.

'You want a beer?' he asked.

'Yes, please.'

He went to the fridge and removed two frosted cans of Lion Red. He knocked his head on the light shade again when he stood up and fingered it hurriedly to stop it swinging. He placed a can in front of me and ripped the tab on the second. He turned away from me, leaned against the bench and took a long pull.

'Did he go quietly?' he asked.

I popped my beer. It opened with a hush and a thin foam swilled out to the lip.

'Not really,' I said. 'One of them attacked me with a sledgehammer and set his dog after me. Your son escaped in a four-wheel-drive, but I managed to stop him on the next block.'

He turned his eggs and bacon off, then came and sat down opposite me at the table. He flicked the edge of the can gently with a fingernail. It was clear and tinny against the quiet. 'So now what?' he asked.

'So now he's in custody. He'll spend the night in a cell; he'll be interviewed tomorrow morning. Depending on how much information he can provide about the shooting the other night, the prosecutor might be willing to let everything else slide.'

He raised the can and killed the rest of the beer with two gulps, throat pulsing. He tossed the empty in the sink with a clatter and then got up and took a fresh one from the fridge. He pulled the tab. He took a small mouthful and sat down again.

'Do you see this sort of thing much?' he asked.

'What?'

'Kids getting caught up in bad things.'

I shrugged. 'I see kids do bad things and I see bad things happen to kids. This is far from the worst.'

He didn't seem to have heard me. 'If you knew about everything that was going to happen. Like, you could read the future, and knew what sorts of thing your kids were going to get into, do you think you'd still have them?'

I didn't answer.

He cast his eyes around. 'I guess the lead-on to that is, if you knew you were going to hit a patch of real rough luck — ' he gestured vaguely at his surrounds, 'would you still want to live the life that got you there?'

I said nothing.

He laughed. 'Because I think I would definitely be *no* on both counts. What about you?'

'I don't have kids.'

'Doesn't matter. You can still decide.'

'Life's a one-time-only offer,' I said. 'May as well buy up big.'

He smiled and twisted the pull-tab off his can. 'One-time-only offer,' he mused. 'I like that.'

I finished my beer, took a business card out of my jacket pocket and slid it to him across the table. He took it without comment.

I pocketed my wallet and thanked him for the drink and let myself out.

The patrol car that had dropped me off was waiting for me at the roadside. The driver was a Korean officer in his late twenties. He blipped his lights at me as I came down the drive. I climbed into the passenger seat beside him. Console glow tinged his face light green.

'They found a golf club in that place off Weymouth,' he said.

'A lot of people have them.'

'It was buried in the back yard.'

He started the engine and moved away from the kerb.

'Is anyone talking?' I asked.

'Not yet. Do you want to come and have a look?'

'Yeah. I probably should.'

P-lab examinations are never low-key. Fingerprint and physical evidence recovery require specialist Scene of

Crimes officers. Chemical retrieval calls for Environmental Science and Research technicians. Gang connections to the drug business mean an Armed Offenders Squad callout. And Class-A narcotics constitute major crime, so invariably a CIB detective will be directing operations. My Manurewa manufacturer had been blessed with all four. There were vans, a fire truck, marked and unmarked patrol cars, people with gas masks, people with guns, and a generous display of crime scene tape.

We parked. I got out. Thankfully, the dog seemed to have been evicted. A Scene of Crimes sergeant saw me and approached, pale with the evening chill. He introduced himself and we shook hands over the emergency tape stretching the frontage.

'We sent a team around the back to have a look at things,' he said. 'There was a patch of dirt there that looked as if it had been dug recently.'

He held the tape for me as I ducked under. We followed his jittering torch glow around to the rear of the section. It was a complete dump. Two busted stoves and a dishwasher were backed up against the wall of the house. A bicycle lay wheel-less on a bed of plastic downpipe. The rear boundary fence was brown corrugated iron. Just short of it was a hole, approximately a metre and a half long by half a metre across. A small pile of fresh-dug earth lay beside it. A series of three arc lamps bathed the little arrangement in gold. At the base of the hole lay a partially exposed golf club.

'Are the occupants still here?' I asked.

'No.'

'Did anyone question them about it?'

'No, we only just found it.'

'Did you find a spade?'

'I don't think so,' he replied. 'Does it mean anything to you?'

'It's a TaylorMade nine-iron. Those are good clubs.'

He said nothing.

'Bag it up, and I'll ask them about it in the morning,' I said.

The patrol car that had dropped me off had left, so I caught a lift with a SOCO team back to town. Taser disadvantage number three: paperwork. Don't ever shoot someone with a taser unless you really like writing.

I filed my incident report on the discovery of the missing Nissan. I filed my incident report for the Manurewa lab. I wrote up my taser report. I drank a cup of coffee and tried not to think about cigarettes.

The night shift replaced the day shift at a trickle. Darkness crept in as desk lamps died. Nine-thirty ticked around: forget twelve-hour days, try sixteen. At twenty minutes to ten, a dozen phones rang in unison. Bleary day-shifters weren't interested. Lazy night-shifters couldn't be bothered. I picked up and the racket ceased.

'Who've I got?' a voice asked.

'Sean Devereaux.'

'It's Pollard. I've got a multiple eleven-ten.'

Which meant: murder of the plural variety. Which explained the phone call, because multiple homicide is not the sort of thing suitable for a radio broadcast.

'Where?' I asked.

'Bell Ave, out past Great South Road. Can you give me the number for Manukau CIB?'

I checked my lists and told him the number. I looked at my watch again. Nine forty-one. Definitely bedtime.

'I'm going to come out and have a look,' I said.

I took a marked patrol car. It was a brand-new Commodore. A little smoother and quieter than my chariot of days past. It had low-profile LED roof flashers, which were not only brighter, but thought to reduce fuel consumption due to lessened wind resistance. I felt very mod.

I took the Southern Motorway down to the Mount Wellington Highway, exited at Sylvia Park Road, then made a left on Great South Road. Bell Ave was on the right, stretching west to where the railway line paralleled the eastern lip of the harbour. The area was mainly low-rise industrial warehousing and storage yards.

The street dead-ended ten metres short of the railway. An unmarked Commodore and a blue Mazda station-wagon were parked side by side, blocking access to a huge, undeveloped section on the northern side of the street. I pulled in behind them. Grassland pooled with shadow extended northwards, stalk-like forms of power poles marking the path of the railway on the left.

I buzzed my window down. The air carried a cocktail of ocean and engine odour. Pollard waited a moment and got out of the Mazda. He measured in at about six-foot-six and was garden-hose narrow. He was back on the beat after a stint in communications working off a broken leg, courtesy of a drunk more agile than usual.

He came and stood with his pipe-cleaner fingers gripping the sill. His belt was cinched to the first hole and the top of his trousers was ringed with a lip of excess material from being too tightly bunched. He leaned back from his arms, jutted his bottom jaw out and nodded.

'This is nice. I like it.'

I shrugged. 'Yeah. I don't know. Kind of flashy. What have we got?'

'Two dead males and one female. Ditch the car and I'll show you.'

I parked on the opposite side of the street and got out, folding my arms to wrap my jacket tight. Cold, but no threat of rain. I crossed the street and followed Pollard as he headed across the tufted lot. He removed a torch from his jacket pocket and snapped it on. Strips of shadow stretched away blackly into the beyond. We rounded a gentle hump, throne to a lone, naked lemon tree, and came to a dark blue Subaru sedan. Three shapes inside.

We stopped. A breeze gusted. Grass lolled. The headlight beams from the street threw sharp and narrow cuts of light, the lemon tree a stricken silhouette. Our breath steamed whitely and dispersed into the blackened overhead. We could have been the last two people on earth, stumbling upon remnants of pre-apocalyptic existence.

'How did you find it?' I asked.

'A train driver saw it, called one-one-one, my unmarked guys out at the street were called to have a look, and after that they called me.'

203

'Give us the torch.'

He gave me the torch and I shone it in through the driver's window. The glass had been broken. Glittering angular shards protruded above the doorframe. I checked the driver. He had no face. His features had been melted into a smooth plastic mess, his nose scorched flat to his cheekbones. I checked the back. The rear window was also broken. A man and woman sat in a similar condition to the driver. Their clothes had melded with their skin. Ruined lips left tortured grimaces.

I stepped away. 'Molotov cocktail,' I said. 'In through the driver's window.'

'Drug deal?'

'Maybe. Drug deals don't normally end so heatedly.'

'Clever. You and your words.'

'How many tyre tracks do we have coming in?'

'I don't know,' he admitted.

'Try not to scuff your feet. You called forensics?'

He nodded and blew steam.

'The car didn't catch fire,' I said. 'He must have extinguished it. Didn't want it noticed.'

'How do you hide a Molotov cocktail and a fire extinguisher?'

'You only need to hide the Molotov. One in through

the driver's window, maybe another one in through the rear, or just some gasoline. Once everything's nicely ablaze he can walk back and grab the extinguisher.'

Pollard said nothing.

'It's probably a neat and tidy way of doing things,' I said. 'It'd be the way you'd do it if you didn't have a gun.'

A locomotive passed in a wave of light and heated diesel fumes. The vibration tinkled glass free from the rim of the door. I looked at the driver again. He was a tall, lean-looking guy. Or cadaver. You couldn't tell much about the back seat passengers other than the fact they'd been living people once upon a time. I shone the torch in the rear passenger window. The man looked older, remnants of short grey hair in the waxy mess. On the back of his left hand he had a tattoo of a rose encircling a burning arrow.

'Passenger's got some pretty distinct ink,' I said. 'I might check it out.'

I gave him his torch back.

'You look a wreck,' he said.

'I'm not surprised. I've been up since five.'

I walked back to the car. I had a reasonable description: white male, mid-forties, medium build, grey hair, tattoo on left hand.

I got on the phone and called night-shift detectives, gave my description and requested database searches. I was put on hold, then transferred to organized crime cops. I re-gave my description, including details of the tattoo, speculating that it was a prison job. Keys were tapped. Databases were accessed. I slouched back in my seat. The car had an on-board computer system, but phone calls were easier than learning new-fangled gadgets. Ten-thirty approached. Ten-thirty went. I was transferred. I was put on hold. I re-re-gave my description.

Finally, I struck gold. I got a name. I got an address.

John Hale arrived.

▪ EIGHTEEN

The Escort expanded to fill my wing mirror. Hale slowed. He drew level and recognized me. He parked the car and came and sat beside me on the passenger seat.

'How're things?' I asked.

He twisted the rear-view mirror towards him. He inclined his head and checked his hair. 'Moderate. Yourself?'

'Middling. What are you doing here?'

He told me. He told me about the kidnapping he'd witnessed, about avoiding police custody, about tracing the EFTPOS to Geoffrey Gage, about his meeting with Cedric.

'And now said kidnap victim is dead,' he said.

'You could have told me what you've been up to,' I said. 'You don't have to go all Lone Wolf.'

He sucked a tooth and looked out his window. 'Figured you had your hands full.'

'Yeah. But not that full.'

He put his elbow on the sill, fingered his temple. 'Technically, I escaped lawful custody. I wouldn't be doing you a favour if I came running to you afterwards.'

I didn't answer. He turned and looked at me. 'You look horrific,' he said.

'Thanks. How did you find out the girl was dead?'

'I eavesdropped radio chatter. Ambulance was responding to three K.I.A. found in a blue car. I deduced shit.'

'What's her name?'

'Christine McLane.'

'What's she done?'

'Nothing worth being burned to death for.'

I said nothing.

'The girl was a contracted grab,' he said. 'But I don't know why. I have the time of the incoming call for when the job was requested, but that's it.'

I pocketed my phone. 'Maybe your investigative skills need a touch-up.'

He shook his head. 'Most of my not inconsiderable finesse has been occupied with evading the law.'

'There'll be an alert out on your car.'

Pollard folded himself back into his Mazda. The interior light blinked on and then vanished.

'One would imagine so. One would imagine the car is positively sizzling right now.'

'I imagine you're right.' I said.

He returned the mirror to its original orientation. An ambulance approached from behind, emergency flashers bestowing hard crimson edges on the scene ahead. 'What's it like?' he asked.

'They were Molotoved,' I said. 'Burns are extensive.'

'How many?'

'Two, plus the girl.'

'Someone wanted her dead,' Hale said. 'The others are just collateral.'

I said nothing and looked out my window at the corridor of white leading out over the lot. I cracked the door to stop the windows fogging.

'I did a bit of a ring-around before you got here,' I said. 'One of the guys in the car is called Ward Luvis.'

'Who's he?'

'Manukau CIB reckon he was a Mongrel Mob sergeant-at-arms. Apparently, he was the go-to man for all your revenge-slash-violent-takedown needs.'

'What's he look like?'

'Forty-something and grey.'

'He'll be the gentleman I encountered on Friday evening.'

'Probably.'

Hale fell quiet. At length he said, 'We should check his house. Glean some additional info.'

'Could do. But imagine the sort of company a fellow like that would keep.'

'Doesn't bear thinking about,' he said. 'Although they'd probably look like Little Miss Muffet next to us.'

We took Hale's Escort. Its wanted status didn't deter his desire to drive it. The rear-guard of emergency vehicles passed in waves of siren wail.

The late Ward Luvis had occupied an address on Don Buck Road, Massey West. We took SH1 north then turned off onto SH16. His home was located in a two-storey block of redbrick flats situated amidst a fairly ordinary slice of suburbia.

The building was at right angles to the street. The upstairs units were fronted by a narrow, cantilevered concrete walkway, accessed by a stairway at each end. A driveway scribbled with jagged cracks stretched down to a parking bay at the rear of the building.

Hale parked at the kerb and we got out and started checking door numbers. Ward Luvis had occupied the central upstairs unit. TV noise penetrated the front door. Blue light flickered weakly behind a curtained window.

Hale knocked. The TV was muted. The curtain edge tugged and then went limp. Deadbolts slid free. The door inched back against a security chain.

'Who is it?' a male voice asked.

'Police,' Hale said.

The door remained in place. Patter of feet, the sound of drawers being opened and shut. An unseen window scraped noisily open. Traffic hushed.

'What do you want?'

'Just to ask a few questions about Ward,' Hale answered.

'Ward's not— I mean, I don't know a Ward.'

'Open the door or I'll ping you for the drugs you just hid.'

The door began to close. Hale gripped the handle and pushed until the chain went taut. I heard feet scrape carpet. 'Hey, man—' Hale raised a bunched fist and struck the door panel level with the chain, stripping the bolt out of the adjoining wall. The chain slackened and clacked and flopped loosely. Hale one-armed the door through its full arc as if it was weightless and stepped inside. I followed.

The room was set up like a motel unit. There was a divan against the wall beneath the front window. Behind it stood a small circular Formica-topped table with two plastic chairs. A low grey couch spouting white stuffing sat against the left wall. Opposite were a widescreen plasma television and an X-Box console. Maybe a dozen DVDs littered the worn carpet. The kitchen was in the rear, a bedroom area right. Access to it was hampered by a pool table, claiming almost half the width of the room.

A kid of about twenty-three or twenty-four blocked our path. He wore a white T-shirt maybe three sizes too large, and black jeans above bulky, unlaced sneakers. He was half-turned, poised to grab one of the wooden cues that lay discarded on the pool table's green baize. He hesitated, then decided he couldn't go through with it. The fact one of his visitors had just broken his security chain without any visible exertion whilst maintaining a perfect deadpan had sapped his bravery.

Lights were off, but pornographic TV imagery provided sufficient glow.

A shape appeared at the bedroom door, and then a woman scrambled out around the pool table, fingers trailing across the baize. 'What're you guys up— for *God's* sake, Alan, what are you watching? I mean, jeez.'

She was probably twenty-five. She wore a low-cut, sleeveless top above a frayed denim skirt. Her hair was a bedraggled brown and her eyelids held different altitudes. Freshly woken.

'Who are you guys?' she asked.

Her words arrived in an emphysemic wheeze. I showed her my badge.

'Police,' I said.

Police is a good word, because it can imply singular or plural. In the company of John Hale, most people assume plurality.

'Got warrants?' she asked.

'We just want to talk,' I said.

'Oh,' she said. 'Well, phew.'

I took a step back and closed the door. The security chain clicked sadly. I found a light switch and flicked it on. Alan and Ms Bedraggled nailed a perfect synchronized squint. I moved sideways and stood in front of the table. Alan closed in on his snooker cues.

Hale said, 'Touch them and I'll throw you off the balcony.'

He used his quiet voice. Hale's quiet voice sounds sincere. People take it seriously. People who've just had their front door broken take it even more seriously. Alan stopped. He put his hands in his pockets, sidled over to the television and turned it off.

'You guys know Ward Luvis?' I asked.

Bedraggled nodded. 'He's my boyfriend. Where is he?'

I ignored the question. 'Can I get your name?' I said.

'Nadia.'

'Nadia, when was the last time you saw Ward?'

'Friday morning. I haven't seen him since. What's happened?'

She'd raised her arms and clasped a knotty hairdo.

'You know where he was going?' I asked.

'No. He never tells me.'

'How long have you known him?'

'Maybe two weeks.'

She looked straight at me. She didn't think about it. It felt pretty genuine.

'And who are you, Alan?' I asked.

Alan said nothing. He looked at me with his hands in his pockets, bottom lip pouted.

'Alan's Ward's cousin,' Nadia explained.

Hale draped himself on the couch and watched the blank television.

'Ward have a phone or anything he left behind?' I asked.

'No,' Nadia said.

'How about a computer?'

'Um, yeah, in the bedroom. But you can't just go and poke through it.'

I looked at her. I gave an exaggerated sniff. 'Whatever that is,' I said, 'I doubt it's legal.'

She didn't reply.

'We'll trade,' I said. 'I'll look through his computer, and in exchange, I'll pretend I can't smell anything.'

Glances were exchanged. Alan's lack of denial seemed to confirm the odour's illicit status. I sidled around the edge of the pool table and squirmed around the far side to the door leading to the bedroom. I flicked the light on. A double bed with skewed and wrinkled covers occupied centre stage, the headboard against the right-hand wall. On the far side of the bed, a computer console was set up on a small metal table. Space was so tight there was no room for a chair. The wink of LED from the PC's tower unit told me it was on, had probably remained so since Ward had departed on Friday. To the left of it, another door led through to the bathroom. I gave his toilet and shower stall a habitual once-over, then took a length of toilet paper off his roll, and draped it over the computer's mouse. The slight nudge caused the screen saver to withdraw. His desktop image was a nude blonde on a beach. I opened the web browser. The computer struggled with the request. It was a ten-year-old clunker faded to a shade somewhere between margarine and mustard. Basic operations were accompanied by prolonged chattering. We got there eventually.

I pulled up his history. His last online access had been Google Maps. He'd queried a Union Street address. I brought up the page. The address in question was an apartment block, corner of Nelson. I closed the window, dumped the paper in the toilet and left the room. It wasn't the sort of place you'd want to linger. Days of airlessness had fostered a rankling B.O. pungency.

Nadia watched me closely as I re-entered the living room. Alan was still looking glum. Hale was still on the couch. He affected Mr Suave. His hands were linked behind his head, legs stretched, feet propped heel-toe.

I removed my wallet and dropped forty dollars on the edge of the pool table.

'I'm sorry we had to break your lock,' I said.

Nadia shrugged.

'You can bog the damage with some filler,' I said. 'Drill another hole for the bolt.'

Nobody said anything.

'Maybe open a window,' I continued. 'There'll be more of us on the way. They might not be so lenient about the drug possession.'

Nobody said anything. Hale and I left.

I called Pollard and relayed my findings, outlined John Hale's movements for the last couple of days. The cellphone he'd recovered from Cedric was in the glove box. I found the number and recited it.

'So,' he said. 'Definitely not a drug handover.'

'It wasn't an anything handover. Luvis must've been contracted to kidnap the girl we found with him in the car. For some reason, whoever recruited him decided to top all of them.'

'You know the girl's name?'

I told him. 'Luvis had checked out a Union Street address before he left his house on Friday, so hopefully it was hers.' I gave him the details. He recorded wordlessly.

'Does anybody owe you any favours?' I asked.

'Potentially. Why?'

'I was hoping you might be able to extinguish any active warrants on John Hale.'

'Don't you have any favours owed?' he asked.

'No. Other way around. I've hit a real bad patch.'

'I make no promises,' he answered.

Wasted effort. He'd devoted two days to a cause that proved ultimately worthless. Molotov cocktail. What an exit. Would the burns themselves do it, or would the nerve overload induce coronary failure? Didn't matter. He'd chased leads on a woman who'd died without knowing he cared.

Which begged the question, if ends were supposed to justify means, were the means to an essentially fruitless result defendable? Was it sufficient to argue that because it was a just pursuit, his course of enquiry was reasonable? Maybe. But the implications were that any action was excusable, provided the existence of a righteous mandate. Success was a non-issue, provided you gave it a good shot. He struggled to see the truth in that.

He liked this: his efforts had pitched him against the ethically defunct, but he still felt guilty. It had to be a good thing. Guilt implied a positive quality. It implied he wasn't one of them: the lost souls so unhinged they lacked even the loosest connection to a moral reference frame. The people outside the grasp of redemption. The nowhere men. His tongue traced the words on sighed breath: *I am not a nowhere man.*

Relapse: I found a petrol station on the way home and bought cigarettes. Even the government health warning couldn't quell the urge. Who needs healthy teeth and gums when you can bask in the grey tendrils? Nothing sounded better than the plastic wrap coming off. The pop of glossed cardboard. Match scratch. That idyllic nicotine nocturne.

I went to bed and smoked a couple. Maybe I lacked tenacity, but burn victims will kill your resolve. And so will twenty-hour work days. So will multiple homicide investigations.

A couple became a half-pack. The night table grew ash dunes. I thought about Joseph Te Awa. I thought about why some people come off the rails and some don't. I thought about Mrs Carson and her daughter on the mortuary table. I thought about the Molotoved Subaru, and what sort of person you'd have to be to conceive of something so despicable. Were late night cigarettes a vice of the decent and the damned? Or were people who tossed bottles of burning chemicals into cars more closely aligned with Jeffrey Dahmer, and kept human heads and organs in their refrigerator?

I stubbed out and slept with suffering on my mind.

■ NINETEEN

You're the guy from yesterday.'

'Correct,' I said.

Joseph Te Awa formed an air pocket in his cheek and squeaked it out slowly between pressed lips. It was like a nominal admission that the game was up. Middle ground between a full-blown defeatist sigh, and stony, impassive silence.

We faced each other across a plain interview room table. No one-way glass, but a camera lens maintained a static vigil. Te Awa was six-foot and solid. His hair reached his neck and was waxed into a heavy part either side of his face, which was dotted with dense black moles, like a flick of oil. Purple acne scars scored his cheeks. He wore frayed jeans below a green hooded jumper.

'I thought you quit smoking,' he said.

'What makes you think that?'

'You got bird shit eyes, and you smell like smoke. It looks like you tried to give it up, but couldn't hack it, and got back on it *real* hard. Did a whole pack or something.'

'Maybe I didn't quit. Maybe I smoke whole packs all the time.'

'Nah. Otherwise you wouldn't have the shakes.'

I said nothing.

He smiled. 'My old man used to do that all the time.'

I didn't reply for a moment. The room was silent. Thick walls deadened hallway murmur. The lighting was a top-shelf brand that didn't hum and the light didn't flicker. A pleasant interrogation environment.

'I want to talk to you about Friday night,' I said at length.

'OK,' he said.

I opened the manila folder I had with me to reveal camera stills of the Nissan heading north on Albert Street. I selected the topmost shot and spun it round for him to see.

'Is that your car?' I asked.

'Probably.'

'Well, on Friday evening, at the time shown in the

221

picture, were you driving north on Albert Street through central Auckland?'

He nodded.

'Say yes, if you agree, just so there's no mistaking it on the camera.'

He said yes. I got up and held the image he'd been shown to the camera lens, then sat back down again.

'I need to know who shot the bus driver,' I said. 'And I want to know why you ditched your car.'

'I don't know who shot the bus driver,' he said.

He ducked his face to his shoulder and thumbed a corner of hood against his nostril. I fanned the photos and found one of the Mercedes sedan. I showed it to him. 'The shot was fired from this car,' I said. 'Do you know who was in it?'

'Not really.'

I tamped the pages square. I slipped them back in the folder and closed it and pushed it off to one side, long edge flush with the end of the table.

'How long you had that suit?' he said.

'I scavenged it this morning.'

He rocked his chair back on two legs, caught himself with his knees beneath the table to stop a fall. 'You look like you slept in it. You look like you lay awake smoking and thinking about what you were going to say to me today.' He laughed. 'You're a douche bag, bro.'

I smiled. 'And you're a paradox. You pick up stuff like that and it makes me think you've actually got a brain. And then I remember I found you living in a P-lab, and you couldn't even set fire to a car properly.'

He shrugged. 'I'd rather be a paradox than a douche bag. And the car didn't burn because we put the fire out.'

'Why did you put the fire out?'

He just looked at me and said nothing.

'You need to talk to me,' I said. 'Withholding testimony obstructs my investigation.'

'I haven't done anything wrong.'

'Maybe you're right. But someone fired at you with a shotgun, missed and killed a guy, so you need to answer my questions.'

'Will I get my car back?'

'If you talk to me there's a good chance you will. If you don't talk to me, there's a substantially better chance that you won't.'

'Nobody likes a fuckin' snitch.'

'I'll tell that to the dead man's mother when she asks why I haven't got anywhere,' I said.

'Piss off. I don't know the guy.'

I opened the folder, thumbed my photo stack and took out the bottom image. Robert St George, in situ, jawless.

'That's what happened to him,' I said. 'His face got torn off. It took him less than a minute to die. All for something he had nothing to do with.'

He said nothing. His cheeks paled, highlighting his acne. His lips parted. A saliva film stretched and broke. He licked his lips.

'Start chatting,' I said. 'And don't faint. It wouldn't be good for your street cred.'

He said nothing.

'Why did you try to hide the car?' I asked.

He pinched his nose and laid his hands palms-down on the table. When he removed them the finish was left oily and whorled.

'Because we knew someone would have seen it getting shot at,' he said slowly. 'It would've picked up some pretty sweet heat; we didn't want the cops onto us.'

'Who's we?'

'Me'n Eugene.'

'Eugene's the guy with the short hair and the rings in his ears.'

'Uh-huh.'

'And you dumped the Nissan on Highbrook Drive.'

'Yeah,' he said.

'So why did you set fire to it and then put it out?'

He thought about it. He clonked his seat forward and then leaned back again. His eyes panned the line between ceiling and wall. He made fists around his thumbs and cracked his knuckles crisply.

'Good game's a fast game,' I said.

'We called Lee,' he said finally.

Lee: the one with the dog and the sledgehammer and the free taser trial.

'We were going to drop the car off and he was going to pick us up. So we sorted that out, except we got there and Eugene said we should set it on fire, so we did. But then Lee turned up and said that was the most dumb-as-fuck idea he'd ever heard, and put it out.'

'Lee wasn't impressed.'

'Yeah. Not really. He reckoned it was a stupid place to leave it anyway, and burning it made it like, retard-grade. But anyway. We had to just leave it there.'

'All right. Let's go back to the beginning. Why were you and Eugene shot at?'

'Eugene had a job.'

'What sort of job?'

'The sort of job where I just drive. You know, Eugene

gets out, comes back a little bit later, and you don't ask any questions about anything.'

'Where did you take him?'

'It was a house. It was, like, Te Atatu or something.'

'And you had to drive him there?' I asked.

'Uh-huh. That's what I said.'

'OK. So what did you do when you got there?'

'Nothing. I just stayed in the car.'

'So what, you just pulled into the driveway and—'

'No, I didn't go into the driveway. We drove past, and Eugene pointed out the place, and I asked him where I should park and he got me to go round the corner a wee bit. So I went round the corner and stopped. Eugene got out and went off and came back a little bit later.'

'How much later?'

'I don't know. Two radio songs.'

'Ten minutes, maybe?'

'Yeah. Maybe about ten minutes.'

'Did Eugene tell you what he was going to do before you left?'

'No. He just said he needed me to drive him somewhere.'

'OK,' I said. 'And what time was that?'

'What time was what?'

'What time did he tell you he needed you to drive him somewhere?'

'I dunno. About four or half-past four or something like that.'

'This was on Friday?'

'Uh-huh.'

'OK. Did he take anything with him?'

'He had a golf club.'

'OK. So he went into the house with the golf club. Did he come out with the golf club?'

'Yep.'

'And what happened when he got back into the car? Did he say anything to you?'

'He just said we had to split pretty fast. He was kinda worked up. He chilled out a bit when we got going, but then we picked up a tail a bit later on.'

'How much later on?'

'Like, pretty much straightaway, probably less than two minutes. Eugene told me which way to go. We went on the motorway and I just hammered it as quick as I could. Anyway, Eugene told me to head into town, so I did, but then whoever chased us caught up and boom, just shot at us, like that. But it missed and one-eighty-sevened that bus driver.'

One-eighty-seven. California penal code for homicide. A gold nugget of Americana courtesy of rap music.

'Did you see who was in the car following you?' I asked.

'Nah,' he said. 'I didn't.'

'Can you remember the address you went to?'

'No.'

'Would you remember it if you saw it?'

'Yeah. Probably.'

'Would Eugene be likely to tell me if I asked him?'

'No.'

'Maybe I could beat it out of him.'

'You couldn't.'

'I reckon I could. I took you guys three-on-one. Four, including the dog.'

He went quiet. I picked up my folder and left the room.

■ TWENTY

Google Maps made identifying the address Joseph Te Awa had visited a painless process. He led me on a virtual expedition up SH20 from South Auckland, through Mount Roskill, Avondale, Kelston and Glendene. Our trip ended at an address just off McLeod Road in Te Atatu. I knew he was telling the truth because the Mercedes was visible, parked in the front yard, partially obscured by a tarpaulin rain cover.

The house was a single-storey brick unit. A wooden fence bordered it on the left. Waist-high hedge traced the right-hand boundary and property frontage. I did a lagged, stop-motion neighbourhood tour. It was pure residential for several blocks. Streets were narrow and unmarked. Sufficiently quiet that a visit from Eugene and his golf club could go unnoticed.

Te Awa hadn't disclosed the nature of the visit but it didn't take too much insight to fill the blanks. They were in the business of drug distribution. A furtive visit involving a golf club normally means a debtor won't pay. A furtive visit involving a golf club, followed by a car chase resulting in a shooting, would indicate debtor and golf club didn't get along well.

I opened the Telecom database. The phone number at the address was registered to one Carole Kennedy. The Habitation Index told me she was in the company of three additional Kennedys: Jared, Ethan and Troy. I pried on. Carole was forty-six. The others were twenty-two, twenty-four and twenty-seven respectively. I ran a firearms check. Nothing on Carole. Nothing on Ethan or Troy. I got a hit on Jared.

He'd held a gun licence for the past three years. He had a '91 C-Class Mercedes sedan registered in his name. Progress. I picked up the phone.

The evidence was good. The chain was coherent. My witness's account of the crime synced with the evidence. He'd provided me with a suspect's address. An occupant of the address was licensed to operate a firearm. The prospect of murder weapon recovery solidified.

Enthusiasm rekindled. A previously dispassionate situation room of twenty-five cops discovered new vigour. Water cooler chat dispersed, screen savers were banished. Driver's licence photos were pulled and printed. Calls were placed. Meetings with prosecutors were scheduled. Warrants were written. Judges were contacted, filled in and asked to sign.

We went at two o'clock in the afternoon. An illicit check of IRD records showed no income for the three Kennedy boys for the last financial year. Unemployment was not only an ideal breeding condition for mischief, but significantly improved the chances of at least one of them being in on a weekday afternoon.

The possibility of a shotgun on the premises called for a bulk turnout: we took a ten-man team. I rode with a bleary Pollard in one car. Three uniforms tailed us in a second unmarked. A five-man Armed Offenders Squad unit followed in a black Nissan Patrol. We went west on SH16. It was light overcast, holding at about twelve degrees. Good indoor search warrant weather.

Pollard wore a light green suit over a canary yellow polo shirt. His neck cantilevered straight out in order to accommodate his head below the roofline. His crown rubbed the roof. His left palm draped the gearshift, fingers pattering as if the hand wanted to scuttle free.

'Ward Luvis wasn't always called Ward Luvis,' he announced. 'He shortened it from Luvinski.'

'Russian, Polish or Latvian?' I asked.

He shrugged. He leaned back and drove with his right thumb snagging the bottom of the wheel. 'The driver was a guy called Jamie Kilcullen,' he said. 'Then we had Luvis and the girl in the back. Kilcullen was six months out of prison following an assault charge. Luvis's file reads like the Devil's Confession. He's got ten years' worth of minor drug offences. He's done time for assault, separate stay for manslaughter after he stabbed a taxi driver in the throat with a pen.'

'Epitomes of good behaviour,' I said.

'Absolutely. Tragic losses.'

'What about the girl?'

'I have her name and address. It matches the place Luvis checked before he left on Friday. There's meant to be another guy in there with her, but it was empty when I went for a look.'

I didn't reply. We hit traffic choke and slowed. He slipped a plastic thermos from the drinks holder between us. He popped the cup, splashed out a steaming taster so small it could have been a cap of gin. He downed it, replaced the cup and slotted the thermos home. We accelerated.

'Technically, it probably wasn't a Molotov,' he said. 'If the accelerant was in a bottle, it would be too difficult to get it to break just by throwing it inside a car. More likely he walked up to the car, used a thermos or something to slosh petrol in through the windows, sent a cigarette in afterwards.'

'A gentleman,' I said.

He touched a canary-yellow shirt button. 'Yeah, a gentleman. I think the driver got it worst. He took a full load of petrol down his throat, so they don't reckon he lasted very long. The two in the back only had exterior burns, but the kiddie locks were on for taxiing the girl, so they couldn't have gone anywhere. Probably been there since Friday.'

We hit a silent patch. I watched the view. Patrons of SH16 looked back with caution. Unmarked police cars aren't that inconspicuous. Most people know to treat plain Holden sedans with extreme caution. Everyone within a fifty-metre radius maintained a conservative ninety-five.

We got onto McLeod Road and turned back east, made a left turn moments later. The real-life neighbourhood experience didn't differ much from the Google Maps version. We kept to thirty and traced the narrow, unmarked road to the single-level brick place on the right-hand side of the street. It appeared as Googled, except the Mercedes was no longer in residence. A tarpaulin chrysalis lay heaped in its absence. Pollard slowed and pulled us up twenty metres short. The two-way on the dash chirruped three times in quick succession. It was a short-hand way of checking we were good to go, without broadcasting something that could act as a tip-off to anyone eavesdropping our frequency. I unclicked my belt and glanced around. Single-storey houses sat shoulder to shoulder behind shallow frontages. No traffic. Footpaths and front yards were empty; kids were still in school. Low risk of unintended collateral.

'The car's out,' I said. 'So I'm guessing our suspect is, too.'

'What do you think?'

'Let's just bust it while things are quiet. It'd be good to grab the gun while nobody's home.'

'There's supposed to be four of them living there. They might not all be out.'

'We still need to go in.'

'Block the street off?'

'Nah, just send them in quick.'

He raised the handset and did as advised. We pulled to the shoulder. The back-up unmarked rolled on as arranged. The Patrol tailgated it for a few metres, then stopped and ejected three AOS cops in black fatigues. They sprinted the remaining distance, hurdled the hedge and hit the front yard. Two broke left and disappeared down the far side. The third guy kept right and hugged the boundary line towards the back yard. The Patrol accelerated and came to a stop nose-in to the kerb beside the unmarked. Doors flung and cop cargos disgorged. Two AOS officers with Bushmaster assault rifles and three uniforms with Glock handguns fanned wide and struck a beeline for the house. They crouched, keeping their heads below sill level. When they reached the front wall they flattened back-to against it. An arm stretched from behind cover and fingered the bell. Crouches held.

Nobody answered.

The arm broke cover a second time and rapped on the door.

'Police. Open up.'

No luck.

An axe was baggage-chained in. The guy on the door had no inhibitions: he butted the top of the blade into the wood below the handle and sheared the deadbolt. The other four funnelled past, AOS leading. Axe man went in last. A breeze eased the door closed behind him. The dropped tarp heaved in restless slumber.

A minute. Two. Three.

Nothing.

'Let's go have a look,' I said.

Pollard let his foot off the brake. We rolled forward at idle speed and stopped behind the Patrol. I took a pair of gloves from a dispenser on the back seat, then got out and tracked across a soggy lawn to the front door. The break-in crew filed out as I arrived. The guy with the axe emerged last. He held it one-handed, blade propped on his shoulder.

He beckoned me inside with a head-jerk.

'You can come in,' he said. 'Take a deep breath first.'

A uniform lurched past him and retched. He made it to the lawn and launched a spew. Axe man fanned his nose and chuckled.

I entered. A ripe organic odour hit me immediately. Exiting cops blocked the main corridor. Towards the rear of the house, a bathroom door stood open. Bundled towels lay in a creased pile adjacent. I shielded my nose and mouth as I went in.

A body sat crumpled in the shower stall, face pulped, flailed limbs in static disarray. The wide eyes, the mouth slightly ajar, he seemed surprised to see me.

▪ TWENTY-ONE

The break-in crew held a perimeter while we checked the body. Pollard led the way back into the house. He crouched elbows-on-knees beside the metal shower stall, right fingers spinning his wedding ring, a grimace aimed at the mildewed shower curtain as he considered things.

'It's lucky we came in,' he said at length.

I made no reply.

He sucked a front tooth. 'This is the younger one,' he said. 'Whatshisname.'

'Jared,' I said.

'Looks as if he's been crowbarred or something.'

'Crowbar's too wide. Probably a golf club. The boy told me Eugene had one when he visited on Friday. They dug up a nine iron at the place I went to yesterday.'

He turned his wedding ring full-circle.

'I'm sure it's a drug issue,' I said. 'Unsettled debts somewhere.'

He stood and jiggled his trouser cuffs down over his exposed ankles. 'And retribution was a botched shooting on Albert Street,' he said. 'Bus driver for drug addict.'

I didn't answer.

'Leaves the question of who did the shooting,' he said.

'Older brothers, probably. They must have chased the guy into town, then come back and put little brother in the shower until they decided what to do with him.'

He cupped his shirt to his face, spoke through his collar. 'God knows how they managed to go this long living with a dead body.' He cracked a smirk. 'You'd think by Sunday you'd have at least called an undertaker.'

I ignored him and stepped back into the corridor. Air quality was better. I made a right off the entry hall into the living room. Body odour tang replaced decomposition gasses. An unzipped sleeping bag was draped across the couch. A PlayStation console was rigged to a 21-inch CRT television opposite. Cans of drink stood at random. The kitchen was across the hallway. A stainless steel bench stretched the width of the far wall. Stacked dishes teetered. To the right was a stove and an old single-door fridge with a huge silver handle that could have been

239

taken off a '66 Thunderbird. The lino was maroon-on-white chequerboard blistered with smooth irregular lumps. The table was Formica, the chairs metal tube and cracked vinyl. I had a look in the fridge. The Kennedys liked Export Gold. There were two stacked six-packs and a half bottle of milk and not much else.

Best bet for weapon storage would be a bedroom. I headed for the back of the house. I checked the master bedroom first. There was a queen-sized camping mattress with the linen torn off and heaped in the centre. A spread-eagled *Woman's Day* occupied the nightstand. I checked the closet and the dresser. No guns, no ammunition.

I crossed the hall to the second bedroom. Twin bunks were set up against the far wall. A pair of cupboards adjacent. A now-familiar rankness prevailed.

I toed through garment clutter to the cupboards and opened them. I knelt and nosed. A cardboard box on the floor contained twelve-gauge buckshot shells, both packaged and loose. And: an owner's manual for a Remington 870 shotgun. *And*: a discarded trigger lock.

I left the room. Pollard was back in the corridor, twisting his hands in his pockets to make his trousers flutter.

'Call Scene of Crimes?' he asked.

'Not yet. Tell the guys out front to pull back. We'll wait for somebody to show up here.'

'What are you going to do?' he asked.

I paused. The deceased's bowel had yielded, representing the primary odour source.

'I'll wait in the house,' I said.

I went into the living room and watched the roadside clutter disperse. The AOS guys got back into the Patrol and headed right. Pollard and the unmarked headed left. The scene resumed its prior typicality.

I walked down the corridor. The bathroom was opposite the master bedroom. A toilet sat below a frosted window against the far wall. Shower stall and corpse were to the right. A sink with a mirrored medicine cabinet to the left. The cabinet contents were stock standard: a tube of toothpaste, two toothbrushes, Panadol and Dispirin, assorted other painkillers. Taped beneath the cupboard beneath the basin I found a first-aid kit. The contents weren't strictly medicinal:

A small glass bong stained with dark residue.

A plastic zip-lock bag with maybe half a gram of methamphetamine.

Five or six 3 ml hypodermics.

A coiled rubber tourniquet strap.

The needles looked new, but based on the condition of the tourniquet, the owner was a frequent user. I re-taped the kit to the bottom of the cupboard where I had discovered it. Smell de la voided bowel and human putrefaction rose up with eye-watering intensity. I left the room. It backed the theory that one of the lads had made the mistake of delaying payments on a covert habit. But beaten to death was rough punishment for a recreational pursuit you could contain in a first-aid kit from your local pharmacy. Life has fearsome fine print.

I walked to the front of the house. The street view remained unchanged. I headed back down the corridor. Another once-over of the bedrooms turned up something that made me stop and rethink everything.

I sat down at the kitchen table and waited. I breathed B.O. and dead body. Four o'clock came and went. I contemplated an Export Gold but voted against it. A light shower flecked the roof briefly and then faded. My cellphone rang.

'You've got a car inbound,' Pollard said. 'Blue Honda Accord. You remember the Mercedes had plates off a blue Honda? This is probably the one.'

'Who's driving?'

'Can't tell. You want us to do anything?'

'If you see a shotgun, help me out, otherwise just stay where you are.'

I ended the call. Suspension heaved as the car traversed the footpath. Tyres spun against a slick lawn. The motor died. A door opened and closed. Bottle chime and plastic bag rustle marked a short walk to the front door. There was a pause as the new arrival considered the busted lock. Silence as scarred wood was inspected. Either it would deter them from coming inside at all, or they'd feel bound to investigate. I imagined if you possessed the qualities necessary to commit murder you'd match the latter category.

The hinge squeaked. Footsteps padded, and a woman appeared in the entrance to the kitchen. The broken door proved inadequate preparation; she looked up and saw me sitting at her kitchen table and stopped with a jolt, as if she'd nudged a live wire. She dropped the bag with the bottles. They plunged and grounded with a clunk, then toppled and rolled inside the plastic.

The woman's features went slack. Her jaw sagged and she pressed bunched fingers to her mouth and slouched against the doorframe.

I stayed in my seat. The woman looked at the floor.

'Carole Kennedy?' I said.

She nodded. 'I thought you'd turn up,' she said. 'Didn't think you'd be this fast.'

'Would have made it eventually,' I said.

She gripped the doorframe and used it to propel herself into the room. She was maybe five-seven. Medium build, very thick from the waist down. Blonde hair reached her shoulders, falling around a face that was dry and cut with sharp lines.

'You mind if I get a beer?' she asked.

'Go ahead.'

She stepped to the fridge and took an Export Gold from an open six-pack and sat down with it at the table, across from me. She cracked the tab, but didn't drink any. She sat staring at the top of the can as if it possessed prophetic qualities. Her hair hung in knotted ripples and her eyes bore a jaundiced tinge. In the middle of the table were a glass bong in a transparent plastic evidence bag, and a digital voice recorder.

She took a hit off the beer. It chilled sizzled nerves. She exhaled shakily, tilted her face back and blinked, pressing her lips together. Condensation on the can grouped and dribbled. She nodded at the pipe.

'I forgot about that one,' she said.

'It had rolled under your bed.'

'Well fuck,' she answered, and had another drink. Her voice came tinder-dry, as if her throat was scorched.

'Eugene was your supplier,' I said.

She didn't answer. The dew on the can dropped as the contents decreased.

'How much did you owe him?' I asked.

She swallowed. 'Where are you from?' she asked finally.

'Excuse me?'

She took a hand off the can and gestured circularly. 'Yeah, like, are you a cop or—'

'My name's Sean Devereaux. I'm a police detective.'

I showed her my badge and ID. Her reaction was a single eyebrow bounce.

'Five,' she said.

'You owed him five thousand dollars?'

She greased her vocal cords with a sip. 'Mmmhmm.'

I sat and said nothing. I watched her work the beer down to almost-empty. The familiarity of the action kept her calm. 'He wanted me to pay,' she said. 'But I couldn't. I didn't have it. I told him. I don't work, I draw a fuckin' benefit, I can't just hand over that sort of cash, you know. I mean, God.'

I didn't reply.

'That was almost three weeks ago,' she said. 'He rang me up, and he just said, Carole, you've got such-and-such amount of time left to come up with what I owed him, and after that it's …'. She paused and clicked her fingers softly. 'You know, you're done.'

She finished the beer in a relatively composed manner. She raked her hair back, held the can between thumb and index finger and tapped it gently against the table.

'But I didn't pay,' she said, 'because I couldn't. So Eugene comes round with his golf club and my boy answers the door, and Eugene just comes inside and pushes him into the kitchen and beats him dead. And then he goes over to the fridge and takes a beer, and he's sitting right where you are now, opening up his beer, when I come in. And my boy is lying on the floor, with his arms and legs spread everywhere, and his face all bleeding, but his mouth going like he's still kind of alive, and Eugene just sits there and has a mouthful of beer and says something like, no good for payin' when you're dead, so I had to have him instead. And then he just leaves his beer on the table and goes out, using his golf club like it's a walking stick or something.'

She was back to looking at the top of the can. She

stared at it and worked the pull-tab free. She glanced at me, lids laden to overflow, as if daring me to console her, to say anything at all.

'So then what did you do?' I asked.

'I got the gun out of the bedroom. I loaded it up, and I chased that piece of shit halfway across town, and then I took a shot at him. And after that I drove home and parked the car and came in and cleaned up my boy. Just around his face and stuff. And then I just sat down next to him on the floor and told him how sorry I was.'

I said nothing and just looked at her. She scrubbed her face with her hands, pushing her knuckles into her eyes.

'But it's like, too little too late when your little boy is dead,' she continued. 'I told him I was sorry I took a wrong turn and got him into this. But that was shit, because I could just imagine him saying something like I'd been taking wrong turns the whole time. Like, I never made a single good turn in my whole life. They'd told me to not do the drugs, but I couldn't stop, couldn't stop, couldn't stop, even after his brothers left, I just couldn't stop, I had to have more. God.'

She fixed me with a stare.

'I loaded the gun up again and sat on the floor and tried to work myself up to do it. But I couldn't. Because

I knew I'd just be sending myself to an even worse hell than I've already made for myself. And that's not a nice thought.' She smiled. 'Like, the place I'm going to arrive at is going to be even more shit than where I am now. And it's going to last forever. A forever and ever and ever of flames.'

She lolled her head as she said it, highlighting the monotony, then raised the can and lobbed it towards the sink. It hit the cupboards below and clattered to the floor and dawdled back and forth before settling.

'A good prize for a crap life,' she said, and flicked the pull-tab onto the floor.

I said nothing. She sat with head and shoulders forward, picking a stray shirt thread. A fitting metaphor: normal existence tragically unravelled.

I went into the corridor and called Pollard.

Pollard made the arrest and I made the calls. I asked for a Scene of Crimes team and a forensics unit from Environmental Science and Research. They showed by quarter to five. Come five, those not wearing nylon coveralls were a minority.

We ringed the place with emergency tape. The Mercedes was apparently abandoned plate-less, on a street near Swanson and Universal. We sent a patrol unit and a tow truck to pick it up. Neighbours arrived home and began to clot the perimeter. The media showed up and mingled with the hubbub, prowling for tattle.

Another CIB sergeant and two detective constables arrived at six that evening. Pollard and I left. Dark had settled like draped velvet on the surrounding rooflines.

We retraced our McLeod Road route back to the North-Western Motorway. City-bound traffic was thin, but the opposing flow looked standstill. I freed a cigarette from my jacket pack and ignited. It was the best thing I'd had all afternoon. Raindrops struck the car with flat clicks, marring the windscreen with dollar-sized distortions.

'Going to be a crappy night,' Pollard said.

I consumed some cigarette. 'Better than no night at all,' I said.

He clucked his tongue in admission. 'Hot gossip of the week was you'd quit,' he said.

'I have quit. This is just a momentary relapse. I'm weaning myself off them.'

'Momentary relapses will still kill you.'

'Yeah, well. A couple more aren't going to tip the cancer scales much more than they've already been tipped.'

I cracked my window. To the left the harbour lay as flat and perfect as greased slate. A twin crimson trail curved the way ahead.

'I packed them in because I was scared of dying,' Pollard said.

'Yeah. That'll do it.'

He glanced at me. 'Don't you worry?'

'About what?'

A weave of the head as he searched for examples. 'Emphysema. Heart disease. The Big C.'

'Yeah, fairly regularly. But I'm addicted. So I try to live on the assumption I'm one of the numerous people who will never have a major health issue. I see the glass of life as being half-full.'

'The odds don't exactly tilt your way,' he answered.

'Worst-case scenario, I'll die sooner rather than later. But you can't reflect on earthly existence and think oh I wish I'd given that up sooner. You live, and then there's blissful, guiltless death.'

'No heaven?'

'No heaven.'

'Why not?'

'I don't know. Celestial residence just doesn't strike me as plausible.'

He checked his wing mirrors for a counterpoint. 'Maybe it doesn't work like that. Maybe heaven's just reliving your time on earth.' He went quiet. 'Maybe it's just an infinitely repeating life–death loop. Maybe we're in heaven now.'

'You might be,' I said. 'I'm not.'

Pollard said nothing.

'Maybe you've been sent to heaven and I've been sent to hell,' I said. 'And they overlap the same territory.'

Pollard considered that. Buildings sharpened out of the city's incendiary haze. He left his knees in charge of driving while he stole a hit off his thermos, head turned so he could still see the view ahead.

'I swing one way and then the next,' he said. 'But then I see something like that kid in the shower, and I think I'll spend the rest of my life as atheist as a post.'

I said nothing. Smoke trickled out the window and rode the slipstream back the way we had come.

■ TWENTY-TWO

Hale left the Escort straddling the footpath down on High Street, and took the stairs up to his office. The door was ajar. He stood in the corridor and listened, watched the strip of yellow glow that cut the carpet. No movement. He waited ninety seconds. His stereo played Wilco's 'Sky Blue Sky', soft as deathbed breath.

He went in. Music volume jumped as he pushed the door back. Reception was empty. His study door was open. The sergeant from Friday was seated behind his desk. A two-page spread of the *Herald* was open in front of him, William Dart's classical CD review his article of choice. He looked up.

'Got a warrant?' Hale asked.

The guy smiled. 'This isn't a search.'

'A friendly pop-in, then.'

'Yeah. A friendly pop-in. To let you know you're off the hook.'

Hale looked around. Blinds obscured a street view. The stereo's display maintained its careful count. Atop a speaker: his wallet and cellphone, confiscated after his arrest on Friday.

'You want a drink?' Hale asked.

The offer surprised his guest, but the pause was only momentary. The smile soon regained hold.

'What have you got?' the guy asked.

'Struck me as a fine night for whiskey.'

'All right. Good.'

The John Hale grog coffers: a half-full bottle of Jim Beam in a cupboard beneath the stereo. He levelled off two shot glasses. He moved slowly; the epitome of the undisturbed. He replaced the bottle and set the glasses on the desk. No surface wobble. A good, calm placement.

He drew up a chair and sat down. The stereo switched track. Quiet claimed the interlude.

'Haven't heard this one in a while,' Hale said. 'You'd have to have a pretty good hunt through my things in order to find it.'

The guy breathed a half-laugh out through his nose,

as if he was brushing off praise. 'I saw them live last year at the Civic,' he said.

'So did I, actually.'

'I thought "Impossible Germany" was played beautifully.'

'It was.'

'And "Jesus, Etc." A stunning rendition.'

'I agree. I'd venture as far as saying "Spiders (Kid-smoke)" surpassed it.'

The guy smiled. 'Hate it Here' began. The stereo settings had been switched to random play.

'You broke in,' Hale said. 'It tripped my alarm. I might have to bill you for my time.'

'How about I don't bring you in for escaping lawful arrest and we call it even?'

Hale took a sip. Smooth and warm on the ride down.

His guest mimicked him, upped the ante with a double swallow. A smack of lips signalled satisfaction. 'There's a guy we like to keep an eye on,' he said. 'He's a piece of shit. Gang ties, in and out of prison, you know the deal. Uses the name Cedric.'

'I may have met him,' Hale said.

The guy resampled the Beam. A haughty swig, but the burn didn't faze him. He put the glass down, pushed his chair back a fraction. He folded his legs knee-on-knee and passed his tongue across his top lip.

'And the guy's missing, which is a worry.'

Hale got his whiskey down to half-empty. 'Why were you after him?'

'Present tense. Why *are* we after him. Because we followed up on your kidnap complaint. Because we worked the info you'd given us and the name Cedric came up. And your name came up as well, courtesy of a guy called Geoffrey Gage who'd mentioned you'd paid him a visit. So we check out this Flat Bush place Cedric's been known to show up at — it's cleaned out and there're half-a-dozen bullet holes in the south wall.'

'Goodness,' Hale said.

The guy folded the newspaper. It was at least a week old. 'It makes me think,' he said, 'that you blew a lead.'

'I didn't blow anything. I acted on something you'd denied occurred. I told you I'd witnessed a kidnapping. You ignored me. So I did something about it.'

The guy leaned back in Hale's chair. He pattered his fingertips on the armrests. He was wearing a black jacket over uniform blues. He re-read the week-old headline, raised the paper and flipped it so he could see below the fold. 'Imagine if I had a gun with me,' he said conversationally. 'I could kill you without anyone knowing.'

His eyes moved to Hale's face as he said it, searching for unsettlement. Hale polished off his whiskey. The stereo stayed discreet. A breeze from the door made the window blinds tick faintly.

'Try me,' he said.

The guy gave a little shrug and fingered the folded newspaper to one side. 'Maybe I could pull it off,' he said.

Hale put his empty glass on the near edge of the desk. His eyes wandered with feigned musings. 'You couldn't clear beltline before I made it across the desk,' he said. 'I'd break your neck. It would be very fast and clean. I'd put you in the bath and dissolve you in sulphuric acid and then just rinse you down the drain like a hangover.'

A measly twinge of smile. It was like pencilled-in emotion; change it as you please. 'Part two of the pop-in goes like this,' the guy said. 'I'm paying you special attention. You're kind of like my pet project. You fucked up my kidnap lead, so I feel compelled to check you're squeaky clean.'

'Positively spotless. And I didn't admit to anything.'

'No, of course not. But a man's entitled to his suspicions.'

Hale didn't answer.

'I'd be careful,' the guy said. 'Otherwise things might go missing. Your P.I. licence for a start. That wouldn't be good, would it?'

Hale said nothing. The guy stood up and came around the desk. He patted Hale on the head as he passed. 'Be good, little Johnny,' he said. 'I appreciate the whiskey.'

'Only temporarily,' Hale said. 'You don't know what I spiked it with.'

The guy paused, a slight hiccup in his stride, but he didn't take the bait. He headed through reception, and a moment later the door to the hallway closed and he was gone.

We went back to the station. I did incident report paperwork. I made copies and added it to case files. I drank coffee. I did more paperwork. I went into Claire Bennett's office and found her similarly occupied.

'You're always in here,' I said.

'An apt observation.'

'I guess it's the point of having an office, isn't it?'

'I'd say so.'

She put down her pen and squared up a papery shambles, nudged her computer mouse and glanced at the screen.

'You look horrific,' she said.

'Thanks.' I took a seat. 'Did you hear I semi-cleared up your bus shooting?'

She surveyed her office disarray. Ring binders occupied the floor. Curled Post-it notes topped her monitor in a rag-tag row. Filing cabinet drawers stood fifty millimetres shy of flush. 'Semi-cleared up?' she asked.

'We made an arrest. I got an un-coerced, recorded confession.'

She didn't answer. She looked too tired to care.

'I'm going to work the Molotov case,' I said. 'What's happening with the girl's place?'

She leaned forward and skim read something on her monitor. 'We've done fingerprinting and photos, but we haven't taken anything off-site yet.'

'I'll go and have a look. Do we have a key?'

'You look as if you need to call it a day.'

'Maybe. I'm on a roll, though. I may as well ride the good luck.'

A key was found. I went back to my desk and ran background checks. Victims with their own history of offending aren't uncommon: Christine McLane, D.O.B. 1989, had done two months for possession of

P, and another thirty days for receiving stolen goods. I delved on. McLane's address was an apartment up the top end of Union Street. The only other occupant was one Ellis Carlyon. Outstanding speeding tickets, but nothing prison-worthy.

I went downstairs and checked out a marked patrol car, even though the address was close enough to have walked. Eight o'clock in the evening. Nightfall glossed the city to red-and-yellow-daubed obsidian. The Sky Tower stood sheathed in green glow, alone among neighbours reaching only waist-high. Light traffic scuttled randomly. I went west on Cook Street and south on Union. Residence de la McLane was in a medium high-rise complex on the last lot before Nelson and Union Streets merged. The building was ten storeys of two-tone grey, stilted on concrete columns to enable ground-floor parking, with narrow concrete balconies below each window in a weak offering of outdoor living.

I left the car on the road, took a pair of latex gloves from the boot and headed for the stairs below the building. Security lights clicked on and a shadow crucifix mapped my progress.

Christine McLane's unit was on level eight. My key didn't grant elevator access, but an echoing ascent of a concrete fire-escape got me there. I snapped on my gloves. There was nobody guarding the door, so I unlocked it and went in. The light had been left on. A yellow document on the floor in the entry requested the still-absent Ellis Carlyon to contact Auckland CIB. I moved into the room. The kitchen was to the left, the living room to the right, with a single bedroom beyond. A ranch slider opposite the entry gave out onto the balcony and made a feature wall of Spaghetti Junction and Ponsonby. I went to the window and opened it. The gentle white-water whisper of traffic rose up off the motorway and rode the cold air inside. That's the thing about city living, the traffic's always there. It adjusts your reference for silence.

The unit had already been searched. Fingerprint powder traces dirtied smooth surfaces. Friday's *Herald* occupied a wooden coffee table standing between the couch and television. I checked the bedroom. A double bed sat with covers pulled back, wrinkled linen exposed. A laptop computer occupied an adjacent desk. A curled power lead lay disconnected beside it, a line to an ADSL modem similarly truncated. To the left of the desk, a door led through to a bathroom en suite.

I sat at the desk and opened drawers. I found a calculator, a single packaged Durex condom and an empty container of Augmentin antibiotic pills. Bank statements betrayed a fast-food fervour, but there was nothing of interest in the dresser opposite the foot of the bed, other than men's clothes. A couple of yellowed paperbacks occupied the nightstand. Beneath the bed, a duffel bag spilled scrunched women's garments. I took it as a sign Christine McLane had only planned on being in residence temporarily. But there was nothing to indicate she subscribed to the same thoughts about her existence in general. I closed the bag and placed it on the bed, then stepped through to the bathroom. Crisp white tile everywhere. The reflections were cornea-sizzling, but a quick perusal unearthed nothing illicit.

I went back to the bedroom. It carried a faint perfume trace, as if its owner had simply stepped out, return pending. Death comes unexpected, even if you're a hygiene product. I powered on the laptop and it booted immediately. It would have left Ward Luvis's PC for dead. When it reached the log-on screen, I tried to log in as *Ellis*, but it prompted me for a password. I hit restart. The average computer isn't built to withstand break-ins, by virtue of the fact few people think to set an administrator password. I pressed F8 as the system ran its start-up protocol. A boot menu appeared, and I selected

Start in Safe Mode, then logged in as the computer administrator.

I turned on the modem and ran the web browser. The homepage was set to Facebook. Clearly, Ellis Carlyon was a social networking convert. His personal page loaded. His profile photo had been taken with the laptop's webcam. Hyper-contrast lighting left his facial features delineated by deep shadow, elongated slightly by the low-angle perspective.

The screen sidebar boasted 338 friends. I scrolled his personal page, trying to identify the people he communicated with most frequently. Of his 338 friends, he only touched base with about twelve of them on a frequent basis. The other 326 were fillers, social padding, people objectified into collector's items like baseball cards. I started clicking names randomly, accessing their personal pages. Most were blasé about the risk of Internet predators; I found phone numbers and addresses for six out of the first ten people I tried.

I removed my cellphone and dialled the first person generous enough to provide a phone number. A man answered. I identified myself.

'Do you know where Ellis is?' I asked.

'No idea,' he said. 'Is he in trouble?'

I hung up so I wouldn't have to lie. I tried a second number. Another man answered. We ran through the same dialogue. I called a third person. A woman, this time.

'How do I know you're a police detective?'

'I can give you a number to call, someone can verify I'm not having you on.'

She opted not to, and hung up instead.

I tried another number. Another woman answered. I ran through my introduction for the fourth time.

'What time is it?' she asked.

Background interference from her end. It sounded like several people were enjoying themselves.

'Half-past ten,' I said.

'I dunno. What did you say your name was again?'

I told her. Deadened booms reached me from elsewhere in the building. Concealed pipework sloshed.

'Have you tried the casino?' she asked.

'Sky City?'

'Yeah. I'd say if he's not at home he's probably still there.'

I thanked her and ended the call. Fingerprint powder rimed the phone keypad. I locked the apartment on my way out.

■ TWENTY-THREE

I called Comms when I got back to the car. Ellis Carlyon drove a white 2000-model Lexus Altezza. I went south on Union Street to the intersection, then made a left back down Nelson.

I indicated and turned right into the Sky City parking building and accepted a ticket from the machine. I'd searched for cars in Sky City before. At six floors, it's not the easiest place to check. But with the time required to pore through surveillance data, a manual search is often more efficient.

I cruised aisles slowly. My window was still open. Exhaust tang and concrete dust entered with the squeal of damp tyres on polished floor, and the reflected booms of door slams. It wasn't a busy night, but a disproportionate abundance of white cars offset that benefit.

I found it on level three. I slotted myself in a vacant park three spaces down and waited. I checked my watch. Five after eleven. Potentially, I had a long wait. A wait elongated by the fact I was without CDs. Radio chatter would have to suffice.

I buzzed my window up and watched.

He showed at midnight.

He weaved as he walked, but he had his cellphone out, checking messages. Interpretation: he'd had a few, but probably wasn't sloshed. He had black hair buzzed short around the sides and gelled stiff on top. His grey suit bore an affluent gleam, and that combined with his haircut made him look like a greaser or a loan shark.

He slowed when I climbed out of the car.

'Ellis Carlyon?'

He looked confused. 'Yeah?'

I tried to play it discreet. I asked him to come with me. He refused. Alcohol had worn his patience thin.

I gave him the news: Christine McLane, dead. His knees went. He collapsed vertically, his legs a crooked shambles beneath him. He pressed his palms against his ears and his jaw went slack. When he vomited it spread smooth and wide.

I drove him back to central. The vomit had missed his clothes, so the trip was tolerable. He sat inert, non-communicative, his head slumped against the door pillar, a spew string swinging from a slack lower lip. The news had induced a mental whitewash, as effective as a lobotomy. Light from the street passed across his face without drawing his focus. He was a man absent, his consciousness withdrawn to depths where the fear of his and others' mortality couldn't reach him.

I dropped the car off and took him up to CIB. He followed like a pet zombie, mindlessly obedient. I put him in an interview room; two chairs on the same side of the table, door open as I went to get coffee. Minor details he probably wouldn't appreciate, but the sort of subliminal gesture that differentiates witness from suspect. He sat with his arms heaped in front of him, head turned to study his reflection in the one-way glass in the right-hand wall.

I dosed his cup with two sugars and set it on the table in front of him. The sight of it perked him up. He took a sip and swallowed cautiously, as if his experience of caffeine was long ago and ill-remembered. I drew a chair out and sat down beside him.

'I'm sorry you had to find out the way you did,' I said.

The apology seemed to restore his focus. He wiped his

wrist across his mouth and shrugged. 'Yeah. Well.'

I looked at him. He was probably in his late twenties, two gold studs through his right earlobe, stubble dusting his cheeks.

'Could you tell me what your relationship to Christine was, exactly?' I said.

He stared down at his watch face. Maybe he was logging minutes since I'd broken the news. Tracking time elapsed since The Moment.

'We were together,' he said.

'How long had she been living with you?'

'About a year and a half or something, on and off. She was with me about a year, then we broke up for about two months. But she's been back with me for about three months, I think.'

He was still watching the time. The second hand swept a smooth quarter-turn. Another fifteen seconds of silent prayer that the nightmare would dissolve.

'She was found Sunday night,' I said.

He looked up and spun his coffee mug slowly with his fingertips. He exhaled smoothly, as if a return to introversion seemed an attractive option. The smell of his bile rose. 'Where?'

'In an industrial lot, off Great South Road.'

He looked away from me, his eyes flickering across the opposite wall, mouth ajar, trying to rationalize the information. He shook his head. 'OK. But. How did she … you know?'

'We don't know the cause of death at this stage,' I lied.

'Yeah you do. Of course you do. Don't bullshit me.'

I didn't answer.

'C'mon.'

'She was found in the back seat of a car that had been set alight.'

His features went slack and he gazed at the opposite wall and gave a low moan, pressing his fists against the sides of his head.

'Hey look, we can give it a break for a minute or two. I'll get you a drink of water.'

'No. No, I'm fine. Just don't touch me. I'm sweet.'

'Nobody's touching you.'

'Yeah, OK. Cool.' He scrunched the heels of his hands into his eyes and patted his jacket pockets, careful to look away from me.

'What was she doing there?' he asked at length.

'I think she may have been abducted.'

I described the kidnap John Hale had witnessed on Friday. He closed his eyes and shook his head rapidly, as if ridding water from his ear canals 'Shit. God. Why would someone want to take her?'

'I don't know. It might be something you can help us with.'

He didn't answer. He raked his hands through his hair, and when he placed his palms on the table, I could see his fingers were shaking.

'Where were you on Sunday?' I asked gently. 'Six p.m. through to midnight?'

A common response to such a question is an earnest declaration of innocence. But Ellis Carlyon just cleared his throat and said, 'I was in the casino from about half-past six.'

'When did you leave?'

'I don't know. Half an hour ago.'

'You've been in there over a day?'

He cleared his throat again and blinked twice. 'Well. Yeah.'

I drank some coffee. 'Is spending that long in the casino pretty standard practice?'

He licked his lips and shook the tremor out of his hands. 'Not really. I lost three grand. That's not really standard practice either.' He cleared his throat.

I didn't reply. Corridor murmur filtered through

to occupy the quiet. The weight of it built slowly and persuaded Ellis Carlyon to continue speaking.

'I had this foolproof system,' he said. 'For roulette.'

I looked at him and said nothing. He cleared his throat again. Gambling tactics might have appeared a strange topic, but I imagined he considered it infinitely more preferable to discussing murder by Molotov.

'It's fifty-fifty, right?' he said. 'Red or black. You keep the bet simple, red or black.'

'OK.'

'So I figured, well, you know, if it's fifty-fifty, even if you lose once, the chances of losing again are only twenty-five per cent, and then again twelve-and-a-half per cent and so on. Smaller and smaller as the number of spins goes up.'

He sat hunched as he spoke, his elbows pressed to his sides, palms upturned and gesticulating. New-found animation to illustrate his foolproof system.

'I understand,' I said.

'So then what you do is, if you lose, you just place enough on your second bet so that your first is covered.'

'Except you hit a bad spell and lose four times in a row, and you don't have the chips to cover it, and you end up dealing with big money really quickly,' I said.

'Well, yeah. And then you're done.'

He cleared his throat again. He took a hurried sip of coffee, ducking his head to the mug as if it was an activity at which he didn't wish to be observed.

'When was the last time you saw Christine?' I asked.

'Umm … Friday morning, I suppose.'

'OK. So tell me what you did on Friday.'

'I got up in the morning, Christine was still in bed, and I went to work.'

'What time did you get up?'

'Sevenish.'

'Where's work?'

'I work for a travel agency.'

'Where?'

He frowned and closed his eyes and flicked the fingers of his left hand. 'Fanshawe. I'm down on Fanshawe Street.'

'Did Christine have a job?'

'No. Jobs are kinda tight, you know? It's sort of why she moved back in with me. She was on the dole.'

'So what time did you get home on Friday?'

He cleared his throat. 'Eight.'

'OK. Did you see Christine on Friday evening?'

He cleared his throat again. 'No. I didn't.'

'But you didn't wonder where she was?'

'No.' Soft, like the admission was a guilty one. 'Well,

we'd had a bit of a fight the day before. Nothing big, I just wanted to know when she thought she might be able to put a bit towards the rent, nothing major, just, you know. Anyway she kinda went off at me, about having no cash at the moment, ra-de-ra-de-ra, and I got a bit wound up. So I guess she didn't really want to talk about it, thought it'd be best to be out when I got in.'

I sat quiet. He rested his elbows on the table top and pressed this thumbs against the bridge of his nose. His suit creases caught the light and shone.

I said, 'Has there been anything in the last couple of weeks that struck you as out of the ordinary?'

'Like what?'

'I don't know. Can you think of any reason why someone would want to harm Christine?'

He didn't answer. A tremor started up beneath his right eye, like a moth trapped beneath the lid.

'How often did she use drugs?' I asked.

His thumbs left his nose and his forearms thumped against the table. 'What?' he hissed. He spoke with his head ducked low, face upturned, as if my mere suggestion of the fact was a grave offence.

'She never used,' he insisted. 'Why the hell would you say something like that?'

I didn't answer. As far as I was concerned, the drug angle wasn't too far below the belt. Christine McLane had a prior conviction. And a cynic might peg Ellis Carlyon as a user. Ritalin abuse can lead to behavioural tics, like repeated throat-clearing. He studied me as I finished off my coffee, disgust at my question still present in the narrowness of his gaze.

'Sorry,' I said.

He shrugged it off, touched a thumbnail against a straight-edged sideburn. He finished his coffee with a careful mouthful, rocked the mug gently to and fro on the table top, watching dregs play chase.

I said, 'During the last four weeks, has there been anything at all to indicate Christine may have been in trouble?'

'I don't know what you mean.'

'Well, did you ever get the sense either of you was in danger?'

'No.'

'Has there been anything at all that's struck you as unusual?'

He cleared his throat. 'I don't know. Not really, I guess.'

'You seem a bit unsure.'

He paused. Shadows passed in the corridor behind us;

he tracked their movement on the opposite wall.

'Anything at all,' I prompted. 'Anything strange, anything you thought didn't fit the norm.'

He drew breath. He held it in one cheek and released it slowly between pressed lips.

'There's stuff on the computer,' he said.

'What do you mean?'

'She's got a file on my laptop. It's password protected. But I know the password, and I snooped it.'

'OK. What's in the file?'

'Just a photo.'

'Of what?'

'A house.'

'A house where?'

'I don't know. It's just a picture of a house, taken from the road.'

'When did it turn up?'

'I dunno. I found it maybe a week ago or something. It could've been there ages.'

'Did you ask her about it?'

He nodded. 'She didn't tell me what was in it. She just said something like, Ellis, you gotta understand I'm allowed a bit of privacy, and blah-de-blah. You know. So I didn't push it.'

'OK. What's the file location?'

He told me.

'What's the password?'

'Ellen. It's her mum's name,' he added.

I clinked the two mugs together and stood up. 'I've got to go,' I said. 'A lady called Claire Bennett will be through in a minute to speak with you.'

He didn't answer.

'Your apartment is still being examined,' I said. 'We'll check you in to a motel.'

He nodded. 'OK.'

He dropped his hand on the table. He watched blankly as it traced a slow, damp circle, as if its motion was beyond his control.

■ TWENTY-FOUR

Pull Ward Luvis's driver's licence photo and see if he recognizes him,' I said.

Bennett's office. An eight-hour day with the door closed had hot-boxed the temperature to stifling. She got up from her perch on the desk and cranked the fan dial. Loose paper shimmered.

'You didn't ask for an alibi,' she said.

'He doesn't need one. If his shock was faked I'll nominate him for an Oscar.'

'So what are you doing now?'

'I'm going to go and check out that file.'

'It's after midnight.'

'It's urgent.'

I walked back up the street to the apartment building.

The air was so cold it ached on intake. My breath smoked thinly. A croaky Toyota SUV dribbling white smoke constituted the only uphill traffic.

I took the stairs to level eight and unlocked Ellis Carlyon's front door. I coaxed on a fresh pair of gloves, flicked the lights and went through to the bedroom, where I booted the laptop. Christine McLane's quasi-secret folder was located in the My Documents directory. I double-clicked and typed *Ellen* when prompted. The folder contained two items: a JPEG image file, and an icon for a program called giggles.exe.

I checked the JPEG first. It was a photograph of a single-level weatherboard home, taken from the roadside. A letterbox bearing the number '12' sat on a low wire fence. To the left of frame, the rear of a grey Mitsubishi station-wagon was partially visible, all but the last numeral of its licence plate cut off. I studied the image. It could have been taken literally anywhere. Subject-wise, it seemed insignificant, but password protection obviously implied some measure of importance.

I clicked giggles.exe. A black window flashed briefly on the screen, and then vanished. I clicked it again and was met with the same result. Giggles seemed ineffectual.

I sat in the quiet a moment, listening to the traffic and

hard disc hum. Maybe it was innocuous. Or maybe it was something worth examining further. I checked my watch. Maybe it was even something worth examining at ten minutes to one in the morning.

I opened my phone and called John Hale.

They'd tossed the house: crowbarred the front door and ransacked his living room, just for the hell of it. The television screen was a crack jigsaw. Wall art had been de-glassed. His book case had been toppled; Norman Mailer, John Updike, Katherine Mansfield, spread-eagled with crumpled pages fanned. They'd ripped the fan out of the ceiling. It occupied centre stage, blades bent, plaster clinging to its support like some uprooted bulb. The photo albums pissed him off the most. Pages had been torn free, pillaged covers dumped; his only tangible link to boyhood scattered across his carpet.

He sat down on the couch. His motel-hopping had been a drawn-out affair: he hadn't been home since Friday. He hated the thought of his prized possessions being neglected, in disarray. The ranch slider to the deck was ajar, but thankfully unharmed, the clean odour of damp fern and manuka swirling in with the breeze. He pondered their decision to leave the slider intact. For someone drawn to TV screen destruction, it must have posed an enticing target, and its demise would have gone unnoticed: his home was on the northern side of Scenic Drive, his closest neighbour five hundred metres away through dense West Auckland bush. A miracle survivor, if there ever was one.

He got up and gathered photographs. Childhood revisited in faded three-by-five. A perfect kitchen snapshot: six-year-old John Hale, replete with grin, clean plate and clean conscience. A fragment from the Northland days. He remembered the evenings after his father returned from work, mill colleagues in tow. The hubbub of easy chatter, the scratch of matches, the waft of cigarette smoke and the wet slap of the fridge door. More faces; a mother-father-John triptych. Cancer had claimed his mother in her thirties. He couldn't remember her, but recollections of his father filled the mental void. He'd been a foreman at a now-defunct premises in an always-defunct town. Poor health caught him early. Daily exposure to harsh timber additives stamped 'lung disease' on his departure ticket. He died three weeks before Hale junior was sworn in as Constable John Hale.

He stashed the stack inside one of the discarded album covers and set it on the couch. The fan had been torn down with such force that the wiring had detached, blades awkward and twisted like some abused bird. He picked it up and set it outside on the deck and went to check the rest of the house. The kitchen was fine, the hallway had escaped brutality. His bedroom and bathroom showed no injury. He went downstairs. He had a partially restored '66 Ford Anglia in his garage. He turned on the overhead lights and looped it. No damage that wasn't pre-existing. The radio was on, *Classic Hits* reaching him faint and tinny.

He went upstairs and took a Speight's from the fridge, pried the tab with a hiss and stood in the wedge of glow from the open door and sank half the can. He felt the tension receding. He closed the fridge door. The cool slap resonated with thirty-year-old memory. He flicked the lights on, took beef mince from the freezer and set it going on low on the stovetop. The message light on his phone was blinking. He raised the handset and called his voicemail. One message received Friday. A now-familiar and exceedingly pissed-off police sergeant demanding his whereabouts. The call had been made from a mobile. Hale dialled it. He stood facing the kitchen window, the pass of headlights bringing branches into jagged relief.

The guy answered. 'It couldn't wait till morning?'

'Got a pen?' Hale asked.

'Who's this?'

Hale laughed over mince sizzle. 'Did you manage to keep the whiskey down?'

The guy didn't answer.

'I asked if you had a pen,' Hale said. 'I don't want you to forget anything.'

Still no answer.

'If you come in my house again,' Hale said, 'I will kill you.'

'I don't know what you're talking about.'

'Yeah you do. You brought me in on Friday. You thought I was bullshitting you about the kidnapping. I slipped your custody. You came here and thought you could get me when I turned up. I didn't, so you took it out on my living room.'

'Threatening a police officer is a serious offence.'

'Wrong answer. You're meant to say you don't know what I'm talking about.'

'That, too.'

Hale stirred his mince. 'This wasn't a burglary. This was just some arsehole venting frustration, who didn't have time to do more than one room.'

'If you want to report a crime you need to—'

'No. I'm not reporting a crime. I'm reporting that if you ever mess with me again, I'm going to break your neck. Check my background and tell me I wouldn't.' He paused. 'Better still, check my background and tell me I couldn't get away with it. Check my psych appraisals and tell me I'd have remorse.'

'You're a weirdo, Hale.'

'Probably. But the upside of it is I always get even.'

The guy laughed, and then he clicked off. The meat continued its gentle, wet crackle-pop. Hale hung up the phone. He opened a can of beans and added them to the pot. The mundaneness kept him rational. He killed the rest of the beer in one hit and went to the pantry. The door was secured with a sliding bolt to keep the dog out, but the dog had been dead six years. He took sheets of old newspaper from a box on the floor and went through to the living room and began gathering glass. The open ranch slider had bled the inside temperature, but he left it open. The phone rang. He walked back through to the kitchen, carpet crunching with embedded shards. It was Sean Devereaux calling.

'That burned girl,' Devereaux said.

Hale took the phone back through to the living room and sat down on the couch. 'What about her?'

'I'm checking out her computer. She's got a password-protected folder. There's a program in it that does nothing, and an image of a house taken from the street.'

'Where's the house?'

'I don't know. It could be virtually anywhere.'

'How did you access the folder?'

'I found the boyfriend. He knew the password.'

'And what does he think of the contents?'

'I don't know. He seems to think they're pretty innocent.'

'And you suspect otherwise.'

'Yeah. Something like that.'

Hale drifted back to the kitchen. The pot burbled. 'What are you still doing up?' he said. 'It's almost one o'clock.'

Devereaux skirted the question with a laugh. 'What are *you* still doing up?'

'I'm cooking mince,' Hale said. 'And tidying.'

Devereaux fell quiet for a moment. 'I tried to quit smoking. It threw my sleep out of sync.'

'How?'

'Kept me awake. Gave me nightmares.'

'What were they like?'

'I got this one where I'm in a room lying on a bed, and

somewhere I can hear someone screaming.'

'Who's the someone?'

'Don't know.'

'Young or old?'

'I don't know. I never find out. I never get off the bed.'

'I'm not that good at dream therapy,' Hale said.

'I think it's some sort of subconscious metaphor.'

'Meaning what?'

'Meaning there's always someone who needs help, and if you don't help out, you may as well pack it in and hand over to someone else.'

'Nobody's holding you to that.'

'My mind seems to.'

'Tell your mind to piss off.'

'I've tried that. Sometimes it works. Sometimes it visits at night and tells me to load up a pistol and take route .45 out of town. If you get my drift.'

Hale was quiet a long time. 'So did you manage to quit?' he said.

'I don't think so. I'm having a cigarette right now.'

Hale laughed. 'Email me the contents of the file. I'll check it out and get back to you.'

'Cheers. Appreciate it.'

■ TWENTY-FIVE

Hale closed his busted front door as best he could and took the Escort out onto Scenic Drive, heading east on SH16.

He got off at Nelson Street and cruised a clockwise loop from Fanshawe to Customs, to Gore, and then turned onto Fort Street and parked. The area was semi-reformed red-light. Upscale apartments and office space had claimed the south side of the street, but the harbour side was still seedy. Low-rise, low-rent, with correspondingly low appeal. Windows had blinds and grime with ground-floor porn ads floating in pink neon bubble-writing. Varied building heights combined to form a khaki, gap-toothed outlook.

Hale got out and crossed to a premises in the bottom of a two-storey building just west of Gore. Black paper backed the street-facing windows. Cigarette butts littered the pavement beneath a metal table and chair beside the front door. A bassy thud reached the street in deadened pulses.

A bouncer in a creased black suit stood just inside the threshold. His chin was ducked, a lighter in cupped hands raised to a cigarette clamped in a crinkled lipless grin. Ten bucks moved him. Hale went in. The floor was chequered lino. Neon tubes imparted light pink, putting smoke wafts from the door in hyper-contrast. A bar along the right-hand wall stretched half the depth of the room, truncated to accommodate a low stage where three bikini-clad women gyrated against slick metal poles with feigned ecstasy. At tables fronting the stage, a handful of men drank and lusted, catcalls snatched between waves of stereo.

Hale sat down at the bar. To his right, a guy in shirtsleeves and jeans sat zonked. His shoulders were rounded over a glass of wine, fingertips slowly spinning the stalk, gaze on his drink, as if its random convections possessed some deeply therapeutic quality.

The bartender was a tall Maori guy in his forties, with a shaved head. He stood with his back against the right-hand wall, arms folded, thumbing the cap of a stainless

steel lighter with bored listlessness. He acknowledged
Hale with a flick of eyebrow.

'What'll you have?' he asked.

'Heineken. Thanks.'

'Tap or bottle?'

'Bottle'll do it.'

He took a Heineken out of a glass cooler behind the
bar, de-capped it and set it down in front of Hale. His
fingers left streaks in the bottle sweat. Hale handed over
a second ten, took a mouthful and watched the room.
The bouncer reached for his filter and lit up again, doing
his best to keep the smoke outdoors. A drinks girl did the
rounds of the stage tables. Alcohol-fuelled hands groped
her for free action. The stage girls danced on, detached.
Bikini tops were removed with exaggerated elegance
and cast crowd-ways. Hale watched. The woman on the
left was older than the other two; early thirties, maybe
Korean, hair with orange highlights scissored short, jaw
ajar with pseudo-passion.

Hale lingered over the drink. It took her five minutes to
notice him. She didn't register surprise, but her look was
protracted. She embraced her pole for another minute
before she left the stage, disappearing through a door at
the rear. When she reappeared, she was dressed in jeans

287

and a grey sweater. She weaved her way through the erect fronds of lustful snatches and claimed a stool next to Hale. She leaned close for a shout: 'You after a chat or a lap dance?' she asked.

Her breath warmed his skin. He laughed. 'A chat, technically.'

'Technically. Which means you want something.'

'You always were a bit of a cynic.'

She shrugged. The bartender drifted away. 'Yeah, well. You bring out the worst in people.'

He drank the beer down to half-empty. 'How are you?' he asked.

She smiled. 'Sincerity was never your strong point.'

'No, that's me being genuine.'

She shrugged. 'Well. Since you last saw me, I had a mental breakdown and became a stripper. But you knew that, obviously.'

Hale swivelled on his stool and checked the room. The bouncer was propped against the doorframe. The guy at the bar was still fixated on the swirling of his wine. An on-stage act of lesbianism kept the audience foaming. 'I keep tabs,' he said simply.

She crossed her legs. 'Right. Of course.'

'I've got a case,' Hale said.

She watched him take a swallow and passed a hand through her hair.

'It's a semi-consultation thing,' he added.

'You mean Sean Devereaux asked you for a hand.'

'Essentially.'

'With what?'

'It's been in the paper.'

'What, the Carson thing?'

'No.'

'The burned car?'

He nodded, mid-sip. 'The people who were in it are the primary concern.'

She unfolded her legs and swivelled so she was square to the bar and looked at his reflection in the cooler glass. Acoustics trembled his beer.

'For a moment I thought you were visiting because you missed me,' she said.

'Sorry.'

'I haven't seen you in probably two and a half years.'

'Sorry,' he repeated.

She shrugged at his reflection. 'I'd be lying if I said you broke my heart. I think you're pretty much unloveable.'

He shrugged and took a mouthful.

'So what are you after?' she asked.

'You got a computer?'

'In the flat.'

'I think I need to show you.'

She looked towards the bartender. He floated back towards them, arms folded again, the lighter cap winking pink as he flipped it.

'I need to take off for twenty minutes,' she told him.

He didn't object. Hale finished his beer, and she led the way outside.

Her flat was just round the corner on Gore Street. It was a first-floor unit above a superette decked out with garish neon signage that buzzed like a morgue cooler. The front door squealed when she opened it, and he saw a wide gash arced in the lino. The place smelled of nicotine. Phone books chocked a camping table to waist height. Her living area had a low, worn two-seater couch, and a television set with rabbit ears. A single bulb in a woollen shade shaped like a church bell hung from thick cord. A desk with a laptop computer was side-on to the far wall, the single wood-framed window above it divided in two by a liquor sign that clung to the building's frontage.

She did a bent-over loop of the room, tossing garments

and magazines, eventually unearthing a pack of cigarettes and a lighter in a jacket heaped in front of the television. Shaky hands liberated a smoke from its box. She bit the filter with the bouncer's same toothy grimace and lit up with her chin ducked. Fumes coiled and bolstered the stink. She collapsed in a chair behind the desk, opened the laptop and powered it on.

Hale stayed standing, examining her walls as the computer booted. She had black-and-white framed photographs of three-piece bands he'd neither seen nor heard of.

'Don't look so disgusted,' she said.

'I'm not. I just never really pictured this as your sort of thing.'

'It isn't. This is the sum product of job stress leading to a nervous breakdown. Avoid at all costs.'

'This': a cosy job and a cosy residence, to stripper service and a dairy as a downstairs neighbour.

'I'm sorry. I had no idea.'

'Yeah you did. You knew some of it. You knew enough that you had no trouble finding me tonight. And you're smart enough to realize that me working as a tit-show probably wasn't a good sign. But I haven't heard from you, so don't pretend you care.'

He said nothing.

'Don't worry. Not caring doesn't make you worse than anyone else. Just be thankful you didn't visit a year ago. I still had my P habit. Then you would have felt really guilty.'

He sat down on the couch. Her monologue had numbed him.

'What's your email log-in?' she asked.

He told her. She typed.

'You want the thing from Sean Devereaux?' she asked.

'That'll be it.'

She sat with her legs crossed as she had done at the bar, light from the window outlining her in profile as she typed, the orange cigarette tip fanning vertically as she worked her lower jaw back and forth. He checked his watch: three-thirty a.m. She leaned back and linked her fingers behind her head, jiggling her raised foot as the file downloaded. She slouched forward and double-clicked. He stayed in his seat.

'It's a photo of a house,' she said.

'I know. I need to identify it.'

'Whose is it?'

'That's the point. We don't know.'

'It could be anywhere.'

He got up from the couch and stood behind her at the desk.

'You've got a partial licence plate on the car in shot,' he said. 'And the street number from the letterbox. You can cross-reference stuff.'

'"Cross-reference stuff." And how do you reckon I should do that?'

'I don't know. You're the expert. Can't you just pull the database into a text file and check addresses against licence plates?'

'I told work I'd be back in twenty minutes. And you've got no guarantee the car's registered to that address.'

'Got to start somewhere.'

She tapped ash on the edge of the desk. She closed the photo window and double-clicked giggles.exe.

'He said the giggles thing does nothing,' Hale said.

'I doubt it.'

She closed the window and exited her web browser. She brought up a search window and typed. The hard disc hummed. Foot and cigarette tip jiggled in unison. Hale went back to his couch. The IT stuff evaded him. He sat and watched her profile. She typed. She tapped more ash. She glanced out her split-view window.

'Sean Devereaux hasn't gotten any less weird,' she said.

'I didn't realize he was weird to begin with.'

She shrugged. 'Yeah, maybe not. But that email was sent at two a.m.'

'So?'

'So I wouldn't call working at two a.m. normal behaviour.'

'You do it. They call that irony.'

She ignored him. 'It's funny,' she said. 'I don't think I ever got much of a connection with you. But little Seany asks you to check out an address, and you're up at three in the morning sorting it out for him.'

Hale said nothing. She looked at him, the cigarette held aloft between two fingers, eyes slightly narrowed, amusement sparking at one corner of her mouth. He just sat there unresponsive, hopefully unreadable, waited for her to turn back to the screen.

'The giggles program doesn't do nothing,' she concluded at length. 'It extracts information hidden in the photograph.'

He got up and stood behind her again. She tilted the screen back. 'It's like a sort of security protocol,' she said. 'You send someone information embedded in the pixels of the photograph. The someone has a program equipped with an algorithm that can extract that information.

Individually, they're worthless; you can't extract the information without the correct algorithm, you have no idea what the algorithm is used to decrypt.'

'So how does it all work?'

'Run the giggles.exe program. It strips information out of the image and saves it as a text file.' She toggled to another window. 'It then saves it to an obscure location, so even if someone accesses the image and the algorithm together, as you've done, it's not immediately obvious what's going on.'

She opened said text file. It bore a single line of type:

150 Landon Ave, Auckland.

'Thanks,' Hale said.

'Any help?' she asked.

'I expect so. But I don't know what it means.'

He moved away. She closed the laptop but didn't look at him.

'It was good to see you,' he said. 'I'll visit again.'

She looked out the window. 'Goody,' she answered flatly.

He waited for something further but she stayed silent. He left her there in the neon-edged dark, the cigarette glowing faintly, five minutes before she was due back on stage.

■ TWENTY-SIX

Hale rang at six a.m. Tuesday. I was already awake. My cell was set to vibrate, and the call toppled it off the bedside table. I had to scramble to answer.

'The photo was a semi-decoy,' Hale said.

'How?'

'The image itself was probably of no value, but it had the words *150 Landon Ave* hidden in the pixels. The giggles program extracted the text.'

He explained the process.

'Maybe the house in the photo was at 150 Landon.'

'I doubt it,' he said. 'On account of the fact it says 12 on the letterbox.'

I said nothing.

'Does the address mean anything?' he asked.

'No. It seems a bit over the top as a security measure.'

'It's just an email safeguard. You disguise information in an image file when you send it online; limits the risk if someone's bugged your system.'

'I think the technical term is *hacked*.'

He made no reply. I kicked the covers back and sat on the edge of the bed. My throat felt raw, as if it had been torn with a steel rake.

'It seems a bit paranoid,' I said.

'I guess it would depend on the nature of the hidden information,' he answered.

'Yeah, but she's not selling state secrets.'

'If someone sent her an address, she might be selling drugs. Or sex.'

'Drug users just ring, and sex-for-money is legal. And she might have been the sender, and not the receiver.'

He didn't reply.

'Thanks for the help,' I said. 'I'll check it out.'

He ended the call. I showered, had breakfast and sucked down a dawn smoke. It pacified the nicotine want, but kept the throat scalding.

I'd checked out a substitute Commodore the night before. By seven I was westbound in light traffic on Tamaki Drive, the harbour to my right cool and grey, chopped with crests of white.

Claire Bennett wasn't in when I arrived at the office. I wrote up a report outlining Hale's findings, then went back to my desk and ran a check on 150 Landon Ave. It was a Mangere East address, just south of Middlemore, maybe five kilometres west of the Southern Motorway. It proved a quick query — 150 Landon had garnered no police callouts for any reason.

I checked the Habitation Index. An Alice MacBride, D.O.B. 1972, was said to be in residence. A check of the system yielded a clean slate.

Pollard was at his desk, spooning cereal. A paperwork mishmash had left him pushed for space. A burn victim photo-spread formed a melted tableau in front of him. I gave him the gist of the paperwork I'd left for Bennett.

'What are you going to do?' he asked.

'Talk to Ellis Carlyon, then check out this 150 Landon place.'

'As in do a door knock?'

'As in watch for a little while and see what happens. I've left a note for Bennett. She'll have to decide whether we're going to approach this place straight off, or wait it out a bit. But in the meantime someone needs to keep an eye on things.'

He had an in-one-ear-out-the-other look. Jacket crinkles

and a loosened collar implied an all-nighter. He nodded.. 'All right.'

His plate gave a little rattling pirouette when he dumped it on the desk.

I found a copy of the Molotov case file, located Ellis Carlyon's contact numbers and current address in the Persons of Interest list, and left.

The file had informed me Ellis Carlyon was staying with his sister at a place in Ponsonby. The address in question was a restored two-bay villa just north of Franklin Road. My knock was met with an extended period of silence. At length fingers split the blinds in a front window and the door was opened cautiously.

'You again,' Ellis Carlyon said.

He was wearing a white T-shirt with a stretched neck that gaped to mid-chest, his blue jeans bleeding sinewy strips of white denim at the cuffs. His eyes were scarlet-edged and couldn't settle.

'Yeah, me. Can I come in?'

He leaned out and gave the street a slow look, then stood aside and pulled the door wide. I entered. The place was divided by a wide corridor. It was in a state of mid-renovation. Drop cloths covered the floor, dusted with plaster from walls only recently gibbed. Tongues of looped white electrical cord hung through the raw cut-outs of future sockets. He led me through to a kitchen at the rear, where a breakfast bar split the space lengthways. I stayed in the doorway. To the left, a set of French doors gave onto a deck walled in by dead lavender in concrete planter boxes.

'How are you feeling?' I asked.

He removed a mug from a cupboard and dismissed the question with a half-shrug. His pants were beltless and slopped on his hips.

'I checked out that computer file,' I said.

'Oh yeah?'

He trudged at half-speed. Bad news leaves a numbing hangover. He slotted bread in a toaster and poured himself coffee from a glass plunger. The thirty hours' casino time had caught up and aged him a decade overnight.

'Any idea where 150 Landon Ave is?' I asked.

He was adding milk to the coffee. The question caught him mid-pour. He sloshed it. Tan fluid crested the rim.

'No idea,' he said.

There was a ceramic bowl loaded with cigarette butts on the bar in front of him. I removed a smoke of my own from a pack in my jacket and stuck it my mouth. Quitting wasn't going to happen.

He'd barely looked at me. He turned down his toast a fraction.

'Did Christine ever use drugs?' I asked.

He cleared his throat. 'You asked me that before, and I told you no.'

I shrugged. 'Details sometimes change after a good night's sleep.'

He capped his milk and put it in the fridge. He liked it sideways on the shelf, not upright in the door.

'What's that supposed to mean?' he said.

'I spoke to you last night, I was tired, you were strung out; sometimes stuff can get told a little differently in the morning.'

It did nothing to coax forth anything fresh. He popped the toast to check progress and then set it going again. He went to the fridge and removed margarine, made a separate trip to collect the jam.

I wagged my cigarette on my lip.

'I'll be in touch, Ellis. Answer your phone.'

I got on SH1 and inched south with rush-hour traffic. It took me forty minutes to clear Otahuhu. I exited at East Tamaki Road and went west through nondescript residential, then hit rag-tag retail at Hunters Corner. I stayed southwest and crossed the railway line at the bridge on St George Street, then headed back north and made a left off Gray Ave onto Landon.

Number 150 was a single-level pink weatherboard place on the right-hand side of the street. There was a ranch slider at the left, with a wooden step below it. The front door was at the right-hand end, in a second wing set back to accommodate a lumpy brick patio in front. The yard held a small above-ground swimming pool. Twigs and an empty beer can lolled with random currents. Next to the pool, broken sections of wooden fencing formed a ragged stack.

Curtains were in place behind the ranch slider. An old red Chrysler Cherokee was also parked next to the pool. The street was quiet. I rolled on at idle speed and made a U-turn and parked so that 150's frontage remained visible. I couldn't door-knock just yet. Watching was the only option.

I turned the engine off.

Nine o'clock arrived without excitement. A black cat slunk past on the opposite side of the street, eyeing me sternly. A postie slotted mail. Cars emerged from driveways, cautious and leaking smoke, reluctant to face the day. The Cherokee stayed in place. Nine-fifteen. I sat and thought. Nothing cheery: the deceased constitute my client base. Everyone who came to mind was dead.

My vigil lasted until nine twenty-two, when my phone rang. It was Claire Bennett.

'What are you doing?' she said.

I told her.

'You need to move now.'

'What? Why?'

'No. Shut up. Turn the engine on, and drive away, nice and carefully.'

I didn't reply. I did as directed and twisted the key and moved off the kerb. The rear of the Cherokee slid past in the passenger window. I made it to Gray Ave and went right.

'OK, done, what—'

'No, Sean. You don't just go and do whatever the fuck you want.'

'What? What are you talking about? I don't know what you're on about. Explain what—'

'Keep driving,' she answered. 'You're phone's going to ring in a minute. Answer it.'

■ TWENTY-SEVEN

I got back onto Kolmar and made for the motorway. Red lights at Hunters Corner stalled me. My cellphone rang as predicted.

'I hope you're not driving,' the caller said.

'Stopped at a light, so we're all kosher.'

The guy gave a quiet laugh. 'Still illegal, I'm afraid, detective.'

'Who am I speaking with?'

'Nobody spooky. Claire Bennett gave me your number. We need a face to face. Where are you?'

'Coming up on East Tamaki Road, eastbound.'

'There's a liquor place called The Mill, left-hand side of the street. It's got a big red sign. You know which one I mean?'

'Uh-huh.'

'Be there in twenty minutes.'

And then he hung up on me.

The tail end of rush hour meant it took me fifteen minutes to get along East Tamaki Road. The Mill was on the left as described, located on the eastern fringe of the retail stretch before development switched to residential. I drove past the customer entrance and turned into the wide service access down the right-hand side of the property. I parked against the eastern wall, facing the street. Dense traffic flowed stop-start; customers trickled in ones and twos. I turned the radio on and watched the street. I'd been pulled off a surveillance job on an address that had shown a clean file. The tip-offs would have been minimal. Pollard wouldn't have snitched me. Therefore someone had red-flagged the computer system.

The dashboard clock showed ten. One minute past, and an olive-green Honda Civic sedan turned into the service lane and pulled to a stop nose-in to my Commodore. A grey-haired guy in his early fifties with wire-framed spectacles was driving. There was a Korean guy about my age in the passenger seat beside him. The rear door behind the driver opened and a third guy in his early forties wearing jeans and a T-shirt climbed out. His scalp and jaw were fuzzed with dark stubble, and he had silvered aviator sunglasses swinging around his neck from a length of black elastic. He looked agitated.

I got out of the car and squirmed along the wall to the front bumper. The two remaining guys in the Civic climbed out. The driver moved unhurriedly and appeared calm, but the passenger was of a similar disposition to the back seat guy. His door knocked the wall solidly when he opened it. It slammed and rocked the chassis when he closed it. He was under six foot, but he was carrying weight.

'Idiot,' he said to me.

The guy in the jeans and T-shirt chased the insult up by stepping forward and shoving me. He did it one-handed, open-palm, more irritated gesture than intent to injure. I leaned into it and took it in the centre of the chest, but putting my weight forward meant it didn't knock me back. I caught his wrist with my right hand and pulled him towards me, then spun and used my left hand on the back of his elbow to drive him into the bonnet of my car. His forehead boomed on the sheet metal. His glasses sandwiched between his chest and the top edge of the grille and emitted a crunch.

I released him and stepped back.

The guy went down on one knee. Back of his right hand against his forehead, left arm still draped across the bonnet, the skin of his forearm squealing softly as it slid limply off the paint job.

The Korean guy's expression was a blend of impressed and pissed off. The older man had one arm raised, stymieing any potential retaliation. He elbowed his door closed just enough to catch and stepped forward on one leg, his trailing foot stretched to tip-toe. He appraised the bonnet victim, grimaced and sucked air through his teeth.

'What do you do if someone's trying to kill you?' he asked.

I recognized his voice from the phone.

'No survivors to comment,' I answered.

He stood straight. He wore a green shirt the same shade as the car and an orange tie beneath a grey suit. 'Yeah, very clever,' he said. 'Congratulations on almost letting the cat out of the bag.'

'I didn't know there was a cat to let out,' I said.

He didn't answer.

'I'll need to see some ID,' I said.

He glanced at me, but seemed to dismiss the instruction. 'Hop in the car,' he said. 'We'll fill you in.'

■ TWENTY-EIGHT

I got in the back seat of the Civic. The grey-haired guy from the phone got back in the driver's seat. His hair was combed in a neat part that cut a flesh-tone razor line through the left side of his scalp. The Korean guy sat beside me on my right with his elbow on the sill and his chin between his thumb and index finger. It took my bonnet victim a minute to recover. His glasses resembled a fiddled-with paperclip. He was still holding his head when he climbed in the passenger seat.

I said, 'Shall I grab you a Nurofen?'

'Fuck you, Devereaux,' he said. 'Maybe next time think twice before you try and run covert surveillance in a police car, you retard.'

'I hope they were cheap sunglasses,' I said.

Nobody spoke. The Korean guy gazed out his window

308

at nothing. He had a navy hooded jumper above khaki cargo pants. The jumper had ridden up to reveal handcuffs clipped through a belt loop on his hip. The grey guy at the wheel sat mute, waiting out the conflict. The rear-view mirror was full of traffic motion.

'I want to see some ID,' I said at length. 'And an explanation would be good.'

The grey man twisted the mirror until it framed his gaze for me. 'My name's Roger Buchanan,' he said. 'DIA.' He had a quiet, neutral tone, as if he was delivering an oncological diagnosis.

'You got ID on you, Roger?'

He held a Department of Internal Affairs ID up to the mirror that confirmed his name, and that he held the rank of inspector. The introductions worked clockwise: the Korean guy leaned towards the door and slipped a badge holder out of his left pocket and flipped it open without looking at me. It was a silver detective's shield, which meant he was police as opposed to DIA.

'You can call me Choi,' he said.

'Is that your real name?'

'If you like.'

The guy with the broken glasses showed me another DIA

identification card. It gave his name as Dennis Willard.

'Why did you pull me off my surveillance?' I asked.

Buchanan looked at me in the mirror. He was a squared-away type of character, window-mannequin neat. His shirt cuffs cleared his jacket by about ten millimetres, his collar flaps were crisply-ironed and buttoned down. He wore his watch on the underside of his wrist. 'This is all hush-hush,' he said.

'I can keep a secret.'

His mouth hooked wryly. 'Maybe you could take a couple of guesses, so we don't have to tell you outright.'

'Nobody's going to know, even if you do.'

He looked away and shrugged, but said nothing.

I said, 'Two Department of Internal Affairs staff with a police detective on temporary detached duty: could be a lot of things.'

Nobody spoke.

'Probably not fraud,' I said. 'Probably not gambling infringement.'

Nobody spoke.

'Computer crime,' I said.

'Warmer,' said Buchanan.

'Sex crimes,' I said.

'Getting there.'

'Child porn.'

Buchanan nodded. He ran a fingernail through the razor-edge hair part. 'Essentially.'

'Internet-based child porn on a huge scale if you pulled me off it as quickly as you did.'

'Your database search of the address tipped us off,' Buchanan said. 'We've got surveillance on the house as well.'

'So why does 150 Landon need four people watching it?'

'There's only three of us here.'

'But you aren't stupid enough to leave the surveillance unattended so you could come and chat to me. So there's one other person keeping shop. Five would be a bit excessive.'

Nobody spoke. Buchanan thumbed the handbrake button as he looked out his window. Willard's forehead had stamped a dish in my bonnet. It caused a dip in the band of sunlight reflecting off the metalwork.

'We've got an ongoing op,' Buchanan said. 'We're in the process of identifying users of a particular network. The guy at number 150 is one of them.'

'My info said there's a woman living there. Alice something-or-other.'

'Not any more. One guy. No woman.'

I didn't answer. Willard removed his sunglasses from around his neck. They tinkled.

'What's your interest in the place?' Buchanan asked.

'You know the homicide case of the girl found in the burned car?' I said.

'Yeah.'

'On her computer there was a JPEG image with that address encrypted.'

Buchanan mused. He ran a thumbnail through the hair part. 'It's probably a precaution for sending email,' he said. 'Disguise information in an innocuous-looking photo.'

'I'd gathered that.'

'What else is on her computer?'

'It's not actually hers. It's the boyfriend's. It hasn't really been checked.'

The car fell quiet.

'Well, you've put us in a pickle,' Buchanan said at length.

'For what reason?'

'Because if you poke around in this it could screw us.'

'I'm not *poking*. I'm investigating a homicide.'

'Still. This goes way above you. We have to obstruct

your progress until we've moved in at our end.'

He propped his wrists on the top of the wheel. He inspected them one at a time, checking to see if his cuffs were uniform.

'The place get many visitors?' I asked.

'Not really. Some. We can't identify anyone.'

'It would be good to see if my victim actually visited the place. You got tape recordings?'

'They're digital, but yeah.'

'I'd like to check them out.'

Buchanan thumbed the handbrake button some more. Traffic noise stayed steady. Choi looked out his window. Willard sat mute.

'If you've got the time, we'll take you over to the observation point,' Buchanan said.

'OK, good,' I said. 'We'll do that.'

Rush hour had cooled off, so the drive back to Landon was much more petrol-efficient. Chat ceased. Buchanan didn't strike me as a socialite. Choi apparently disapproved of me. And Willard's broken sunglasses meant he and I would never be chummy.

Buchanan wound a clockwise route through the suburbs and entered Landon at the western end.

Four doors short of 150 he turned into the driveway of a property across the road. It was a cream, single-level weatherboard unit skirted by long grass, with an unpainted picket fence stretching the frontage. A jumbled television aerial had relinquished its perch and lay in the yard.

Parallel bald strips in the lawn reaching down to an open-end carport constituted the driveway. Buchanan drove in and parked. I waited for them to climb out, then followed them to a side door secured by a digital combination lock. There was a hunched pause punctuated by soft crunches as Buchanan thumbed in the code: bottom row, top row, third from bottom. We filed in, and Choi triple dead-bolted and chained the door behind us.

I followed Buchanan through a small kitchen into a living area which was more command-post than lounge. It was exposed to the street on three sides, so the curtains were duct-taped to the window surrounds. A ceiling light in a glass shade speckled with fly shit offered weak illumination. To the left, a long row of desks was mounted with half-a-dozen computer terminals. Far from high-tech: the monitors were pale-yellow cubes, showing blurred images that cast a blue strobe flicker across the walls and ceiling. The desks were all different heights. To the right, a row of television monitors mirrored the computer set-up, split-screen security-camera recordings enhancing the flickered images. On the floor, thick ropes of snaking data cables were taped to the carpet. Computer units lay stripped of panelling and innards, while DVD recorders and server and router boxes sat in blinking towers that hummed with voltage. The whole room smelled of warm plastic.

A heavy-set, red-haired woman in her mid-thirties sat slumped in an office chair mounted on casters. She had one foot propped on the edge of the desk, rolling herself back and forth listlessly in front of one of the computer terminals. A pyramid of three empty coffee cups stood to the right of the keyboard, a cereal bowl flecked with chip crumbs on her left.

'What's happening?' Buchanan asked.

'Nothing,' the woman answered. 'His phone line's inactive, his computer's running, but sitting idle. He hasn't come outside.'

She dropped her foot to the floor, threaded hair behind her ear and looked back over her shoulder at us. Stereo speakers were mounted on the sides of her monitor. Elbow's 'Fugitive Motel' played low.

'Hi,' she said to me. 'Darlene.' She had too many teeth, like kids crowded for a photo.

'Sean Devereaux,' I answered. 'I recommend track six.'

She honoured my recommendation and cycled to 'Not a Job'.

Choi and Willard took seats at the television monitors and mimicked Darlene's slouch. Buchanan touched his tie knot, stepped gingerly through the mess of cables and smoothed the tape beneath the window in the far wall with the back of his hand.

'Must get a bit cosy in here,' I said.

The other three ignored me.

'We normally run a team of two,' Buchanan said. 'But we boost things if we think something big's on the way.'

'And is something big on the way?'

He fingered his collar buttons and shrugged. 'Maybe. Maybe not.'

'But you've got him bugged in any event.'

Buchanan put his hands in his pockets and looked at the techno chaos around him. 'He's more than bugged. He's infested. We've got his phone. We've got his computer. We've got cameras on him. We can track his car. We pressure-tapped his plumbing so we know when he takes a shit.'

He saw my expression and smiled. 'Kidding about the plumbing.'

'What's his name?' I asked.

'The registered occupant dashed about six months ago. The guy in there we're watching is called Jon — no H — Edward.'

'Does he get many female visitors?'

He shrugged and removed his glasses and gathered some shirt tail. He dabbed lint off a lens. 'I guess. People visit him at night. Our night vision's not that flash, so specifics are never that good. What time-frame are you looking at?'

'I don't know. Whenever.'

Willard gave a little smirk. I said nothing. The memory of his sunglasses would keep him in line. Darlene licked her finger and chased chip flavouring around the empty bowl.

'What's the description?' Buchanan asked at length.

'Young, blonde and attractive,' I said.

'We review footage fairly regularly. I don't remember anyone like that.'

'Does your Jon Edward have a propensity for sending messages encrypted in photographs?'

He ducked his chin and re-spectacled carefully, gaze

tilted upwards to check the frame was level. 'We haven't detected anything, but it's possible. Bear in mind this guy lives on his PC. He's sending and receiving huge quantities of data on a daily basis. We're talking upwards of ten gigabytes, sometimes. We intercept piles and piles of his shit, more than likely a decent chunk of it is image files, conceivably with hidden data, but we simply haven't checked.'

'You cottoned to the idea of him using data in images as email security pretty quickly, so I thought maybe it's something he's done before.'

'Potentially. Probably. A lot of these guys are justifiably paranoid, so it's possibly something he does regularly. But we haven't been specifically looking for it.'

I nodded. Darlene was still slumped in her chair, gaze rigid, tongue slowly prowling her molars for chip traces. Willard's status was similar. Choi clattered a DVD onto a disc tray and ignored us.

'Have you got footage I can look at?' I asked.

Buchanan took a seat at a computer terminal beside Darlene, shook the mouse to clear the screen saver and began cycling through a file directory.

'How long have you got?' he asked.

'A while. Why?'

'We've got him on twenty-four hour watch. We've got a lot of data.'

'Maybe if we could just check out his visitors.'

Buchanan pinched his nose. Hardware hummed. The plastic smell was headache-inducing. Migraine mitigation would likely require a cigarette.

'We log all the visits he gets to the house,' he said. 'As I told you, most of them are at night, so the detail isn't all that great. How far back do you want to go?'

'I don't know. How far back have you got?'

'A month. The actual video feed is stored off-site, we've just got some stills we keep for reference.'

He double-clicked a file and a picture-viewer opened. A four-way green-tinged image of 150 Landon's frontage filled the screen.

'Where are the cameras?' I asked.

'We've got one on our roof aimed down the street. Another in a power pole, another in a tree, another in the back seat of a car we keep parked down there.'

He cycled images. 'Any of this helpful?'

The images were just blurred snapshots of vehicles parked at the kerb and in 150's front yard. Licence plates weren't visible. People weren't visible.

'Not really,' I said.

He cycled on. More blurred cars. Some blurred in-motion shots of faceless people. The bad light made me squint.

'You identified any of these people?' I asked.

He shrugged. 'Maybe,' he said vaguely. 'Not really my job. I just record and send people the stuff I've recorded.'

He cycled faster. The increased speed reduced the images to a blurred montage.

'Hang on, hang on. Stop.'

He stopped and cycled back a couple of frames. 'You recognize that?' he asked.

A white Toyota Altezza parked at the kerb opposite 150. A white Toyota Altezza like the one belonging to Ellis Carlyon. Two of the angles showed the car front- and end-on, but the licence plate wasn't discernible.

'Can you get any more resolution out of this?' I asked.

'Don't think so. What you see is what you get.'

'Can you print me a copy?'

He could. A laser printer at the far end of the desk fed me a single curled monochrome sheet.

'I'm going to need access to any footage you've accumulated.'

'I'll see what I can do,' he said.

'Murder investigation, it's kind of urgent.'

'I'm sure it is, but I'm not the one in charge.'

I didn't answer. Willard might have given another little smirk. I folded the print-out twice and slipped it in my jacket pocket. Buchanan seemed to interpret some measure of finality in it.

'I'll run you back to your car,' he said.

■ TWENTY-NINE

It was approaching eleven-thirty by the time he dropped me back on East Tamaki Road. I crossed the street to a petrol station and stocked up on smokes, bolstering my nicotine levels as I drove east towards the motorway. With regard to 150 Landon, Ellis Carlyon had feigned ignorance. So the fact his car was visible in security footage of the property didn't bode well for him.

I called his cellphone. It rang through to voicemail. I didn't leave a message. People in adjacent lanes waggled forefingers at me for phoning while driving. I called his sister's house, hanging up after fifteen rings. I called his office and got more voicemail.

I exited the motorway fifteen minutes later and headed north on Ponsonby Road towards Franklin. At just after midday, I parked out front of the villa I had visited earlier that morning. Ellis Carlyon's sister answered the door. She was tall and fortyish, with grey hair coiffed up in a loose perm, like a swirl of iron candyfloss. She had a ballpoint pen trapped crossways in the fingers of one hand, and a cordless telephone in the other.

'Are you the cop?' she asked.

'I'm *a* cop.'

'Ellis isn't here.'

'Do you know where he is? He's not answering his phone.'

'No, I don't know where he is. He reckoned you were rude and threatened him, so he was going somewhere else for a little while.'

She dumped it in one breathless spiel. She had the door half-closed as a shield against potential blowback.

'So you do know where he is, then.'

She didn't answer. She was wearing a blue woollen turtleneck sweater above dark grey trousers. She leaned back from the waist to see behind the edge of the door. She pocketed the phone.

'Mr Carlyon has connections to a homicide,' I said. 'It's not inconceivable he's in danger. If something happens to him, and you withhold knowledge of where he is, there's going to be strife.'

She flicked the pen against the edge of the doorframe. 'Don't take that tone with me,' she said.

I didn't answer. I removed another cigarette from my new pack and put it in my mouth, and looked at her down the barrel. Her eyes tracked the movement. Her mouth showed unwavering contempt. The frequency of her flicking dropped.

'Is he in trouble?' she asked.

'He will be when I find him. The question is whether someone more malevolent finds him first.'

'Well, I don't know where he is. He said he was scared of you.'

'He's not scared of me. He's scared of what I represent.'

She smiled thinly, gave a little amused sniff. 'That's a good line. What do you represent?'

'Being truthful, honest, all that palaver.'

She didn't answer.

'What time did he go?' I asked.

'This morning, probably not long after you left. Work's given him leave, so he won't be there.'

'Where did he say he was going?'

'He didn't tell me.'

'Did you ask him?'

She didn't answer. Her gaze was narrow, laden with

disapproval. Her mouth was hooked at one end, as if my questions represented an irksome foolishness she was patiently tolerating.

'I'm sorry,' I said. 'I think you're lying to me.'

'Go away,' she said quietly.

She threw the door closed. A through-draught assisted, and it slammed in my face. The rush of air blew my trousers against my legs. The brass knocker clacked once. I lit the cigarette, and then walked back to the car.

I drove back to the station and tried Ellis Carlyon's cellphone again. It went to voicemail. I tried his office line. He wasn't there. I Googled his employer, and got a number for reception. I called and asked if Ellis Carlyon had a business cellphone I could reach him on. He did. I dialled, and got lucky.

'Hello?'

'Ellis, it's Sean Devereaux. Where are you?'

He didn't answer.

'Hey, are you there? Don't hang up. Where are you?'

'Look, man. I just need a breather, OK? This whole thing's strung me out, and I just need some space.'

'Yeah, look, I understand that, but I need to know where you are.'

He cleared his throat. 'I don't think I have to tell you.'

'All I want to do is go over your story.'

'We've been over it. Twice.'

'I just need to clarify some stuff, that's all.'

'What stuff?'

'It's complicated.'

A long pause. 'Are you tracing this?'

'No.'

'Because if you are, I'm going to hang up right now.'

'I'm not tracing the call.'

He didn't answer.

I gambled: 'Ellis, why have you gone to a motel?'

He exhaled. The electronics translated it as three seconds of crackle. He started to say something, then caught himself. It sounded like the letter 'B', maybe not even that, maybe the prerequisite pursing of lips. Maybe the beginning of an aborted 'because'. A fraction of a syllable before the subtext of the question reached him, and he realized I hadn't asked *why have you gone to a motel?* but rather *are you at a motel?*

'I haven't,' he said.

'I reckon you have. I need to know where you are. You told me you didn't know anything about 150 Landon but I've a got a photo of— '

He hung up. The dial tone flat-lined in my ear.

'Shit,' I said aloud.

Hush took hold. Activity paused as people took the opportunity to crane over dividers and glimpse the source of my displeasure.

Twelve fifty-five p.m. I'd seen Ellis Carlyon's bank statements when I checked his apartment. I Googled the bank's call centre number, and dialled it. Account checking the fast way: ring the bank and play it smooth.

A young guy answered. I told him my name was Ellis Carlyon. I supplied his address and D.O.B. details, sifted mental clutter and quoted a fast-food purchase when asked for a recent transaction. No issues. I laid out a bogus predicament: my EFTPOS card was playing up, could he check if a payment had gone through?

'No, sir, we've got no record of it.'

'You sure? The guy ran it three times.'

'Our records show your last transaction was a five-hundred-dollar ATM withdrawal.'

'The Ponsonby one?'

'No, that was in Warkworth, just this morning.'

I ended the call. Carlyon was playing it cautious, verging on paranoid. The large cash withdrawal would eliminate the need for electronic transactions. No record, no risk of a trace. His ATM visit told me he'd driven north out of Auckland for an hour, but not much else.

I looked up Warkworth motels. They weren't abundant. Nothing is abundant in Warkworth. It's a little town on SH1, just south of where the Auckland region officially terminates. I found two bed and breakfasts and a motor lodge. I called each of them in turn. None of them had an Ellis Carlyon in residence. None of them had a white Lexus Altezza. Meaning if he had a motel in mind, he probably hadn't lingered. And he wouldn't have driven north for an hour just to withdraw money and then turned around and driven south. So excluding the possibility of a U-turn, essentially he had two options: continue north on SH1, or head east towards the coast. I Googled the eastern option. South to north, he had Snells, Matakana, Omaha, or Leigh.

I compiled a list of potential accommodation. Motel-checking constituted another thirty minutes of phone enquiry. Nobody had an Ellis Carlyon. Nobody had his white Lexus.

I checked maps. I re-Googled. If he'd headed north, his options opened up, and probability was tilted against me. The next significant feature on SH1, northbound, was the town of Wellsford, twenty minutes from

Warkworth. I found two more motels and called them. No Ellis. No Lexus. The next place north was Te Hana. It's a tiny industrial settlement straddling the highway, bordered to the east by the northern railway line. It's not prospering, and I didn't think it had a motel. Just north of it, Mangawhai Road forked northeast out towards Mangawhai Heads. I called a couple of bed and breakfast places. No luck. Further north, and the map turned nasty. His chances were good regardless of whether he chose SH12, west, or SH1, north.

When in doubt, check the subject's back story. I logged into the Department of Internal Affairs system and brought up Births, Deaths and Marriages Online. Ellis Carlyon had been born February 1981 to Marguerite and Brian Hugh Carlyon. Dad was dead, mother wasn't. She was listed at a Waipu address, about one hour north of Warkworth.

I opened a reverse telephone directory, found her number, and called it.

His mother answered. I came on friendly. We shot the breeze. No, she didn't know where Ellis was.

I ended the call.

He wasn't with his mother. Waipu felt good, though. It matched his apparent northbound trajectory and it had familial importance. I consulted my phone book again, and found a number for a motel on Cove Road. A man answered, and I identified myself.

'Have you had an Ellis Carlyon check in this afternoon?'

'No. We've had an Ellis Jones, though.'

'What sort of car was Ellis Jones driving?'

Paperwork riffled. 'White Lexus Altezza,' the guy said.

I checked the time. It was one fifty-six. Call it a sixty-one-minute track down.

■ THIRTY

Claire Bennett wasn't in her office, so I called her cellphone.

'I almost blew a DIA stakeout this morning,' I said.

'I know you did.'

'They've got surveillance of a car that looks like Ellis Carlyon's parked outside 150 Landon.'

Silence as she assimilated. 'I'm not following.'

'He told me he knew nothing about the place, said he'd never heard of it. His dead girlfriend had the address encrypted in a photo inside a password-protected file. He claims he had nothing to do with the place, but his car's been there at least once.'

'The girl might have driven herself there.'

'Maybe. He's panicked, though. He's not answering my calls, he's left town. Which means either he's telling the truth about not knowing the address, but has some idea of what she was doing there; or it was him driving the car. '

'Or a combination of the two.'

'Yeah. Or that.'

'Ah, shit,' she said at length. 'So when did he AWOL?'

'This morning. I think he's set himself up in a motel in Northland.'

'OK,' she said. 'Go and get him. Take some back-up.'

'Yours truly should suffice.'

'OK,' she said. 'Just get him back.'

I checked out my replacement Commodore and took SH1, north. Early afternoon traffic was light. A fine time for homicide investigation.

North of Albany, the outlook turned to lumpy rural. I turned right off the highway an hour later and detoured east on the scenic route towards Mangawhai. The fields were rich, the grass as heavy and dense as a spread of wet cloth, road a graceful sketch across gently moulded hills. I passed the township at the Heads and took the curling two-lane highway north through a dense backdrop of native forest, emerging back on the coast south of Lang's Beach. Holiday homes flecked the undulating surrounds, sudden flashes as the mid-afternoon caught hillside windows. I followed the coast road through wrinkled and flowerless pohutukawa, a slight onshore stirring foam-edged ripples in the tide.

Waipu was another fifteen minutes north. The motel was on the eastern town fringe on Cove Road. Painted road signage announced its presence. I slowed and surveyed the topography. It was flat and unremarkable. Across the road to the north, beyond a deep ditch, fields formed a flat seam with the horizon. Ahead of me the road extended straight west. A shallow hump sheared the far-off alignment, power cables sagging deeper with distance.

It was four twenty-five p.m. I stopped the car on the verge and turned the engine off. The organic smell of silage and manure had infiltrated the aircon. I got out and locked the car and walked along the road to the motel. It was a two-storeyed structure of about fifteen rooms, neighboured east and west by a stretch of low housing. The building faced the street end-on, a smooth black pool of asphalt parking adjacent. I couldn't see a white Lexus.

Reception was located in the central ground-floor unit. Pushing the door set a bell chiming. The carpet was worn, the weaves troughed with grit. A faded aerial photograph courtesy of a bygone era occupied the far wall. To my left a man in his fifties sat reclined in an office chair behind a tall counter, his attention on a television mounted on a bracket on the right wall. His shirtsleeves were pushed raggedly to his elbows, forearms folded across his stomach. His crown was bald, the remaining hair forming a uniform band of grey, as if a strip of animal pelt had been moulded to the sides of his skull.

The television showed provincial rugby. The ring of the bell had died before he looked at me. His eyes panned first, and then the head followed.

I showed him my badge. 'I called and spoke to you earlier this afternoon,' I said.

'Oh yeah.' His eyebrows rose. 'About the white car. And Whatshisname.'

'Is he still here? I can't see his car.'

The eyebrows resumed normal altitude. 'He hasn't paid, so I suspect he's just popped out.'

'Have you got a key for his room?'

He meshed his fingers and twiddled his thumbs and glanced at the game. 'Have you knocked on his door?'

'No,' I said. 'And I'd prefer not to.'

'What's this guy wanted for?'

'I don't know. I'm just the getter.'

He paused. The television volume was low.

Commentator chatter came at a murmur. 'Do you have some paperwork?'

'No.'

'Then I don't think you can just walk in.'

'I can. It's just a question of whether or not you want to end up with a broken door.'

I smiled as I said it, to take the edge off it. His eyes went to the rugby. The glassed photo frame offered a peripheral reflection. The defending team was inside its own twenty-two.

'We've got insurance,' the guy said, still with the game.

'Insurance is a hassle,' I said. 'You have to file paperwork, you'll lose your no-claims bonus. And the kerfuffle might unsettle other guests.'

He glanced at me and offered an extended exhalation. He drummed netted fingers lightly on the tops of his hands.

'I'd probably need a down-payment,' he said. 'There's risk in giving you a key. For you, there's a lot of convenience associated with having one. That shouldn't just come for free.'

I shrugged. 'Police questionings can get messy. TVs get broken, shit gets thrown through windows. People can get hurt. It's the sort of behaviour that scares the hell out of guests. It can really detract from your upscale image.'

The guy nodded slowly, as if he was carefully considering my strong counterpoint. He clucked his tongue and made a face, eyes still with the game. 'Is there any way these risks can be managed?' he asked.

'Oh, absolutely. I think if you were to part with the key without the implied fee, I'd keep things scrupulously tidy.'

He thought it through. He watched the television. A lineout was thrown. A try was scored. He rolled a drawer open and removed a key, attached with green twine to a yellow luggage tag. It flipped a lazy vertical three-sixty as he tossed it over the desk. He adjusted his posture and re-netted his fingers.

'Bottom floor,' he said. 'Far room. Key's a master, so I'll need it back.'

The door dinged as I left.

■THIRTY-ONE

Bottom floor, far room, was Unit Six. A blind backed a single window. Balcony shade gave the frontage a two-tone colour scheme. I let myself in with the master key and locked up behind me.

There was a small circular table below the window to the right, and a single bed flush against the right-hand wall. The kitchen was in the rear, behind a breakfast bar that stretched half the width of the room. To the left, doors led through to a bedroom and bathroom respectively. I stood and observed. The fridge interrupted its own rhythmic hum with periodic shudders. A dripping tap tinked. Beneath the table, the carpet was stamped with indentations where a chair had once stood but had since been moved. I glanced in the bedroom. A large duffel bag dented the quilt of a queen-size bed. In the bathroom, a drinking glass held a toothbrush and razor. The toilet cistern hissed faintly.

No Ellis.

I went to the kitchen and checked the fridge. Opening the door released a breath of glacial coolness, but margarine and milk were the only things on offer. I chose milk. I poured some in a glass I found beneath the sink, and sat down at the table to wait.

The Lexus rolled into the carpark at idle speed just before quarter to five, grit crackling beneath its tyres. It was equipped with an aftermarket exhaust, and the low-rev throb rippled my milk. A brake ratcheted. The engine quit. A door thumped, and Ellis Carlyon approached the door as shades of grey through the blind. He paused. I finished my drink. Keys tinkled and found the lock. He came in and elbowed the door closed. Nobody expects an intruder. Nobody looks for one. Therefore, he didn't see me, sitting at his table at the limits of his peripheral vision.

'Ellis.'

He lunged sideways into the wall and raised his left leg defensively, cowering behind his hands, as if preparing to defend against a blow. He recognized me, and regained composure. Decisiveness took hold. He stepped forwards, gripped the edge of the table and thrust it back into my ribs, his jaws etched with clenched muscle. It caught me hard in the stomach, and I coughed milk beads. I tipped myself backwards onto the bed. He came around the table, lining me up for a straight right. I pushed up and took two blows on a raised forearm. I feigned a left hook and he brought his hands up to catch it, and I stomped the outside of his left calf. The contact sagged him like a burst tyre. Breath hissed between gritted teeth. His guard dropped. I opened my hands and landed him a straight right with the heel of my hand on his jaw. His features went slack, like sedative onset. His gaze lolled skywards, he staggered two steps sideways and collapsed on the bathroom threshold.

He coughed and propped himself up on one elbow, immobile from the waist down, his legs splayed crookedly. His chin dropped to his chest and he looked like the aftermath of a serious session of binge drinking. He retched and spat a thick cord of scarlet saliva. It swung and snagged tile work and hung shivering from his lower lip.

'Good rule of thumb,' I said. 'Don't ever mix it with a cop.'

He didn't answer. I picked up my glass from the table and took it through to the kitchen, rinsed it under the tap and set it in the sink. I took a coffee mug from the cupboard, filled it with water and took it back to the bathroom. By now he'd crawled to the toilet. He had the lid up and was hawking bloody saliva into the bowl, fingers white-knuckled on the rim. His path from the door was sprinkled crimson.

He glanced back at me and reached up. I passed him the mug. He took a mouthful, rinsed gingerly and spat light pink.

'I think you broke my jaw, man.'

'I doubt it. There's probably a lesson in it somewhere if I have.'

He held me with one eye as he took another sip, before spitting again. 'How'd you find me?'

'Phone book, a telephone, and a bit of cunning. Primarily the first two.'

He put the mug on the floor. He squirmed and rolled over, shuffling until he was propped against the wall. His jaw was slack, a tide of blood pooling behind a shining lower lip and spilling in a drip line from the corner of his mouth.

'You know why I'm here?' I said.

'No,' he said sloppily.

'This morning I asked if 150 Landon Avenue meant anything to you. You told me it didn't.'

He made no reply.

'I've got a photo of your car parked at that address,' I said. 'Which leads me to conclude you lied to me.'

He had some water.

'You need to explain,' I said. 'The guy at that address is under investigation for child pornography.'

He gulped the mouthful and coughed a fine spray. 'What? I never knew — I mean, she never … Jesus.'

He stuffed fingers in his hair and stared at the ground. I waited. He started to hyperventilate.

'I haven't done anything illegal.'

'You just assaulted a cop. That's a good start.'

He took his hands out of his hair and massaged his brow. He panted as if I'd told him the motel bathroom was the only place left on earth. 'God. Do they think I'm into child porn or something?'

'Nobody knows what to think.'

'Oh, God, man. I don't do that sort of thing.'

His fingers went back in his hair.

'Don't panic just yet. They don't know it's you.'

That offered some relief. The breathing subsided. He

wiped his forearm across his mouth and surveyed the result. I stepped to the toilet and pulled a strip of paper off the roll and passed it to him. He bunched it and dabbed cautiously at his mouth.

'Why did you let loose on me?' I asked.

'I don't know. 'Cause you won't piss off.'

'Right,' I said. 'Play the Q-and-A game with me and we won't take it any further.'

He got his breathing under control. 'I don't want to talk to you.'

'You're in a pickle, then. When people don't want to talk to me it generally means it's important that they do.'

'You punched me in the face,' he said.

'You assaulted me first,' I said. 'Makes for a good health and safety disclaimer.'

He said nothing. He took a mouthful of water, swilled slowly, and spat back in the mug.

'You've got two options,' I said. 'Keep quiet, and I'm going to take you in for assaulting a police officer, and you can deal with a painful jaw from the comfort of a cell. Or we can chat, and I'll do my best to forget what happened just now.'

He added another red smear to his forearm. 'OK. But, before I get into anything, I just want to make it clear that

I didn't know about any of this, you know, paedophile stuff. All right?'

He chopped his palm on the tile work to reinforce his point.

'All right,' I said.

He lobbed the paper in the toilet. The water in the bowl drowned it gently. 'Christine had a thing going with him,' he said.

'Who?'

'The guy who lives at that address.'

'What's his name?'

'Jon Edward.'

'OK. So what was the thing?'

He shrugged. He tilted his head back against the wall, closed his eyes and exhaled gently as he worked his lower jaw carefully from side to side. 'She went to his house and he paid her to have sex with him.'

'She was doing this while you were together?'

'Yeah. I was the one who took her there. I was the bloody chauffeur.' His mouth hooked upwards at the uninjured end.

I leaned against the doorframe. He drew his knees up and tapped his feet gently against the floor.

'Why didn't you tell me this before?' I asked.

He shrugged again and opened his eyes. 'I dunno. I guess because you'd think it was a bit weird or something.' He said it as if categorizing his confession as 'weird' was simply absurd.

I stared down at him for a long moment. He looked terrible. His eyes were red, his hair was a bird's nest. A clenched jaw kept his narrow face drawn and hard-edged. He wiped his mouth again. 'Christine met this guy in a chat room or something,' he said. 'Don't know what they got chatting about, but anyway, the guy said if Christine was keen to make a little extra money, you know, he'd get in touch.'

'And she was, and he did,' I said.

'Yeah.'

'So he emailed her his address, hidden inside that photograph?'

He nodded. 'He was a bit of a weirdo. He wouldn't just, you know, give out his address online. Had this funny precaution thing where he emailed it, like you said.'

He tilted the mug off the floor and eyed the contents. 'Can you get me some more water?'

I picked up the mug and tipped his backwash in the toilet. The bowl was streaked pink with his saliva. The sink was too small to accommodate the mug beneath the tap.

'If you try and make a break I'm going to knock your jaw the other way,' I said.

He just sat there — deflated, blank and unresponsive. His arms lay limp at his sides, pale palms upturned like some offering to an unknown deity. I walked through to the kitchen, filled the mug and brought it back to him. He drank carefully, with two hands like a kid, rinsed and spat. His eyes closed in a wince as his tongue checked dental damage.

'How many times did Christine visit this man?' I asked.

'Only twice.'

'When?'

'I dunno,' he said.

'Try and be a little more specific. Are we talking days ago, weeks ago or months ago?'

'The first time was probably a couple of months ago. Then the second time maybe a couple of weeks ago.'

'How did he contact her? Did he ring?'

'I think he just sent an email. Not much to it, just the time and date.'

'And what did you think of it all?'

'What do you mean?'

'You didn't mind dropping her off so she could have sex?'

He shrugged and took a drink and swallowed slowly. 'It's just money. Nothing serious or anything. I didn't give a shit.'

'Right. You could have saved yourself the cost of a motel and a sore jaw if you'd just told me about this to begin with.'

He didn't reply.

'So what did chauffeuring involve?' I asked.

He thumbed his nose. 'I drove her there, and I drove her home. I waited out front in the car in between.'

'How long did you have to wait?'

'About an hour.'

'What time of day did she visit?'

'Night-time.'

'As in late evening or early morning?'

'Late evening. Ten or eleven o'clock.'

He took a small drink and rinsed and aimed a projectile spit for the toilet. He missed and doused his trousers.

'Did you see anyone else there when you visited?'

'No.'

'Did Christine see anyone else when she was there?'

'I told you I didn't go in with her.'

'You must have talked about it afterwards.'

'Uh, no. That would be a bit weird.'

'How much was she getting paid?'

He bit his lip and scanned the opposite wall. 'Not very much the first time. A couple of hundred. The second time she made loads.'

'How much is loads?'

'Like three grand.'

'The same three grand you blew in the casino the other day?'

'Yeah. Pretty much.'

'So how did she manage all that in one night?'

'There was this other guy there, I think. He was full of loot.'

'Who was the other guy?'

He stirred his hand mid-air to aid recollection. 'A business fat-cat, finance company director or something ... name was Ian Carson.'

I didn't answer. My pulse ramped up. It fluttered butterfly-light. I felt dizzy and held the doorframe to keep the floor in place. He gave me a strange look.

'You look as if you're going to cark it,' he said.

I stared at the carpet. Regurgitated milk spray had stained my shirt. My arm started to ache where I'd been hit. The jaw shot had jarred my forearm. Carlyon drank water.

'She saw *the* Ian Carson?' I said.

'Uh-huh. Only the second time.'

'The same Ian Carson who's been in the news?'

'I don't know about him being in the news. But he's got heaps of money.'

I looked up. The floor and walls stayed steady. He lined up another drink but dropped the mug. It cracked and clam-shelled open lengthways, water spreading slow and smooth. He watched it all with a flat gaze, letting his head knock back against the wall. His lips parted, his eyes slid back and forth beneath hooded lids, his face betraying neither displeasure nor satisfaction. He looked like he'd blown an emotional fuse. I see that look a lot. He thought his life was coming apart. The question was whether it was because he saw himself as a victim, or his burned girlfriend.

'Don't go missing again,' I said. 'Finding you was a hassle.'

He didn't answer.

I palmed milk residue off the table on the way out the door.

■ THIRTY-TWO

I dropped the key off at reception and went back to the car. The sun was in pink descent. Power poles cast rippled strips of blue shadow on the verge. I opened my cellphone, cycled through the calls register and found Buchanan's number from earlier that morning. I dialled. He didn't answer. Voicemail invited me to leave a message.

I said, 'I don't think you gave me the whole story today. Give me a call.'

I clicked off and dialled Claire Bennett. She was still in her office.

'I found Ellis Carlyon,' I said.

'Where?'

'In a motel, as I thought. He's changed his story slightly. He says Christine McLane went to 150 Landon to engage in prostitution.'

'With the occupant?'

I dropped my visor. 'Apparently. He also told me she said she'd seen Ian Carson there.'

'What, *the* Ian Carson?'

'Yeah. Department of Internal Affairs has Landon under surveillance, so I'm sure they were aware of it, but nobody mentioned Carson. And if they didn't mention him, he's probably of some value to them, which means they could well know where he was the night his wife and daughter were killed.'

'That's a big extrapolation.'

I didn't reply.

'If Carson had an alibi he would have told us,' she said.

'Depends. If said alibi implicates him in something else objectionable he wouldn't necessarily let on.'

'What's more objectionable than killing your family?'

'I don't know. Maybe he was trying to preserve his professional image. And if his alibi was that he was engaged in sex with a prostitute at an address under investigation by the Department of Internal Affairs in relation to child porn, it wouldn't look so good.'

She made no reply.

'We need to get in touch with Internal Affairs,' I said.

'See if you can get hold of this guy Buchanan.' I gave her the number.

'If DIA are looking at a major paedo bust, they won't want to cooperate with us and run the risk of undermining their own interests,' she said.

'That'll be their problem. Both Carson and Christine McLane had an association with this place on Landon Ave. We can't ignore that kind of overlap.'

The phone went quiet as she thought about it. 'I'll call his lawyer and get Carson in for an interview tomorrow,' she said.

She hung up, and I started the car and headed south.

I drove to Hale's place. I didn't arrive until after eight. His house is up a steep gravel driveway, protected from Scenic Drive by a thick belt of foliage. He refuses to have the accessway concreted. Crunching aggregate is claimed to provide good security. Fine, except when winter renders it un-drivable.

I parked at the top behind his Escort. His garage door was down. I went up a set of steps that chirruped beneath my weight, and knocked on his front door. He made me wait a minute before opening up.

'Visiting hours are almost over,' he said.

'Maybe let me in anyway,' I said. 'You enjoy the banter.'

He stood aside and I went past him into the house. Omelette smell greeted me.

'You're only a bantam-weight banterer,' he said.

I went into the living room. It was barer than usual — no paintings and his television was gone. His ceiling fan had been torn free of the plaster, leaving a hole as jagged as chipped glass.

'I had a break-in,' he explained.

'They do some remodelling for you?'

'Yes. They were quite thoughtful.'

'When was this?'

'Couple of days ago. It's under control. They busted my CD player, though.'

I glanced at the shelf beside his sofa. His record player had come out of retirement and an old John Cooper Clarke LP spun slowly beneath the glass hood, the volume at a murmur. Thirty-year-old vinyl snagged the needle with an occasional tick.

'Did you make a report?' I asked.

He smiled and inspected the wound in the ceiling. 'No, but I'm pursuing a promising lead.'

'You know who it was?'

He didn't reply. Kitchen heat had fogged the top half of

the ranch slider. Pete Dexter's *Brotherly Love* was draped open across the arm of the sofa, the spine wrinkled in thin strips.

'Do you think it would be possible to split that omelette in half?' I asked.

He clucked his tongue. 'Don't know about half,' he said. 'But I'm sure we could come to some arrangement.'

I followed him into the kitchen and opened his fridge. His fridge likes me. It offers good things. I took a Mac's Gold.

Hale appraised his omelette. It was still foaming and he let it be. He went to the fridge and claimed a Mac's, opened it with a hiss and tossed the pull-tab. It tinkled into the sink. He leaned back against the bench. The first mouthful was a thoughtful one that rolled back and forth behind his cheeks before descending.

'You have anything else damaged?' I asked.

'They tossed my photo albums.'

'Is anything missing?'

'No.'

'So you cool?'

He clicked his tongue behind a thin smile, tipped his bottle towards me, two fingers snagging the lip. 'Frosty.'

'So what's the promising lead?'

He brushed the question off with another mouthful. Home invasion discussion was over. 'What are you doing in my house at this hour?' he asked.

I repeated what I had told Claire Bennett. His eyes traced patterns in the lino as he listened. Pensive swallows dropped his beer level. He waited for me to stop talking, then diced a tomato and distributed it through the omelette.

'How long has internal affairs been watching the place?' he asked.

'They seem pretty well set up. They've definitely been there a while.'

'What have they got in there?'

'It's a full-on surveillance post. They've got computer terminals, cameras wired through to recorders, up to four people watching.'

'How bored are they?'

'Quite. The novelty factor's worn off.'

'And you think they might know what Carson was doing there?'

'Possibly. I hope so.'

He finished the beer, tipping the bottle high to get the last of it. The dregs are always shy. John Cooper Clarke's lyrics reached us faintly.

'So what do you think Carson was doing there?' he asked.

'I don't know. Probably something he shouldn't. They're trying to set up an interview with him for tomorrow.'

His bottle tinked when he put it on the bench. He took plates and cutlery from separate drawers and divvied up the omelette, spooned potatoes out of a pot, and allocated one per plate.

'Ring ahead next time,' he said. 'I'll think of something less bland.'

'This is high-class by my standards.'

He slid a plate to me across the table. I picked up my fork. It accentuated my hand tremor. My nicotine credit was set to expire, but the omelette would pacify it somewhat. Hale does a good omelette.

'So what are you going to do now?' he asked.

'Question the Department of Internal Affairs about Ian Carson.'

'Maybe easier said than done.'

'Probably. The guy I met this morning isn't returning my calls.'

'So who else was there? You said there were four of them.'

'I didn't get their details. I don't think they like me.'

'Why?'

'They weren't happy I almost blew their surveillance. We scuffled.'

John Cooper Clarke played 'Beasley Street'. Hale mused and chewed. 'You were always a pretty adept scuffler,' he noted.

'Indeed.'

He finished his potato, then chased tomato cubes but didn't spear them, fork whining on the plate.

'So what do you think about Carson?' I asked.

'Do I think he killed his family?'

I nodded.

He shrugged. He propped an elbow on the table, thumbed a sideburn for the answer. 'Statistics would say he probably has. It's always the husband. And the fact he can't offer an alibi definitely isn't in his favour. If he's not guilty of murder, he's probably guilty of something else.'

I said nothing. Raindrops clicked against his roof.

'Two options,' he said. 'You can obey convention and wait until Internal Affairs gets back to you. Or you can pre-empt the contact and revisit them and check the surveillance for yourself.'

'Pre-empting the contact might not be that easy.'

'It probably would be. If there's nobody there you can

check it yourself. Or if there's someone still in residence, you can persuade them to cooperate. Indisputably lawful.'

'Do you want to come along?' I said. 'For the banter?'

He shook his head. 'I'm going to follow up on my promising break-in lead.'

'And what will that entail?'

He laughed but didn't answer. I checked my watch. It was nearing nine.

'I enjoyed the omelette,' I said.

'Yes,' he said. 'I did, too.'

■ THIRTY-THREE

I left at eight fifty-five. Anders Osborne's *Ash Wednesday Blues* served as score. I went east on Scenic Drive and skirted the southern lip of Waitakere, got on the South-Western Motorway at Dominion Road. Night dehumanized evening bustle to neon montage. I entered the western end of Landon just before nine-thirty.

Fastidious concealment made the surveillance house look obvious. Duct-taped curtains sealed all. While neighbouring windows leaked yellow, the DIA watch station stood out — amongst conspicuous, unfettered dark.

The carport was empty. I dimmed the lights, turned into the property and stopped beside the side door I had used earlier that day. I turned the engine off and slid out. A stiff easterly kept trees on a slant, and a jumbled mess of limbs showed where the downed TV aerial slumped exhausted.

I inspected the lock. It was a brushed steel plate inset with twin columns of keys. The bottom four were alphabetic, A, B, C, Y; the remainders numeric, 1 to 9, followed by a 0, in a crisp lime green typeface.

I dredged up the glimpsed finger sequence: bottom row, top row, third row from bottom. Left to right, two punches per row, except on the third, which was only a single. C and Y, followed by 1 and 6, followed by either a 5 or a 0.

I tried CY165.

The lock held.

I tried CY160.

I turned the lock. It opened.

I went in and elbowed the door closed behind me. The living room command post was still lit up. Soft light edged a half-open door at the end of the hallway. It opened fully before I reached it. Darlene's silhouette held back the spill of glow, her shadow on the carpet reaching the entry. Stereo noise called faintly from the room beyond. I palmed the wall for a light switch, found one and flicked it on. She squinted at me. Dark bags looped her eyes. A lock of hair had been twirled into a ragged dreadlock:

incessant twisting for the duration of a twelve-hour shift.

'Bit late, isn't it?' she asked.

'I need to look at some footage. You might be able to help me out.'

She didn't reply. My arrival hadn't seemed to surprise her. Eyeballing a computer all day probably dilutes reactionary capacity.

'You got the short straw, did you?' I asked.

'What?'

'You've got the night shift?'

'Oh. Yeah. The short straw. How did you get in?'

'I know the code,' I said.

She turned back towards the living room. Sitting idle had skewed her balance and she walked off-plumb, brushing the doorframe as she stepped through. Her seat offered a squealed bounce as she dropped into it. She swivelled to face her terminal, propped her elbow on the desk and resumed playing with her hair, index finger tormenting pre-abused strands. She turned the music off. A digital radio scanner tuned to the police patrol frequency sat to the right of her screen. She killed that, too.

'Bit cheeky,' I said. 'Eavesdropping our freak.'

She ignored me. 'You shouldn't be here,' she said.

'Buchanan will show up in a minute. The door's silent-sensored; he's going to have to check I haven't been murdered.'

I took a seat next to her.

'Can't he just ring?' I asked.

'He'll ring, I'll tell him you're here and it'll set him off.'

She was looking at her screen. The television monitors were still up and running: suburban still-life, in monochrome. Our shadows ghosted faint and bloated in the glow against the ceiling. A telephone on the desk beside her monitor started trilling sharply. Her eyes didn't leave her computer screen as she answered.

She listened for a moment. She twirled her dreadlock slowly and said, 'It's Sean Devereaux.'

She hung up.

'He won't be happy,' she said. 'This is a secure location. You can't just walk in.'

'How far away is he?'

'Not far. Maybe two minutes. He only just left.'

'Maybe you could help me with what I'm after and I can skedaddle before he shows up.'

Her eyes panned the screen. It was plain white typewriter DOS script on a blue background. 'Sorry,' she said. 'Not going to happen. It's gotta come from

Buchanan. The best I can do is coffee.'

I smiled. 'Milk, two sugars.'

She glanced at me and cocked an eyebrow.

'Please,' I added.

She rolled her chair back and got up and left the room. I heard soles slap lino, and then a jug click on. A moment later a car suspension heaved on the driveway. A light engine switched off with a rattle. Driver discretion kept door closure inaudible. I heard the lock buttons crunching faintly, and then Buchanan was in the room, all bustle and rapid glances. He looked pissed off about resuming work at quarter to ten at night. He had two fingers on his tie knot like it might drop off.

'You could have just called,' he said.

'Tried that. Nobody answered.'

'That doesn't entitle you to a free visit.'

'You didn't give me the full story this morning.'

He touched his collar buttons. The morning's supply of calm was verging on empty. A clenched jaw conveyed dissatisfaction. 'What did I allegedly omit?'

'You didn't tell me Ian Carson visited.'

Darlene re-entered the room, bearing coffee mugs. She gave one to me and placed the second beside her computer.

'Coffee?' she said to Buchanan.

He toed cables and jiggled his keys as he made up his mind. 'Please,' he concluded.

Darlene left the room again. Digital hum filled the conversational lapse.

'There was a girl found burned to death in a car the night before,' I said. 'Her name was Christine McLane.'

'And you're working the case,' Buchanan said. 'You told me this morning.'

'Right. I found a witness who assures me McLane visited the address you've got under surveillance at least twice.'

'So?'

'So I gave you the girl's description, you said you hadn't seen her. You told me you've got this place under camera surveillance, you've got his phone tapped, his computer tapped, and you weren't aware of this girl visiting? I don't believe that.'

Buchanan made no reply for a moment. Darlene came in with another mug. She passed it to Buchanan, steam wafting above the lip. He took a sip while he thought about his reply. Darlene sat down again and resumed her hair twiddling.

'Full cooperation isn't obligatory,' he said eventually.

'There's a difference between non-cooperation and obstruction,' I said.

Buchanan sipped his coffee. 'We're one part of an international investigation,' he said. 'The guy across the street is part of a global child porn network. This house and this equipment is partially funded by US government money.'

'So?'

'So the financial backing came with the implicit expectation that we don't endanger international efforts by letting you sift around in things whenever you like.'

'I'm not sifting. This is part of an official investigation. I'm attempting to elicit information through proper channels. The alternative is that I get a search warrant for all your intel and an arrest warrant for your friend across the street. And I doubt even the US Justice Department would have success in vetoing a warrant in relation to a murder investigation on foreign soil.'

Buchanan didn't answer. Idle movement kept him calm: he had another mouthful of coffee, ran a thumbnail down the centreline of his tie.

'US Treasury, actually,' he said at length. 'It's a Secret Service operation.'

'You're probably going to have to tell me about it,' I said.

Buchanan swallowed another mouthful. He ran a hand through his hair and looked around as if he'd just realized he was the only one still standing. He drew out a swivel chair from beneath a television desk, bumped it over the taped-down cables and sat down opposite. He leaned forward and rested his elbows on his knees, trouser cuffs hiking to expose narrow ankles. The top of his glasses ran nonparallel to his eyebrows. A dab of knuckle rectified the geometry.

'Think hypothetically for me,' Buchanan said.

'Think hypothetically, or hypothetically think?' I asked.

'What?'

'Forget it,' I said.

'Our information has a federal blanket on it,' he said. 'We can't divulge intelligence without the explicit permission of the United States Treasury Department. It's their case. It's their money. If we mouth off about stuff we shouldn't and blow their case, it's ultimately them who end up looking bad.'

'You showed me that stuff this morning.'

'It's not a full surveillance record. A lot of the good stuff is stripped out.'

'The distilled version,' I said. 'You can hand it over to anyone who asks, so you look as if you're being cooperative.'

Buchanan surveyed his mug and made no reply. Darlene spun slowly back to her monitor and perused the white-on-blue code.

'Can we have an off-the-record chat?' I asked.

'Everything here is off the record.'

I leaned forward in my seat, mirroring his pose. 'Ian Carson is suspected of murdering his family. Christine McLane was kidnapped and burned to death. I need to know whether they visited the house you're watching and, if so, what they were doing there.'

Buchanan didn't answer. He took another mouthful and observed me mid-sip.

'Talking is doing it the easy way,' I said. 'The hard way is doing it with paperwork and subpoenas, and things'll get messy.'

'Anything I tell you is legally inadmissible,' Buchanan said. 'I'll deny things if I have to.'

'Darlene mightn't,' I said.

'I'm good at being temporarily deaf,' Darlene said.

'Whatever,' I said. 'Just talk.'

'Are you wearing a wire?'

'No, I'm not wearing a wire.'

'Turn off your cellphone.'

'You're paranoid,' I said.

'It's a positive attribute. Take out your cellphone and turn it off.'

I rolled sideways in my seat and fingered my phone out of my pocket, powered it off and placed it on the desk behind me.

Buchanan's eyes tracked the little procedure over the top of his mug, and then he said, 'Ian Carson has visited.'

It was a rushed admission, as if it was a relief to get it off his chest. He took another sip of coffee to aid recovery.

'When?' I asked.

'I can't show you video evidence,' Buchanan said. 'It was about two-and-a-half weeks back. It coincided with a visit by your Christine McLane.'

His account matched Ellis Carlyon's testimony. So far so good.

'What was the purpose of the visit?' I asked.

'Our surveillance is exterior only. We don't really know.'

'You can speculate, though.'

He had some more coffee. I saw his carotid pulsing beneath beard shadow as he tipped his mug back. He cleared his throat gently. He looked at the floor. He seemed uncomfortable. 'I imagine it was for a sexual liaison,' he said formally.

'How did you reach that conclusion?' I asked.

'I told you we have access to his computer.'

'Whose computer?'

'The guy in the house across the street. Jon Edward.'

'Right. OK.'

'He participated in an Internet chat room that was used to facilitate casual sex.'

'Nothing wrong with that.'

'Well. No, you're right. But the Internet-based stuff we look at isn't the sort of thing you'd find by running a Google search. Hard porn tends to lurk in areas of the web that have gone into disuse as things have developed. Think of it as a house. There are rooms, closets, whatever, that normal people don't use, wouldn't know how to find. Weirdos stash their porn there so it's out of the way. And while the chat room isn't actually illegal, it's constructed so it's difficult to access without first going through some other stuff that is. Meaning, unless you're familiar with navigating that part of the Internet, you'd never make it to the chat room.'

'OK. So how does it work?'

'The concept is fairly simple. People log in with user names, they communicate, they arrange whatever it is they need to arrange. Our friend Jon Edward across the street is a regular patron. We've got a live hack on the forum. We can view the code in realtime. As I said, Carson's visit was more than fourteen days ago, maybe a week before the deaths of his wife and daughter. I can't give you the exact date because I'd have to access archived data, and I'm not doing that until you present me with a warrant. But, call it two-and-a-half weeks ago, our subject of interest across the street entered a conversation with an anonymous user, and arranged,' he paused, licking his lips, 'an encounter, in which our subject promised a female third party would also participate.'

Nobody spoke. Darlene was facing her computer screen, coffee at mid-tide. Her index finger maintained a firm hair helix, elbow pressure sustaining her chair in a lazy back-and-forth arc. Roof shadows cast an amplified equivalent.

'Anyway,' Buchanan said. 'The following evening Carson shows up, and then about an hour later your McLane girl shows up, too. Five minutes pass, and then Carson leaves, and McLane leaves.'

'Why the timing?' I asked.

'What do you mean?'

'Carson was there more than an hour, the girl was there five minutes.'

Buchanan shrugged. 'I can't explain it.'

'So are all three of them participating in the forum?'

'I don't think so. The initial online discussion was between two people, discussing the presence of a female in a future meeting. So I don't think the girl was a participant, the conversation must have been between Carson and our target. It explains the coded photograph you mentioned. One of them could have made contact with her outside the chat room, told her the time, sent her the location embedded in the image.'

'OK. So if you knew your target's chat name, you must have been able to determine Carson's, once he'd shown up here.'

'That's right. I know the question you're going to ask me next.'

I didn't reply. I waited for him to answer the question I was supposedly on the cusp of posing.

'We're not low-grade,' Buchanan said. 'Our team is Department of Internal Affairs-operated, we have a police sergeant on temporary detached duty, our finances come via Washington DC. We know about Carson. We know he's under investigation for murdering his family. But we don't think he did it.'

John Cooper Clarke had finished. Hale replaced him with R.E.M.'s *Out of Time*. He lay on the sofa listening to 'Losing My Religion', and considered the damage to his ceiling, courtesy of the fan excision.

He sensed things converging. Christine McLane and Ian Carson had been in contact. Three weeks later, the girl was dead, Carson's wife and daughter were dead, and Carson probably wished he was dead, too. They were two seemingly unrelated people: different ages, locations, social strata. Violence seemed the only commonality. It seemed that what had occurred stemmed from their meeting.

Carson would know this. He'd know how the investigation operated. His recent activity was being painstakingly verified. Ditto for the deceased Christine McLane. Merely a question of time before someone discovers the two paths intersect, at a house on Landon Avenue. The fact the meeting had not been declared already was testimony to the fact Ian Carson did not want it discovered. But he would know the find was coming. The knowledge would keep him awake in the dark, heart padding against the sheet, the potency of human worry no match for the humble sleeping pill. And what would happen now? A witness had confirmed the secret conjunction: Carson, McLane, Landon Ave, all superimposed. It was a big find. It was progress. It yielded the crux of the matter: would its discovery provide Carson the impetus to do something proactive?

Maybe. John Hale knew crime. His career had provided front row seating. His recollections were a grim back catalogue from an arm's length perspective. He knew the underlying mechanics of doing something wrong. He felt things coming together.

He removed his cellphone and called his police contact.

'Favour time,' he said. 'Again.'

'Better name it before I commit.'

'Where's Ian Carson living at the moment?'

'I can't tell you that.'

'Yeah you can.'

'You're not going to top him are you?'

'No, probably not.'

'He's staying at his lawyer's place.' He gave Hale the address. 'And you didn't get that from me. Although if you murder him they'll check your phone records and find you spoke to me.'

'I appreciate it,' Hale said.

He ended the call. He took the Escort. The lawyer's

name was Mike Lindley. The house was a low lump of tile swaddled in affluence, on an exclusive stretch of Crescent Road overlooking the harbour. He cruised past, window down. The air was cool, salt spray riding the breeze, trees in mumbled doze. He approached from the west. An unmarked police car was parked on the south side of the street, a lone silhouette at the wheel. Hale rolled past and U-turned. He stopped behind the unmarked, fifty metres east. The house was out of sight, but in the event of action, he'd see the car ahead move.

Two minutes after ten. He turned off the ignition and dimmed his lights. Dark pressed in, dense and uninhibited. Below the cliff edge, the ocean pawed the shoreline with a lolling hush. He shuffled in search of optimal comfort. He was not wasting time. The what-if was a source of immense anticipation. He was eternally content to wait it out.

His cellphone rang. He squirmed to free it from his pocket, managed a third-ring pick-up.

'When are you free for another whiskey?'

'One-time-only offer. Sorry.'

The guy laughed. 'Don't you like being social?'

'You're not really my cup of tea.'

No reply. Ocean noise hid phone crackle.

'I had plans for you,' Hale said. 'But I changed my itinerary.'

'Really? What did you have in mind?'

'Retribution of sorts.'

'I'm recording the call, so don't threaten me.'

'That's the point. Threat's gone. Tonight was going to be the night I avenged my living room, but I've let it go.'

More laughter. 'I don't want you to have to concede defeat.'

Hale paused to draft a retort. He sifted for something of literary merit. 'Normally, I wouldn't,' he said. 'But I'm tied up tonight. Call it loyalty to the nightmare of my choice.'

'Christ. That's deep.' He went quiet. 'Who wrote that? Was it Kerouac?'

'Joseph Conrad.'

'That's right. Conrad. So what nightmare demands your loyalty in favour of visiting me?'

'Bastard-catching. General social remediation. Can't help myself.'

'Right. Were the six bullet holes in the house on Flat Bush Road a by-product of those pursuits?'

Hale made no reply. His silence won a gleeful chuckle.

'I dabble in a bit of bastard-catching myself, actually,'

the guy said. 'Matter of fact, you're my bastard-of-interest at the moment. I'm considering adding your friend Sean Devereaux as a kind of side project. Apparently, this week he tasered a guy, smashed him through his windscreen, then rammed someone else with his car and left them with a concussion and neck injuries.'

'Don't take the moral high ground after busting my lounge.'

'I don't know what you're talking about.'

'And I expect they probably deserved it,' Hale said.

'Now, you see that's the problem. Excessive force versus proper legal procedure. It's iffy.'

'I wasn't arguing judicial dynamics. I was saying they probably deserved what they got.'

'I take it you approve of Mr Devereaux.'

'I've known him a long time.'

'So he's like you then?'

'More or less. Different chapters of the same operating manual.'

'In what sense?'

'He's restrained and I'm not. But we both get shit done.'

A breath of white exhaust from the unmarked wafted skyward.

'He was raised in foster care for a bit,' the guy said.

'Did he tell you that? Looked after by an ex-British air force officer who ended up in prison. Now *there* was an arsehole.' He laughed. 'I'm sure some of his shitty qualities made the generational jump.'

Eighteen minutes after ten. Hale held the phone away from his ear to blunt the malice. The brake lights on the unmarked police car flared. Hale squeaked his window up. The unmarked moved away from the kerb, tail-lights crystalline in the windscreen condensation.

'Keeping with the Conrad theme,' the guy said, 'do you have a heart of darkness?'

'Close. It's certainly shadowy.'

The guy murmured a dry chuckle. 'I went and visited your friend Geoffrey Gage again,' he said.

Hale said nothing.

'He told us about your assault on him,' the guy said. 'That you broke in and knocked his head against a table. That's a serious, serious offence.'

'It's a serious, serious, unsubstantiated allegation. Are you still recording?'

'I am.'

'Good.' He started the car. 'If it comes to it, I can renege on my earlier decision to forget about you. I'm hardwired with the notion of decent payback.'

'That sounded like a thr—'

'Yeah, essentially. I've dealt with people like you for the last fifteen years. I'll deal with them for several more. You're nothing. You can't touch me. I suggest you delete my number.' He paused before closure, engineering the sign-off: 'You don't want to become part of the nightmare.'

He dropped the call, snipped the guy's reply at the first syllable.

He didn't know if the unmarked had moved because it was in pursuit of something, or because its shift had ended. He allowed a five-second cushion, and then moved off up the hill in pursuit. Another five seconds to recoup lost distance. On the road ahead, a 7-Series BMW was holding an easy cruise.

He called Devereaux. No dial tone; his phone was turned off.

He followed the little procession northbound. The BMW made a left at Quay Street and headed for the city centre. Left again and they were uptown through the CBD, then entering SH1 southbound at Hobson. Light traffic melded with the three-car chain. Night-time pursuits weren't easy. Target acquisition was maintained by virtue of diligent car-counting. Sudden lane changes befuddled positioning. Evening chill fogged the glass. He ran his wipers and cleared arcs in the white translucent frost that dusted his windscreen. They were doing one hundred and ten. No problem for the BMW, but the Escort settled into a whining hum that rattled the engine bay and sent judders through the steering column and kept the gear shift shivering. They passed Newmarket, passed Gillies Ave, passed Market Road. Still holding one-ten: the BMW, the unmarked, the rattling black Escort.

One kilometre north of the Green Lane exit, the BMW indicated and slipped across into the left lane. The unmarked allowed a two-second cushion, and then proceeded likewise. Hale accelerated, pushing the Escort to one-forty, chassis rattling like a shaken cage. He moved right to pass a truck, then floated back left across two lanes. He tucked himself in behind the bumper of the BMW just as it moved up the exit ramp to Green Lane East. The four respective north- and southbound entry and exit lanes converged in a roundabout on an overpass. The unmarked was three cars in arrears. The BMW hustled at the top of the exit ramp. It headed straight through the roundabout, and linked with the southbound entry ramp. Hale tailgated it through. The unmarked was too far back to make it. A stream of traffic came in eastbound and it was forced to give way.

Hale fell back once they were on the motorway. The BMW resumed its steady one-ten. Hale raised his phone and called Sean Devereaux again, but there was still no answer. He settled in patiently and allowed a three-car cushion, content to pursue unobserved.

■ THIRTY-FOUR

Buchanan placed his mug on the floor between his feet. He popped a breath mint. It cracked between his molars with a sound like marble hitting glass.

'How good's your evidence?' I asked.

He rocked a hand mid-air. 'Marginal at this stage,' he said. 'But easy to authenticate.'

'How easy?'

'We know Carson's user name for the chat room. We know the date and time of his wife and daughter's murders last week. We know from what we gleaned off the site that he'd arranged for another liaison that night.'

'He might not have showed up.'

He shrugged. 'He showed up for his meeting across the street.'

'All right. So a liaison with who?'

He pocketed the mints. 'With whom, you mean?'

'Yes.'

'We don't know. All we have is the user name. For more info, we'd have to have cooperation from Internet service providers. But that's not our concern at the moment.'

'He hasn't provided an alibi,' I said. 'If you had this information you could have told us.'

'Not really. If we provided it, someone would have to check the validity of the claim. Witnesses would have to be tracked down. Some of the people who frequent that chat room are wanted for serious offences. Police asking them questions for any reason tends to make them a little uneasy. And at this stage we can't allow that.'

I didn't reply. The bank of television screens switched perspective in flawless unison. I'd barely touched my coffee. I turned and placed it on the desk behind me.

'So who's responsible?' I said.

'For what?'

'You just indicated Carson didn't kill his wife or his daughter. The fact he had contact with Christine McLane within the last month suggests the same person maybe killed her, and Carson's wife and child. So who was it?'

Buchanan didn't say anything. He straightened slightly

to release a gentle belch. It swelled behind pressed lips before escaping.

'May I pose a theory?' I said.

'Please,' Buchanan said.

'You've been keeping things close to your chest because you think your target across the street is responsible for both my murder investigations, but you're scared to let us in the loop before your federal backers wrap up their end of the deal.'

He shook his head. 'We're his alibi. He didn't kill Carson's family. He was home, probably asleep.'

I said, 'You've got phone records for your guy across the street, right?'

He nodded.

'There's a number I'd like to see if he's called.'

'Why?'

'The girl was a contracted kidnap. We have the cellphone of the guy who organized the grab team. It's possible the job was requested by your target.'

Buchanan made no reply.

'If we can link that phone number to your target, we can go in and take him down and bypass you completely,' I said. 'If we have evidence that he arranged a kidnapping, we can arrest him without your backing. Your information would be superfluous to an arrest warrant.'

Buchanan was still looking at Darlene. He palmed his tie, checking it still hung plumb. I noticed he had a wedding ring. I wondered if there were children in the picture. He looked worn out; a veteran of long days. He looked like a guy used to cold dinners.

'With that in mind,' he said. 'Why should we be willing to share our information with you?'

'Because I'm suspicious you're actually a decent human being.'

He didn't smile.

'So what's the number?' he asked.

I'd given it to Pollard when I called him from Hale's car, early Monday morning. I thought for a moment, managed to recite the first six digits of Cedric's cell.

Buchanan's attention made a slow drift to Darlene once I'd finished. 'Check the records for him,' he said.

Darlene minimized her blue text window. She left her hair alone as she navigated file directories, entered passwords when prompted. A simple Word document constituted their phone records. She brought up a search box and typed. The screen scrolled rapidly and highlighted a string of text.

'He called it from his cellphone,' she said. 'Three

minutes, eight seconds in duration.'

'So your target set up the kidnap,' I said. 'When was the call?'

Darlene glanced at Buchanan, but he showed no desire to censor any reply. She scrolled. 'It was a while back,' she said. 'We've flagged the date. It was the night Carson and McLane visited. Monday, two weeks back.'

I glanced at Buchanan, but he ignored me. He was looking over Darlene's shoulder at one of the computer screens. I followed his view. Camera feed from the street was displayed. A BMW sedan had come into shot. Buchanan turned to see the expanded version in the television monitors behind him.

'Who've we got here?' he asked.

The car tracked left to right in the bank of monitors. It shrank and expanded between screens as the magnification changed.

'Waiting on a licence visual,' Darlene said.

I said, 'You told me your target has an alibi for the night Carson's family was murdered. What about Friday?'

I was losing him. His attention was with the car. His eyes flicked my way and then back.

'What's Friday?' he asked.

'The night McLane was murdered.'

'He wasn't here,' Buchanan said.

'What? At all?'

'He left around midnight.'

'And when did he come back?'

'Three in the morning. Ish.'

'Well, it's not looking good for him then.'

He glanced at me.

'We've confirmed your man across the street made the call to have McLane kidnapped,' I said. 'Unless you can offer up an alibi for him, potentially he's the same person who doused her in liquid accelerant and set her on fire.'

The BMW stopped at the kerb outside number 150. I pointed at the screen. Buchanan turned in his seat for a better view.

'Something happened in that house when McLane and Carson visited,' I said, 'and as a result your target had McLane kidnapped so he could kill her. Chances are he's also tied up in what happened with Carson.'

Buchanan didn't say anything. He got up and stood in the doorway to the hallway, hands on hips, his back to the room. The car was still at the kerb.

'Corrections welcome at any time,' I said.

Buchanan sniffed a half-laugh. 'Well,' he said, 'good luck with the paperwork.'

'It's Ian Carson's car,' Darlene said.

'What?' Buchanan said. His hands hadn't left his hips. He spun in the doorway, elbows scraping the frame. 'Can't be.'

He frowned, shooting accusation my way. Irritation sparked blathering: 'You— how'd he— you must've—'

'No,' I said. 'Me nothing. I haven't done anything.'

On the video, the car door opened. Nobody got out. Buchanan grimaced and rubbed the top of his head. The movement frizzed his hair. 'Oh shit,' he said. 'Shit, shit, shit, shit, shit! Why's he here? You must have tipped him off or—'

'I haven't.'

'So why's he here?'

'Because he knows this guy's involved with what happened to his family. He knows we're making progress and he's running out of time to do something.'

'And how would he know you're making progress? You don't send him a memo.'

'We send requests for interviews. He probably read between the lines.'

He turned a full circle, checked the status of his surveillance panel. He clicked his teeth behind the grimace.

'Christ,' he said. 'This could be trouble.'

I didn't answer him. He was standing behind Darlene, his jacket pinned back off his waist by his hands on his hips. 'He's going to assault my suspect,' he said.

'Probably,' I said. 'I'm a cop, though. If I have probable cause, which judging by that I do, I can enter the property and protect your suspect.'

'Do it,' he said.

'I need your cooperation. Don't try and wall me out.'

Buchanan looked down at me. 'Just go and cool this off,' he said.

I looked at the television screens. Carson was out of the car. He had a hammer. Negotiation time was set to expire.

'I need your word,' I said. 'I need access to your intel. I don't want any of your files or your testimony to suddenly dry up on me when I need them most.'

He weighed it up. He sucked air through gritted teeth and massaged his chin between thumb and index finger. 'Yeah, whatever,' he said. 'Just go and keep my suspect alive.'

I got to my feet.

'And don't let him get to his computer,' Buchanan said. 'He'll have a hot-key, if he touches it, the computer will dump all his files.'

I headed out of the room.

■ THIRTY-FIVE

Number 150 Landon Ave had a timber front door. Even with a hammer, a break-in was never going to be efficient. Carson was apparently of the same mindset. When I reached the street and couldn't see him, I assumed he must have gone around the back. I crossed at a sprint. Leaf chatter announced a light wind, branches casting contorted, arthritic shadows in the yellow lamplight. The stack of destroyed fencing listed gently, trash in the swimming pool twirling and dimpling the water.

I headed down the left side of the house, heard the brittle tinkle of broken glass. I reached the rear of the property. Beneath a security light, a cracked glass-panelled door hung open above a patch of naked earth.

I entered.

A laundry; the odour of animal urine. Sink and taps to the left, a washing machine to the right. A mesh-sided rabbit hutch on top of it, shredded newsprint littering the floor. Through another door and into a living room. Low light, television flicker etching Ian Carson in silhouette, hammer raised. At his feet, a ruined heap that could only be Jon Edward.

I blew into the room and caught Carson's raised wrist just below the hammer. I gathered a fistful of collar and pulled him off-balance, tossing him sideways towards a sofa against the left-hand wall. His torso was horizontal as it covered the distance, feet skittering to retain balance. He stopped when the crown of his head made contact with the wall. Plasterboard yielded with a crack. He collapsed into the sofa, hammer still in hand, focus wayward.

Edward unwrapped himself. He was tall, late-thirties. Blood ran down his face, courtesy of a long, forehead laceration. There was a computer on a desk against the right-hand wall, opposite the couch. He rolled up onto all fours and made a scramble for it. Blood beaded off his chin and speckled the floor. I made a grab for his arm. He rolled away and snatched free then lashed out and landed a kick to my thigh. I backed off a step. He made it to the desk in a desperate hands-and-knees scamper, spread his hands over the keyboard and pressed a three-key combination. The screen withdrew. A progress bar emerged, below the heading 'DUMPING.'

I grabbed him by the front of his collar. He wore a lumpy, grey woollen jersey, cat hair trapped in the weave. I pushed him back against the edge of the desk. He turned his head away from me, eyelids shivering as he winced.

'Make it stop,' I instructed.

'Can't.'

His lips were parted, his teeth filmed crimson. The progress bar was at ten per cent. Common sense lost its feeble grasp. I held the guy by his collar and knocked his head against the side of the desk. It fuzzed his vision. He shook his head to regain focus. I knocked his head a second time. His eyelids sank to half-mast.

'OK, OK, OK! Control-Alt-Q, Control-Alt-Q.'

I pressed Control-Alt-Q. The progress bar halted. The screen returned to an image of his desktop.

The tension of the moment quietly dissolved. Activity stopped. Carson had dropped his hammer. It was propped up against the base of the couch. Carson himself was lying foetal on the cushions, knees drawn to his stomach, hands knitted behind his head, breathing heavily. Edward was on the floor beside the desk. I took up post in the centre of the room, chin on chest, panting to process the adrenaline.

The far wall was a curtained-over ranch slider, an old CRT television on a small table positioned at the right-hand end. An assortment of plastic trays smeared with food scraps lay on the carpet in front: microwave meals lazily discarded. In front of the couch, *TV Guide* magazines, and beneath the computer desk, plastic milk bottles filled with urine. Apparently, his PC-based activities were so important even bathroom breaks couldn't be spared. I looked at Jon Edward. His lips were ajar, I could see his left incisor was missing. The blood on his face pooled above pre-existing scars that webbed his forehead and cheeks. Aside from that, the Department of Internal Affairs' international child porn-ring suspect wasn't outwardly atypical. His hair was dark, trimmed short, his crown defoliated in an almost perfect ring. On his wrist he wore a red and black plastic watch, Batman's face moulded around the digital display. He wore blue Levis above tan boat shoes, no socks.

Beside the couch, a door led through to a small kitchen. A large orange cat ignored the domestic mayhem and lapped water out of a saucer on the floor beside the fridge.

I took out my cellphone. I was calm, though blood pounded in my head with the cyclic rush of a passing train. I heard a sound like masking tape peeling off a smooth surface, looked up and saw Jon Edward pointing a gun at me.

'Don't,' he said.

It was a black revolver. It was loaded. There was no barrel wobble. I figured the calibre as either a .38 or a .357, but it was a non-issue. Whatever it was, a headshot would be fatal. I looked at the desk. No drawers, but strips of blue duct-tape hung below, curled and twisted.

'Put the phone down,' he said. 'Or I'll shoot you in the head.'

He didn't speak loudly. It was a light, but sincere tone. It was a bank call centre voice, made slightly juvenile by a lisp that turned his *the* into *va*.

I had typed one-one-one. All I had to do was thumb *send*. He read it in my face. He was probably concussed, but the pain didn't appear to inhibit his ability to aim a firearm.

'I'll count to three,' he said. His lisped equivalent of *three* was *free*.

He didn't even start. I dropped the phone on the floor, carpet deadening the impact to a dull thud. It rolled over, luminous screen face-up, betraying my intent. The gun was still aimed at my nose. By now his face was sheeted crimson. Blood ponded in the contours and seemed to deepen them. His eyelashes were gummed crimson.

'Who are you?' he asked.

'I'm a cop,' I said.

'A cop doing what?' he asked. His voice was innocent and playful.

I nodded at Carson, still inert on the couch.

Edward raised his eyebrows, looked at Carson.

'Oh,' he said. 'Yes. He's in a lot of trouble.' He pursed his lips. 'Actually, you're both in trouble.'

The gun dropped to my chest to lessen the angle. 'Move back a bit,' he said.

I moved closer to the kitchen door.

'The Ian Carson tail for tonight, are we?' he said. 'Where's your back-up?'

I didn't answer. Edward squirmed across the floor on his butt to the window, *TV Guides* pushed aside. He fingered a split in the curtains and peeped out, then turned back to the room and raised the gun again. He knew Carson was under investigation. He thought I was a plainclothes officer assigned to tail him and figured I must have followed Carson out here and intervened when I saw the hammer. But with what was stored on his computer, he didn't want his home becoming the scene of an arrest. And the fact I had stopped him clearing his hard drive was evidence his activities weren't a secret. Hence, the gun. Hence, the claim that we were both in a lot of trouble. Point a gun at a cop and things are guaranteed to end badly for someone.

'Here's what's happening,' Edward said. 'In ten minutes, some friends of mine will be here to collect us. Meantime, if I see any blue-and-red lights, I'm going to shoot you. Sound good?'

I made no reply. Carson had waited at the kerb long enough for Edward to have seen him and made a call. Carson was still on the couch, hands wrapping his head. A whimper punctuated his breathing.

'Hear that?' Edward said. 'That whimper? They call that irony.' Eye-winny.

I said nothing.

'Ian's got strange sexual tastes,' Edward said. He smiled sheepishly. 'Which is fine, because I do too. The difference is, when he doesn't get what he wants, he gets violent. Case in point, couple of weeks back, I had a little rendezvous arranged here with Ian and a lovely young woman who is no longer with us.'

He chuckled a little and checked his Batman watch. 'The lovely young woman was running late. Ian got a little angry and, to cut a long story short, ended up cutting my face with a kitchen knife.'

He inclined his head, rolling it side to side, so the blood-rinsed scars webbing his cheeks and jaw were prominent. He was stretched out on his left side on the floor, propped on his elbow, with the gun in his right hand swinging between Carson and me.

'And then to top it all off,' he smiled, 'when the lovely young woman finally arrived, she took the opportunity to pinch all my money.'

It explained the timing: Carson arrives, an hour later Christine McLane arrives. Carson's in a knife frenzy; she takes the opportunity for impromptu robbery. Five minutes later they both leave.

'That's all right, though,' he said. 'I made a phone call and got even.'

Even: he'd had Carson's wife and daughter murdered, and burned his burglar to death.

He fingered the blinds and checked the street again, before looking back at me.

'Maybe we'd better see some identification,' he said. 'ID and badge, please.'

I took my ID wallet out of my jacket and frisbeed it to him. It landed a metre short and slid the rest of the distance like a stone skipped off still water. He levered it open with his thumb, keeping fingerprints out of the equation.

'Sean Devereaux,' he said. 'Good name.'

I made no reply. Edward chuckled to himself. He checked the window again. Carson was still on the couch, but he'd removed his hands from his head.

'Just to reiterate,' Edward said, 'if I see your back-up coming, I'm going to shoot you first. In the head.'

'OK,' I said. 'But there's nobody coming.'

Urban reconnaissance isn't straightforward. Risk of exposure increases as traffic thins. Hale faced this dilemma on the approach to Landon Ave. Quiet streets forced him to slacken the leash out to five hundred metres. He saw the BMW make the left onto Landon at the eastern end and he followed at a trickle. He came around the bend to number 150 at near stall speed and saw the BMW parked at the kerb. He stopped and reversed back to the corner. He knew Carson and Christine McLane had visited the address, but he had no idea what was going on.

He tried Sean Devereaux's number — still no answer.

He dropped the phone on the seat and U-turned. He followed a crooked loop clockwise through the dark and empty streets until he found the western end of Landon Ave, and made the right-hand turn. The Escort muttered as he dropped to trundle speed. He checked left and right, glimpsed the back end of Devereaux's unmarked, lit weakly by lamplight, parked beside a house that was entirely blacked out. He dimmed his lights, turned into the driveway and parked. Chill wrapped him as he slid out. His breath steamed and scurried skywards. There was a side door equipped with a combination lock. He stepped over and knocked, moved back from the door and held up his Private Investigator's licence, making it visible to whoever answered.

The door cracked after half a minute, yellow light warming it along three edges. He kept the licence raised, tilted it forwards into the glow.

A woman's voice said, 'I had a dentist called John Hale.'

Hale didn't reply.

'What do you want?' the woman said.

'I'm looking for Sean Devereaux.'

A pause. 'You'd better come in then.'

He entered into a narrow corridor. A heavy red-headed woman with a knot in her hair closed the door behind him, then led him into a living room decked out with all manner of digital hardware. Bundled cabling crisscrossed the floor. Banks of computer and television monitors served as the only light source, imparting a rapid flicker that made him squint. A digital radio added garbled chatter to the background electronic murmur. A tall bespectacled guy in his fifties wearing a grey suit occupied the centre of the room, hands on hips, jacket tails fanned behind him. He turned as Hale entered.

'Great,' the guy said. 'Now it's a party.'

'Where's Devereaux?'

'I need to see some ID.'

'Where's Devereaux?'

'Across the street.'

'With Carson?'

'Yeah, with Carson. How the hell did—'

'I tailed him here. What's going on?'

'Show me some ID.'

Hale passed him the licence.

'A PI,' the guy said. 'You're not even a proper cop.'

'I'm touched. And you are?'

The guy didn't answer. The woman took a seat at a computer. 'You can call him Buchanan,' she said.

'What's going on?' Hale said.

'Carson arrived and went into the house,' Buchanan said. 'Devereaux followed. He hasn't come out yet.'

'How long's he been in there?'

'Almost six minutes.'

'Have you called him some back-up?'

'No, we—'

'Call one-one-one right now.'

He was out of the room before the guy could answer, through the side door and trotted out to the street. A weak breeze dribbled through. He crossed at a jog. The BMW was out front of a small single-level unit. In the front yard, a heap of fencing beside a trash-filled swimming pool. A feeble glow lit the edges of a curtained ranch slider. He hurried down the left side of the house. Back yard, and he found a fractured glass door spot-lit by a lone security lamp. Shards on the concrete step; he was careful not to make a sound as he entered the house.

The smell of animal urine greeted him as he entered the laundry. The internal door separating the room from the rest of the house was half closed. Voices reached him. A mostly one-sided conversation: an unknown male voice punctuated infrequently by Sean Devereaux's.

To the right, a rabbit hutch sat on a washing machine. He pressed against it and leaned forward to peer around the gap in the door. He saw Ian Carson, foetal on a two-seater sofa, and Sean Devereaux standing in the middle of the room, his back to him.

He heard snatches of a light, lisped monologue: 'The lovely young woman was running late. Ian got a little angry and, to cut a long story short, ended up cutting my face with a kitchen knife.

And then to top it all off, when the lovely young woman finally arrived, she took the opportunity to pinch all my money. That's all right, though. I made a phone call and got even.' Perfect exposition.

Thoughts meshed with mechanical perfection. Colossal implications slotted home.

Made a phone call and got even.

The lisper had coordinated kidnap and murder.

Hale backtracked outside, awkward reverse mincing steps to avoid the glass. He walked back down the side of the property to the street and sprinted back across the road. The side door to the surveillance house opened before he reached it. He hurried in, a bustle of heaving shoulders and steaming exhalation. The woman closed the door behind him. Buchanan was still standing, watching the monitors. He turned as Hale entered.

'What's happening?'

'Did you call him some back-up?'

'Yeah. What's happening?'

'Ring them back and tell them to wait. There's a hostage situation in there. He's got a gun, says he's going to shoot someone if he sees the cavalry coming.'

'Ah shit.'

Buchanan's expression went slack. He wiped a palm across his mouth, glanced around, as if in search of a printed procedure. Panicked fingers slipped and sent a desk phone clattering. He punched numbers frantically, breathing shallow, stooped to let the handset reach his ear. A tense pause before the call was connected, shouted exposition as Buchanan described the situation. He listened quietly for a moment, one hand stuffed in his hair, offered a 'Yes', then an 'OK'. He pulled out a chair and sat down, holding the phone away from his ear, keeping the line open.

'They're going to set up a cordon,' he said.

'How soon?'

'As soon as possible. Within the next ten minutes. The best they can do at the moment is seal the road. AOS is out on another call; it's going to take forty minutes to get another team together. What are they doing in there?'

Hale didn't reply. He was looking at the television

monitors. A black Ford Explorer SUV had come into shot, high beams scalding the screen starch-white. It was moving fast. It pulled to a stop behind the BMW. A heavy Maori guy in his forties climbed out of the front passenger seat. A tall guy with dreadlocks in his twenties got out of the rear behind the driver.

Hale said, 'How the hell did they get that car back?'

'What?' Buchanan asked.

Hale made no reply. He watched Cedric and the young guy approach the front door.

'What's going on?'

'They're moving them off-site,' Hale said. 'These guys were contracted to kidnap a woman last week. She was burned to death in a car.'

'You mean that McLane girl?'

'Yes. *That McLane girl.*'

'Shit.'

'Yeah,' Hale answered. 'Exactly.'

▪ THIRTY-SIX

Go and open the front door. Anything funny, Carson gets a gut shot.'

I did as directed. The cat had finished its meal. It entered the living room, back arched and rubbing the doorframe as it slipped past. I stepped through the kitchen to a small entry hall, and released the deadbolt on the front door. Night air breathed in, and two men followed. The first was a heavy guy in his mid-forties; long hair tied back, black sunglasses that bore a sheen as perfect and vivid as motor oil. The second guy was tall, in his twenties. His hair was in dreads, the individual locks lank and separate from one another, like a limp hand draped over his head.

They closed the door behind them and ushered me back to the living room. Jon Edward was still in graceful repose on the floor beside the window. The heel of one boat shoe-clad foot tapped merrily against the curtained window.

'Evening gentlemen,' he said.

The older guy stepped towards me and cupped my face with both hands. He patted my cheeks lightly. 'Nice to meet you,' he said. 'I'm Cedric.' He took his hands back and glanced at Edward. 'Clean-up job?'

'Yes, please. Where are you going to take them?'

'Don't know. We'll think of something. You wanna come?'

Edward looked positively thrilled. 'Yeah, that would be fun.'

Buchanan palmed the phone's mouthpiece and said, 'They've got half the cordon in place.'

Hale glanced at him. Radio chatter, the security footage and the phone conversation had split his attention three ways. 'Which half?'

'They've blocked the northern and southern approaches of the road this one leads on to at the eastern end.'

Hale closed his eyes briefly and visualized the configuration. He looked at the monitors. A plan of attack cohered. 'How far away are they?' he asked.

Buchanan consulted his phone. 'Just around the corner.'

'Tell them a black SUV is coming their way in the next five minutes. They need to take it.'

'How do you know they're going that way?'

Hale pointed at the television monitors. 'Watch.'

He walked out of the room, down the corridor and out the side door. Darkness met him and drew him deep. He walked along the edge of the driveway, tottering on the uneven terrain. At the front corner of the house he stopped. The street was quiet, the breeze preventing perfect sedation. The Explorer was in view, parked at the opposite kerb. Two people had exited, and neither one of them had been the driver.

He moved right in a crouch. Deep shadows cloaked the motion. Fenceless sections afforded easy prowling. He drew level with the Explorer's driver's door and paused. The window was up, the obsidian-like glass opaque. He straightened, fifteen metres away, across the street. He started across the road — an easy stroll, catwalk cool.

Ten metres. Five. Three.

He reached the truck and twisted mid-step. He raised his left arm and jabbed downwards like a backhand tennis volley, hitting the centre of the driver's window with his elbow. The glass splintered and fell free of the frame like a dropped sheet. He swung with the momentum of the strike and hopped up on the running board beneath the lip of the door, bringing his right arm in through the window frame. He caught the driver by the throat and pinned him against the seat.

Instant recollection: the skinny guy with the tan, from the night he met Cedric. He surged and bucked against Hale's grip. Skin concertinaed beneath his chin. His mouth opened, lips strung with saliva, eyes wide and lightning-bolted with crimson capillaries. He scrabbled and strained wildly, sinew cut crisp, veins barely contained as his left arm clawed for a pistol resting on the passenger seat.

Hale was holding the roof rack with his left hand. It made victim compliance a one-arm procedure. He cinched up the throat grip to ensure firm anchorage. Tongue protruded. The arm flailed for the gun, well wide of the mark. Hale could feel the guy's pulse either side of his neck, heavy and rapid, straining beneath his fingertips.

Spit-laden pleading: 'Stoooop! Please, stop.'

Hale released pressure, but still kept him pinned as he looked inside. Skinny slumped and snatched heaving gasps. His grey, sleeveless sweatshirt was dusted with white shards from the window and his right hand wrapped Hale's wrist. Hale surveyed the cabin. The keys were tinkling in the ignition and the guy had removed his seatbelt. The pistol on the seat was a Glock 19. Hale looked across the roof at the house. All quiet.

'Nod if you understand me,' Hale said. Voice soft as mist.

A stiff nod. The headrest and the pressure from Hale's hand constrained his movement.

'We're going to go for a drive,' Hale said. 'If you reach for the pistol, or if you take us up over thirty, I'm going to bust your trachea with my thumb. You know what a trachea is?'

The nod again. Skinny knew what a trachea was. He knew compromised integrity would make breathing difficult. His gaze rolled south. He could feel the aforementioned thumb. He appraised the wrist it was attached to. It was Herculean: wide, matted with hair, looped with veins, pulsing with thick tissue. It was a wrist from which no threat was idle. It was a wrist that kept promises.

'Turn the ignition on,' Hale said.

A phlegmy swallow. He took his right hand off Hale's

wrist and twisted the key. The motor turned over once, then caught and ran smooth. A weak burble of exhaust misted whitely behind them.

'Leave the lights off and keep it below thirty,' Hale said. 'I'll give you directions.'

The guy slotted the transmission into reverse and nudged back from the BMW. He found drive and took off slowly, lights off, the slipstream lifting Hale's hair. Hale kept the pressure on, in case bravery was rekindled. They reached the eastern end of the street.

'Go right,' Hale said.

Skinny complied. The cordon had killed through traffic. It rendered the indicator redundant. They crawled back up to thirty. Seconds later blue-and-red light bars ignited the middle distance. Shivering pulses brought the surrounding jagged terrain of rooflines into stark two-tone relief. The orbs of colour sharpened into a trio of patrol cars blocking the street.

'OK, stop.'

'What are you doing?'

Soft as mist again: 'Stop. The. Car.'

The Explorer stopped, rocking gently on its springs. Hale stepped down off the running board. Torch lights skittered and honed in. He opened the driver's door with his left hand, pulled the guy out by the throat and dumped him unceremoniously on the tarseal. Police officers were running towards them. He turned away and ducked behind the Explorer, sprinting back in the direction of Landon.

Cedric lay me on the floor, put a broad knee in the small of my back and cinched my wrists together with a plastic snap tie. The carpet smelled dusty and fibrous, flecks of grit biting my cheek. He patted my pockets quickly, found a loose cigarette in my inside jacket pocket. He jammed it in one corner of a thin smile and lit up, leaving a zigzag smoke plume hanging after he shook out the match. The room quietly observed the little routine, me on my side on the floor, Dreadlocks in the doorway to the kitchen, Edward on the floor, Carson on his couch. Carson was upright now, leaning forward with his forearms propped across his thighs, his gaze on the square of carpet framed by his feet. I called it the jail pose. I'd seen arrestees exhibit it on the edge of cell block cots. It signalled a realization things were likely to worsen before improving. The hammer was still propped against the base of the couch.

Cedric flipped another unused snap tie to Dreadlocks. 'Do Carson,' he said.

The cigarette waggled as he spoke. His sunglasses mirrored the smoke plume. He checked his watch. They'd been inside less than five minutes. Dreadlocks moved out of the doorway and approached Carson, who tried to fend; a one-armed, half-hearted effort. Dreadlocks caught his wrist and tugged him heavily onto the floor beside me, kicking him in the side of the thigh to make him docile.

'Thought I heard glass breaking,' Edward said.

He was still on the floor beside the window, curtain corner raised to see outside. Dreadlocks postponed his handcuffing duties and stood straight.

'Is the car still there?' Cedric asked. He took the cigarette out of his mouth. He had an unusual grip, bridging it across his thumb and middle finger, his first finger draped across the top.

'Yeah.'

Cedric went to the window to confirm. He stepped high to avoid the bodies on the floor. His matches rattled softly as he moved. He leaned in across Edward and fingered the curtain aside. He glanced left and right, returned the cigarette to his mouth and inhaled, his cheeks hollowing.

'Could have been anything,' he said.

He tipped his head back and plumed smoke at the ceiling. Dreadlocks glanced down just as Carson swung his leg up and smashed his toe into his crotch. Dreadlocks retched and staggered away, bent double and pigeon-toed. Carson wasn't done. He spun on his back, grabbed the hammer and hurled it across the room.

It was a good throw. It held a head-high trajectory and cartwheeled. Cedric saw it coming. He arched back in easy limbo, the cigarette held to his lips. The hammer spun past his face and thudded against the wall. It bit a ragged chunk of gib-board and hit the floor. Edward whooped like a school kid.

Dreadlocks recovered fast. He didn't take rebellion well. Punishment became a two-man task. Cedric took a long, last drag, and placed his cigarette on the corner of the computer desk. Nonchalant, like the following task was one of little apparent significance. They paused before starting, optimizing their positions, awkward steps in the poky floor space. They set upon Carson in a wordless stomping flurry that no manner of pleading could satiate, observed blankly by the strange man in the corner who tapped a rhythm with the heel of his boat shoe as he watched.

Hale ran back onto Landon and reached 150. He stood in the street, unsure of how to proceed. Movement in the house came through vague and bloated on the backlit curtain. If he went in, there was a good chance he could take them, three on one. Conversely there was a good chance the gun would go off before he could get to it.

He cut across to the verge, into the shadows, and made up his mind about his next move.

Carson wasn't in good shape by the time they'd finished with him. He stayed on the floor, whimpering and bloodied, a crumpled wreck of agony.

His two assailants stepped away, relaxed, unfazed. As if what they'd done to him was towards the more pedestrian end of the assault spectrum. Cedric reclaimed his cigarette from beside the computer and returned it to his mouth. He glanced down at me and gave a grin that was hooked at one end like a knife wound. His face moved in what I thought must have been a wink behind the black lenses.

'Make sure you behave yourself,' he said. The cigarette jumped as he spoke.

He bent down and put a hand on my upper arm and pulled me to my feet.

'Don't speak much,' he observed.

'When I do it's normally worthwhile.'

He gave me a straight right in the gut that collapsed me back on the floor. He saw my phone, still lying face-up, and bent down and pocketed it. Dreadlocks watched with a neutral expression, as if he was waiting in a queue to buy milk. Edward fingered the curtain and looked at the street again.

'Your car's gone,' he said.

They'd want to move them out of the house. It was the basic premise of a clean-up. But with the Explorer gone, transport was limited to either the BMW or the red Cherokee parked in the yard. They probably wouldn't call a taxi.

Hale braved streetlight glare and cut a gangly silhouette across 150's frontage to the BMW. Its presence was a liability. At some stage they would have to get rid of it. Sooner rather than later made a lot of sense.

He reached the car and glanced back at the house. Shadows in the room still changing, but the curtains hung undisturbed. They were clearly all in one room. He couldn't risk an entry. Too many variables in the same space guaranteed bloodshed. He shuffled to the driver's side. Window tint drew him mirror-perfect. He glanced at the curtain. No movement. He tried the door handle. The mechanism released with a dampened pop. An interior light blinked on. He scrambled in on his knees and found the switch and flicked it off. The car was an older model; cracked leather and the chemical tang of cleaning fluid. He palmed button panels and found the boot-release. The rear lid clicked and arched open with a gentle pneumatic hum. He pressed the door gently closed and walked around to the rear. Yellow boot light glazed his torso. The load space held a plastic supermarket bag and a black peaked cap stitched with a silver fern. He turned and shimmied backwards until he was sitting in the boot compartment. He swung his legs in over the brake light panel, lay down and pulled the lid closed on top of himself.

His world dulled to pure black. The confines of the car locked him in a horizontal crouch. It was like a prelude to the grave. The underside of the lid was thirty centimetres from his face. He rolled onto his left shoulder and felt along the carpet beneath the edge of the lid. A lot of premier vehicles were fitted with emergency release handles. He found it after a moment's blind pawing. It was a T-shaped plastic device attached to a length of thin steel cable leading up to the lid mechanism. An abduction countermeasure, redundant in a million cases out of a million-and-one, gratefully acknowledged in this instance. He flipped the handle and found a luminescent image of a stick figure gleefully escaping boot imprisonment. No rush to do likewise. He lay there in the silent emptiness, breathing shallowly through his nose, trying to stay calm.

He checked his watch face, glowing green in the darkness. Two minutes passed before he sensed a door open. The suspension compressed heavily; separate, stiff oscillations as three people entered. Probably dreadlocks in the centre, with Carson and Devereaux either side of him, kiddie locks on for prisoner transport. Thunks of doors closing, and then another two people slid in the front, the dampened vibrations superimposed, reaching Hale as vague shakes through the heavy automobile body. Cedric driving he imagined, the guy with the lisp in the passenger seat.

Doors closed. A devout atheist, John Hale prayed to God that a road block would stop them. The engine started. The car moved off the kerb. He felt a sudden centripetal pressure against his feet as the car U-turned.

Heading west.

Away from the cordon.

They reached the end of Landon and slowed. He felt the cornering force through the top of his skull. They accelerated smoothly. No road block. They were away, southbound and unimpeded.

■ THIRTY-SEVEN

C edric said, 'Where's my driver?'
'I have no idea.'

'Bullshit you don't. Your back-up got him.'

'I don't have any back-up.'

'So where's my driver?'

I didn't answer. The missing SUV had chipped his confidence. Uncertainty kicked in and beaded his brow. He arched up off the seat, freed a phone from his pocket and thumbed a speed-dial. Edward studied him in earnest, lips ajar, complaints imminent. He was sideways in the passenger seat, feet up on the squab, knees propping his chin.

Cedric's call rang through. He lost his patience and skipped the phone across the dash, wiped a sleeve across his mouth. 'Someone's nabbed him,' he said. 'He wouldn't just take off with the car like that.'

Edward dumped his feet off the seat. 'But how could they? How could anyone have known so fast?'

Cedric didn't reply for a moment. He was worried, but chauffeur truancy didn't faze him too badly. A clean exit was now his main concern. He rested one hand on the top of the wheel, reached up and spun the rear-view mirror so it framed his black lenses for me. 'The detective tipped someone off,' he said.

I didn't say anything. I watched his face in the mirror. I saw worry flare in his gut, saw him swallow to douse it. Maybe it had just hit home that he'd kidnapped two people, one of whom was a police detective.

I said, 'It's not too late to stop and let us out.'

The engine tone held constant. The mirrors were dark.

'Don't think so,' Cedric said.

'They've got your driver. He's going to implicate you. They know the house we just left. They'll know the occupant. They'll pull his phone records. They'll trace the calls back to you.'

Edward shifted in his seat. He was unsettled, but he wouldn't say anything that went against the Cedric Code.

'Stop the car,' I said. 'Or you're going to be in shit, from brow to bootlaces.'

'Detective, if you whine again,' Cedric said, 'I'm going to stop the car and cut your throat. OK?'

I said nothing. He gave me that knife-slash grin, skin beneath the lens frame crinkling as he did so. The back seat was quiet. Dreadlocks sat impassive between Carson and me, his fingers linked neatly in his lap. He was calm, quite content to be led. A passenger in more than one sense. Carson's lips were split crimson. One eye was swollen shut, the other was half-closed. Two days from now, the skin beneath them would turn the colour of smoke. Assuming he lived another two days.

'How did you tip them off?' Cedric said.

'I didn't.'

'Bullshit!' he shouted. It was the first split in the calm façade. He swallowed and licked his lips, exhaled to regain control. 'You're not going to die well,' he said. 'I'll tell you that now.'

I made no reply. Southbound on Station Road pulling eighty, the five of us lolling gently, Carson and I leaning forward to take the pressure off our cuffed wrists. Cedric spun the mirror back so his face was no longer visible. I was thirty-three years old. He was probably nearer to forty-three. I wondered to what extent his life experience differed from my own that he was in the front seat and

I was in the back. Did those with the vacuity of soul necessary to kill leave the same station as the rest of us, or were they riding a different train?

Cedric sensed me watching him. He looked out his side window as he drove, switching hands on the wheel to drape his right arm across the top of the door.

'Don't lose sleep thinking about it,' he said. 'I'm just a real baaaaad dude.'

The comment deflated their tension. Dreadlocks cracked a smile. It was contagious. Edward spewed a giggle.

'You've murdered five people,' I said.

Cedric put both hands on the wheel and ran a finger count. 'Carson's wife,' he said. 'Carson's daughter. That's two. The McLane girl, and Luvis and his helper in the car. Yeah. Five.'

He let the statistic sit for a moment. Nobody spoke. Carson was leaning against the door, shattered by the beating. Conversation was beyond him. He probably wouldn't have risked a reply, even if he could.

'Although I didn't actually kill anyone,' Cedric said. 'I'm just the arranger.'

'Why did Luvis have to die?' I asked.

He shrugged, the corners of his mouth downturned,

eyes on the mirror. 'Luvis was a douche bag,' he said. 'He was the guy I hired. It should have been real simple. I told him to kill Carson. Yeah, no worries, he said. I'll do that. But he didn't. He went around to his house, Carson's out, he kills the wife and then kills the little girl. It complicates things, you know? He didn't do what he was supposed to, so I had to get rid of him. I called him up, said I had another job. Told him there was a girl we were having trouble with, she owed us some money, said I needed her brought in. This is the McLane girl I'm talking about. He said that was fine, but he'd need a back-up crew. So I arranged a back-up crew for him, sent them out to grab her on the Friday. Drove her down to a little vacant site beside the railway line, where Jon met them and scorched them all.'

Nobody replied, but he shrugged at the wheel, as if replying to an unspoken challenge. We turned off Station onto St George Street. Shop fronts boxed the narrow traffic lanes, the road a corridor of mesh-backed windows. Veranda billboards advertised takeaways in faded print. 'Gets the job done,' he said.

He checked his rear-view mirror. The road behind was empty.

The boot compartment wasn't built for comfort. Obvious, but riding in one at speed underlined the fact. It was not a good position to be in. The physical constraint reinforced Hale's desire to be back on the offensive. He rolled with the motion of the car, confines invisible in absolute blackness.

He twisted onto his side, coaxed his phone out of his pocket with a thumb-and-index pincer movement, knees and elbows pressing panelling. Screen glow revealed coffin geometry. He speed-dialled Devereaux.

He got an answer on ring four. No greeting. Dial-tone absence signalled the pick-up. He stuffed a finger in his ear to kill background hum.

'How did you get the car back?' Hale said.

'Who's this?' He recognized Cedric's voice.

'We met the other night,' Hale said. 'You pointed a gun at me, so I cut your neck a little bit.'

Cedric didn't answer. Hale lay there, rolling gently with the BMW's row-boat nudging.

'I'm watching you,' Hale said.

'Right. What am I doing?'

He felt the centripetal force kick in, overcoming his inertia as the car turned. 'You just made a left,' he said.

Crackled static on the connection. He pictured the guy checking his mirrors.

'Don't bother looking,' Hale said. 'You won't see me. I'm just too good. And try not to turn so sharply. Your passengers don't appreciate it.'

He ended the call. His terms. His psychological high ground. He returned the phone to his pocket, content he was still in the picture.

We drove north along a quiet SH1. It was nearing midnight, traffic was light. It was obvious to me where we were headed once we crossed the Harbour Bridge and exited at Esmonde. Five minutes later we pulled up outside the Carson house on Hurstmere Road. There was no patrol car keeping watch. It was a crime scene, over a week old. Now that its evidential value had been realized, it was locked up and dormant.

Cedric continued down the street for fifty metres and parked at the kerb. He got out and jogged back to Carson's driveway, where he picked the padlock on the security chain and pulled the gate wide. Edward clambered over the central console to the driver's seat, using his hands to manoeuvre one leg and then the other. He U-turned in the street and drove us back the fifty metres to the open gate and entered the property. Lights off, a neat unobserved operation. Two minutes, from Cedric's door

423

opening to the gates clicking closed again.

The garage door raised obediently as we drew near, triggered by a remote attached to the driver's sun visor. Edward idled in, jerky on the brake, anxious to avoid any incriminating paint trade. Cedric entered the garage behind us. He slapped the boot lid once with a hollow boom, and the door descended smoothly behind us.

■ THIRTY-EIGHT

The lower storey had a lot of windows. Flicking a light would instantly betray occupancy. They herded us along the downstairs corridor and left us in the girl's en suite. Mental correction. Not *the girl*. Amy Lee. The door still hadn't been repaired, the wood surrounding the catch raw and fibrous.

Carson came in at a stagger. He dropped himself on the edge of the toilet, hands still cuffed behind him. His nose bled a steady trickle, crimson droplets clicking wetly on the tile work between his feet.

'I thought I could fix things,' he said.

'I think things are a long way from being fixed.'

His eyes closed. He gave a grimace that cut the skin at the corners of his eyes, traced the bottoms of his front teeth with the tip of his tongue. 'I knew it was him,' he said. 'I knew it was that lispy piece of shit who had my wife and daughter killed. I was going to get him. I was going to kill him with the hammer.'

He choked a laugh.

'Almost got me high, like the thought of killing the guy overwhelmed everything. Like it was OK that my family was dead, because I was going to hammer the guy responsible for killing them.'

I watched him as I stood behind the door and listened. He slopped down off the seat into a pile beside the toilet, rested his head against the rim. Simultaneous balance aid and potential vomit containment.

'What are they going to do with us?' he asked thickly.

'Kill us,' I said. 'Maybe dismember us first, wrap the bits up, get rid of them somewhere.'

He listened blankly, lips ajar, shoulders rounded, legs askew beneath him.

I could hear them outside the door, a three-man conference of war, deciding what to do next.

Edward's voice: 'I thought I heard the boot open.'

Hale waited three minutes, then made his arrival.

The boot lid opened to a blaze of white light. The contrast was dazzling. He had no idea where he was.

426

He winced through a mesh of raised fingers and saw timber roof beams above him. To the left, the interior metal bracing of what was apparently a garage door. He struggled upright, the boot an awkward clutter of knees and elbows as he swung his legs out of the load space. Silence was difficult. He wasn't designed for impromptu contortion. He shimmied over the lip of the bumper and dropped to the ground behind the car. Lack of engine noise had left his ears ringing.

He heard footsteps. He rose to a half-crouch and snatched a layout: opposite end of the room, a door in the corner led to a darkened corridor. To the right, a green Peugeot sedan neighboured the BMW. He crouched and duck-walked round to its far side. Thrill and exertion kept him short of breath. He paused behind the rear passenger door and listened. The footsteps had halted.

Silence.

Hale came up off his knees and stole a peek through the Peugeot's rear windows, saw Dreadlocks paused in the doorway. Hale eased forward, towards the car's front right quarter panel. Two metres from the guy's final place of rest if he moved right along the front wall of the garage. He crouched there on a burning held breath. But the guy didn't move right. The raised boot lid had his full attention. It wasn't a minor oddity. It was a glaring anomaly. He heard cautious heel clicks tracking along the far side of the room towards the offending article.

Hale paralleled the movement. He crawled to the Peugeot's rear wheel. He ducked his head below chassis level and glimpsed ankle: Dreadlocks at the rear of the BMW. Dreadlocks closing the lid.

A sudden spike of noise from the slam, and then the silence again. Pipes ticked.

Hale stayed on the ground.

Dreadlocks moved forward, into the narrow corridor formed between the two cars. Hale's heart tripped against the concrete. He breathed dust. Tension rendered breath shaky on exit.

Dreadlocks turned left.

He walked slow, moving between the cars, back towards the front of the room.

Hale kept his head below window level and circled the back of the Peugeot in a hushed scramble. He unfolded to full dimensions, loomed up behind the guy and closed the distance in three steps.

Dreadlocks heard him.

Maybe a joint pop, maybe some deep genetic trigger that told him danger was near. He was side-on when the swing came. The engagement was artful: Hale caught him with a massive open-hand roundhouse across the mouth. The impact was colossal. The sudden torque locked the guy's spine back in a shallow arch. His whole torso began to flip. His legs followed. By the time the back of his head struck the corner of the BMW's bonnet, his entire body was airborne.

Hale left the guy in crumpled repose and kept moving. He made the door in a crouched scurry, simian-like, knuckles-to-floor. The corridor formed a T-junction with another hallway which appeared to stretch the length of the house. The left-hand side was glass, a series of closed doors in the wall to the right. He saw warm light breathing beneath them. He went left and up a staircase leading off the front entry. He heard downstairs doors opening, the urgent slapping of soles on cool cement. Finding the comatose boot-closer would be a ten-second task.

Upstairs matched the ground floor. A hallway reached front to back. The left-hand side was glass. Doors occupied the wall to the right, all of them ajar. Plans formed within the same frantic half-instant he saw it all. He didn't have long. He set a daunting ten-second deadline. He came out of the crouch and ran to the end of the corridor and into a study, dull in the light from the window. A desk stretched along the far wall, its surface barren save for a desk lamp. He clicked it on, angling the bulb towards the door to maximize the glow in the corridor. He left the room and pushed the first door past the study so that it gaped wide, moved along the hallway and entered the adjacent room, leaving the door ajar.

His watch notched twelve seconds before he heard feet on the stairs. Rapid in the corridor, and then nothing. He waited. The tight space had left him stiff and the crouch burned him. His pulse held back the silence. Yellow desk light leaked in at his feet. Its absence would signal go-time.

He strained for sign of a footstep. Nothing but that fierce, empty quiet, stretching with no sign of breaking.

A shadow crossed the light.

He tracked it and drew breath. A quirk of violence that for different men the same shared instant could mean either death or safety.

The door flung inwards. The plan dissolved with the sudden realization he wasn't in control, that someone else had initiated the contact, driving him from offence to defence.

A gun was the first thing through. He caught the wrist it was attached to and pushed it clear of his body. A shot was fired. The flash held them static in the space of a blink as they fell to the floor.

I was still in the bathroom when I heard the shot. Edward and a kitchen knife were on guard duty. The sound of the gun sent him running. I heard his footsteps on the carpet outside. I turned and felt blindly for the handle with hands still anchored at the small of my back, pulled the door open and chased him along the corridor. I was slower than usual with my cuffed wrists, but I kept pace as he went up the stairs, rounded the corner into the first-floor corridor.

Light in the study. Edward put his head down and made a beeline, slapping a switch on the way through and lighting up the hallway. He crossed Carolyn Lee's open bedroom door just as the second shot rang out. He fell as if he'd snagged a tripwire, one hand clutching his neck. I ran into the room. John Hale and Cedric were on the floor, a heaving mass of wrapped limbs battling for control of the gun. The muzzle roved. Bodies roiled. They bucked and twisted randomly, like taser victims. Hale palmed the gun's frame and managed to ground it. I leapt on the back of his hand to keep the weapon pinned, and kicked Cedric in the face. His nose split and blossomed crimson. He went instantly slack, his head tipping sideways to knock against the floor. His eyelids dropped: end-of-show curtain.

Hale pushed me off and unwrapped Cedric's limp fingers from the gun, tossed it on the bed, onto faded bloodstains. He disentangled himself from the flaccid embrace and rolled to his feet. He made it to the doorway in a zigzagged stagger, head bent and panting, and swiped a wall switch. My shoe-print tattooed the back of his right palm.

'Sorry I trod on you,' I said.

He shrugged and checked the damage, then shook off the sting. 'Lucky it's not my omelette hand.'

He leaned in the doorway and watched Jon Edward bleed out. The bullet had nicked carotid. He wouldn't make it. He lay on his stomach with his hand against the side of his neck, his face against the floor, panicked prayer rippling a growing pool of scarlet.

And that was how it ended: quietly, inelegantly. An August midnight: gunsmoke and blood beneath a pressed palm.